THE

UNDEAD

THE UNDEAD

A NOVEL OF MODERN RUSSIA

SVETLANA SATCHKOVA

MELVILLE HOUSE
BROOKLYN • LONDON

The Undead : A Novel of Modern Russia
First published in 2026 by Melville House

First Melville House Printing: November 2025
Distributed by Penguin Random House LLC, 1745 Broadway, New York, NY 10019
USA. www.penguinrandomhouse.com

Melville House Publishing
46 John Street
Brooklyn, NY 11201
and
Melville House UK
Suite 2000
16/18 Woodford Road
London E7 0HA

mhpbooks.com
@melvillehouse

ISBN: 978-1-68589-219-7
ISBN: 978-1-68589-220-3 (eBook)

Library of Congress Control Number: 2025943095

Designed by Beste M. Doğan

Printed in the United States of America
1 3 5 7 9 10 8 6 4 2

A catalog record for this book is available from the Library of Congress

The authorized representative in the EU for product safety and compliance is Easy Access System Europe, Mustamäe tee 50, 10621 Tallinn, Estonia. gpsr.requests@easproject.com

I dedicate this novel to Russian
political prisoners, past and present,
and especially to Alexey
Navalny, who was tortured for
three years in prison and died there.

THE UNDEAD

CHAPTER 1

aya reached for a branch where a ripe yellow fig was sitting, its honey-like juice trickling out of the hole in its bottom. It came off effortlessly, as if it had been about to fall, and she stuffed it into her mouth. She couldn't get enough of these figs, the likes of which she'd never tasted before. They felt like pure happiness, making her forget, at least for the time being, that life was full of disappointments and nasty tricks. But she had to stop eating them, as dinner was in less than an hour. They'd been asked to come to the table at seven.

"Did you know that wasps can live inside these things?" Dennis said. "You don't want to bite into it. Open it with your hands first."

"You already told me this," Maya said.

Around them, a sprawling fruit garden lay, buzzing with insect life. Dennis was sitting on the ground, his back propped against the old fig tree. Maya and Ksenia stood in front of him, their heads touching its branches.

"So anyway, I was saying," Ksenia continued, fixing Maya with her intense stare. "I see her as this lost, trying-to-figure-things-out type. She has this job she doesn't really care about. She broke up with her boyfriend. She has no idea what she wants from life. I can totally relate to her."

Maya didn't see how Ksenia could identify with this fictional woman she was describing. Ksenia was married to Dennis, who adored her. Also, she knew exactly what she wanted, singularly focused as she was on becoming the best actress of her generation—or at least the most famous. She already played leading parts at the Moscow Art Theatre and had appeared in a couple of movies that made a splash, but this wasn't enough for her. When they met two years ago in their screenwriting and directing program, Ksenia told Maya that she'd enrolled so that she could make movies and star in them. She wasn't shy about saying this out loud. "I'm not getting any younger, you know?" She was thirty-two now, which, Maya supposed, wasn't that young for an actress. Maya was almost thirty-six herself but had no acting ambitions, thank god.

The fictional woman in question was Maya's own creation. She'd made the mistake of letting Ksenia read the script she'd written. Somehow, Ksenia had decided that she would be playing the female lead and was now expounding on her interpretation of the role.

"You know there's no producer attached yet," Maya said. She had to leave herself a way out. "Maybe it'll never get made."

Ksenia had already acted in two of Maya's student shorts. She was undeniably gifted, but Maya resented the assumption that Ksenia would be starring in all of her films from now on, just on the basis of their friendship. There were other talented actresses out there. She was going at it all wrong, too—the Stanislavsky way, when it was really an action role.

"What's that guy's name? Belov?" Ksenia asked, taking a tiny bite from a fig she'd plucked and shoving the rest into the mouth of her husband, who dutifully swallowed it down. "He expressed interest, right? I have a good feeling about this. I'm sure that, when we come back, you're going to get the call."

She was relentless. This was how she'd gotten to where she was. Ksenia came from a small town somewhere down south and was ashamed of her family, who were, according to her, simple people. This probably meant they were uneducated and worked menial jobs, maybe drank heavily. At seventeen, Ksenia came to Moscow and applied to GITIS, the legendary theater institute, to study acting. She got in after several tries, two years later, and in the meantime worked as a waitress, sleeping on the floor of a roach-infested room with three other girls. Maya had never had to go through anything even remotely like this. Born and raised in Moscow, she didn't have to conquer the capital. Her parents, though not rich by any means, had been able to buy her an apartment in the city center so that she wouldn't have to worry about rent.

To steer the conversation in another direction, Maya asked, "What did you guys think of Stasik's movie?"

Stasik was another one of their classmates. Last night, he'd sent them a link to his short film, but they hadn't had the chance to discuss it yet.

Ksenia snorted. "Garbage! Don't tell him I said so, though. Cat, you agree with me?"

Cat was her nickname for Dennis, who was stocky, round-faced, and balding. Maya thought it sounded obscene, for some reason. Maybe it was due to her own perverted imagination that this word coming out of Ksenia's mouth conjured Dennis on all fours, meowing.

Dennis raised his arms, took hold of the tree trunk behind his back, and shook it. A few figs plopped to the ground here and there. "The camera work wasn't bad."

Ksenia winced. "But everything else? The plot's ridiculous, I told him so when he first told me his idea for it. I thought he'd rewrite it, but no. And the acting—come on."

She did an impression of Stasik's lead actress learning that her boyfriend was injured in a freak accident involving a bottle of kefir, a pet ferret, and a dildo, dialing up her affectation a notch. Ksenia's eyes rolled into her skull and her mouth quivered; her hands clawed at her hair as if trying to tear it out. Maya and Dennis burst out laughing.

"I mean, what's the point of studying masterpieces of world cinema for two whole years if you then go and make something lame like that?" Ksenia summed up. Maya couldn't help but feel that Ksenia wasn't speaking only about Stasik and decided right then that she wouldn't be auditioning Ksenia for her movie if she managed to secure the funding.

Dennis got up, and they started walking toward the main house, talking about their last seminar, when they'd watched and analyzed Roy Andersson's *You, the Living*. Their class had divided nearly in half, with one group of people saying the movie was clearly a work of genius and the other claiming it was nothing more than a pretentious load of crap. Some strong opinions had been voiced ("rising tension between the banal and the essential"; "a cheap grotesque!"; "a series of tricks doesn't equal a singular vision"), after which they'd all gone out to their usual haunt, where over burgers and drinks they continued the discussion that eventually devolved into a physical fight. A thin, quiet guy—some of them called him Broomstick behind his back—slapped a beefy loud one across the face, and they ended up rolling on the floor, smashing plates and even a chair.

This only went to show how passionate they all were about making art that mattered—not just to them, but to the people they were making it for.

The past two years had been the best in Maya's life. During this time, she'd done nothing but talk about movies with some of the smartest and most talented people she'd ever encountered and create films of her own. For the longest time, she'd dreamed about this, but in a vague sort of way, never thinking that she would actually do anything to take this idea and turn it into reality. Then, at thirty-four, she'd abruptly quit her magazine job and handed over her savings to VKSR—the best graduate film program in the country—into which, to her own shock, she'd been accepted. Now, she had a whole different life and a whole different self. She was a film director! And, in an even more improbable twist, she was openly favored by her professors, who were certain she would go on to do great things. It was through their efforts that she'd ended up here, in the Italian town of Rimini at the estate of the distinguished writer and director Toni Morino, who was hosting emerging filmmakers from all over Europe for a week. During the day, the guests could do anything they pleased: wander his magnificent property, work in any of the common spaces, or swim in the Adriatic Sea. And in the evenings, they took part in long communal dinners over which Toni himself presided. Maya's heart felt close to bursting from the implausibility of it all. She caught herself suddenly giggling in the middle of conversations when she was supposed to nod her head gravely at whatever her interlocutor was saying and reply with something equally weighty about the nature of art or the human soul.

At moments like these, she sometimes heard her mother's voice say in her head, "The harder you laugh now, the harder you'll cry later." Maya's parents had repeated this throughout her childhood, but it hadn't occurred to her to question the logic of this maxim. The idea behind it was to make you live in a dull, lukewarm state that perfectly matched their colorless Soviet existence. And yet she'd internalized it to the point that her own happiness made her suspicious, leading her to expect some sort of retribution.

Maya was unclear on how Ksenia, who hadn't particularly impressed their professors, had managed not only to come here but also to bring along her cinematographer husband, who had no connection to their program other than being married to her. Though Ksenia did have a way of making people do things they hadn't planned on, which would undoubtedly come in handy for building an enviable career in the film industry. Maya herself had done a few things for her almost against her own intentions, like casting Ksenia in her student shorts and letting Ksenia's friend stay over at her apartment for nearly a month, free of charge. Maya had hated the woman, who casually raided her fridge and left dirty clothes everywhere. She surmised that when she was out, her guest slept in her bed instead of the couch designated for her.

Presently, Maya's phone rang. She signaled to Ksenia and Dennis to walk ahead without her, seeing that her best friend was calling.

"You're still in Italy?" Lena asked.

"Four more days."

"Your life is amazing! Don't you feel any shame?"

"Your life isn't too shabby either."

Lena's work as an editor at a women's magazine allowed her to travel the world, stay at the best hotels, and meet international celebrities, sometimes having meals with them. Maya had gotten a taste of this kind of life before she decided to study screenwriting and directing. "How's the new job?" she asked.

"I haven't made up my mind yet," Lena said. "I've only been here three weeks. But there's this guy I like . . . He's young, though."

"How young?"

"Twenty-three."

"Are you out of your mind?" Maya yelped, surprising herself and a bird that shot out of a tree, flapping its wings frantically. "He's a child! Stop this at once!"

She could tell Lena was taken aback by her reaction.

"What are you, my mom?" she said. "I'll do what I want. It's not like I want to marry him! I'm thinking of a brief, casual relationship with no obligations. I bet he'll like that."

Maya didn't know why she felt so strongly about this. She tried to reason with Lena. "Didn't you tell me you read an article that said you shouldn't have these easy flings with guys who aren't a good match? Because you end up falling for them and getting your heart broken."

"I don't know if I believe that. Why would I fall for someone who's only eight years older than my son?"

Lena was a single mother of a fifteen-year-old who was actively rebelling against her, causing all kinds of trouble. She said after a pause, "Anyway, you're the last person I expected to get a lecture from."

"Why's that?"

"Well . . . you've never struck me as the moral compass type."

Trying to catch up with Ksenia and Dennis, who she could see had reached the main house already, Maya thought about what Lena had said. What could she have possibly meant? Did she have a specific incident in mind that had made her come to this conclusion? Could Maya have done something Lena considered ill-advised or distasteful? If so, why hadn't she said anything right then and there? Maya decided to raise this subject the next time they had a face-to-face conversation, but she still felt unsettled by Lena's statement.

At seven, everyone gathered around a long table composed of smaller tables pushed together in the garden. The air smelled stunningly of different flowers, which were growing everywhere and which Maya didn't know the names of. Bouquets adorned the table, set with vintage silverware and china. Golden sunlight was coming down through tree branches in slanted beams, making the setup look like a scene out of a Zeffirelli or Bertolucci movie. Maya felt an overpowering urge to fix what she was seeing on camera, to not let it go to waste. Had she been ruined by her training? Perhaps she'd lost the ability to simply admire beauty, to take pleasure in it without trying to use it in some way, forever.

Dennis had already pulled out his Pentax and was snapping away furiously, zooming in, out, letting out strained breaths. After taking a few shots of the table setting, he turned his attention to his wife, who had worn a white gauzy dress for this occasion. Ksenia was clearly aware that her smallish features and her thin, dark-blond hair barred her from entering the femme fatale territory, and she worked with what she had. First, she peered into the distance with the expression of a romantic heroine waiting for the return of her sweetheart from a long journey; then she looked at the camera and suddenly flashed a smile at someone who wasn't there, waving at them. Maya marveled at how naturally posing came to her friend. People who chose acting as their profession were definitely not normal. The norm was feeling self-conscious when being looked at, and that was why Maya would always be more comfortable behind the lens. Not that Dennis showed any inclination to take a picture of her.

Finally, everyone took their seats. There had to be more than twenty-five people in all: the great Toni Morino with his white-haired wife, who always wore an aggrieved expression and almost never said anything; a few older Italians who seemed to be their friends; plus a bunch of young filmmakers from different countries. The cook and the housekeeper started bringing out plates of sliced meats, cheeses, and vegetables, covering almost all available table space. There was already bread, olive oil, and plenty of wine. Maya looked forward to the languorous evening, knowing that the dinner would go on for hours, just like yesterday and the day before. Toni and his spouse would retire to their bedroom sometime around ten, but the younger crowd would break up into smaller groups and continue chatting over coffee and liqueurs until the wee hours. She tried a spoonful of creamy Squacquerone cheese and followed it with a sip of chilled white. Both tasted acutely of bliss, and she had to resist the impulse to fill up on just the antipasti. There would be five or six courses, so the best strategy was taking it easy. Next to her, Ksenia groaned, "God, how am I supposed to stay thin with all this food around?" She was constantly trying to lose weight. Grabbing a nearly translucent slice of prosciutto, she took the tiniest bite of it, then placed the rest on her husband's plate.

The general conversation, which had started as a lazy exchange of pleasantries, was gaining momentum. A French director—who looked eighteen but had to be older—declared with an air of defiance that he didn't just want to create films that were formally inventive or put people in a certain mood. As the world hurtled madly toward disaster, he said, he considered it unethical to spend all this money and effort on movies that didn't aim to create real change. Filmmakers, he added, shouldn't be mesmerized by their own uniqueness and try to express it in elaborate ways—they had a moral responsibility as the more discerning members of society. He cast his huge, glistening eyes around the table, as if challenging everyone else to contradict him.

Maya found herself nodding in agreement, even as she realized that his words couldn't possibly have any bearing on her own work. Suppose she decided to make a picture meant to stir people to action. How would she know what to say? She had no idea how to change the world. If she did, she'd likely be somewhere else right now. Also, she had no authority to tell people what to do.

A more pressing question that concerned her was whether she had any uniqueness to express, let alone be mesmerized by. She admired the bizarre imagination of Terry Gilliam and the brilliance of Giorgos Lanthimos, whose movies turned your brain upside down, as much as the next person. But no matter how hard she tried to come up with something equally weird and write a story that would astonish people, what emerged were mostly uncomplicated narratives about the mundane absurdities of life. Which was part of the reason she'd ultimately settled on a genre her classmates considered inferior.

Ksenia poked her in the side. "What's he saying?" Her tone was resentful.

Neither she nor Dennis spoke any languages but Russian. Maya spoke five. As a linguistics major at Moscow State, she'd become fluent in Spanish, French, and English, then in Swedish and Italian. Her first job, which she started in her junior year, had been a translator to entrepreneurs doing business with foreign companies. She'd made tons of money—or so it seemed at the time—but soon found herself working as a reporter, first at a daily newspaper and then at a women's biweekly, where she met Lena. Right now, Maya wondered for what must've been the fiftieth time why Ksenia had even come here if she didn't understand a word anyone said. Had she expected Maya to act as her personal interpreter?

Not bothering to conceal her irritation, Maya gave the gist of what the French guy had said to Ksenia. Let her see that people might not like having extra responsibilities dumped on them! Ksenia assumed everyone was there to serve her, and this really got on Maya's nerves sometimes, even as she was willing to make some concessions to her friend's fragile ego and narcissism.

Ksenia made a face. Maya didn't know if this had to do with what she'd said or with how she'd said it. Dennis, who'd leaned in closer to also be able to hear, commented, "He's probably not even out of school yet! Let's see what kind of movies he makes in five years. If he makes any, that is."

He snapped a photo of the Frenchman, who could be a leading actor, he was so attractive. His bright mouth was large and moist,

Maya noted, then caught herself. What was she doing looking at men nearly half her age?

A young woman from Serbia asked Toni what he thought about films being vehicles for lofty ideas. She also wanted to address problems like inequality and global warming in her work but didn't want to hit people on the head with her political agenda. Was it possible to make people think deeply about serious issues without seeming preachy?

The great master's face was tan and extremely wrinkled, no doubt from a lifetime of sun exposure, and his expression was hard to parse. He replied that movies could be vehicles for whatever one wanted to convey. His own preference, however, was to make films about the transient beauty of the world. "A lot of people seem to like them," he added with a chuckle. "What does that tell you?" On the other hand, as he was nearing the end of his journey (that was the word he used—"journey"), he'd become interested in the question of what makes a good life, he said. "For some of you, the answer to this question could be fighting the injustices you see around you."

With what Maya perceived as a playful twinkle in his eyes, Toni glanced around the table before suddenly fixing his gaze on her. "How's life in Russia nowadays?"

Startled, she froze. She knew what answer he was expecting. Every foreigner wanted to know why her country was becoming increasingly repressive and what she thought about it. They craved details—people thrown in jail after peaceful protests, journalists beaten, corrupt courts issuing unlawful decisions. But Maya didn't follow the news, and what she did know about the current state of affairs came to her in snippets from conversations with friends. She really wasn't the best person to answer Toni's question.

Hoping to strike a delicate balance between sounding polite and conveying that she wouldn't be offering an in-depth analysis, Maya finally mumbled that things weren't nearly as bad as they seemed. Life back home was pretty good. Moscow was amazing—fancy restaurants and public spaces kept opening up, cultural life was flourishing. This drew incredulous looks from the Frenchman, the Serbian woman, and a few others within earshot. Toni gave her one of his cryptic, magnanimous smiles.

"What happened?" Ksenia whispered when he turned his attention to someone else.

Maya realized that she'd blundered. She should've come up with something better to say! She hadn't had time to think, though, caught completely off guard. To Ksenia, she whispered back, "I need to use the bathroom," and stood up.

Two hours later, when dessert had been served and eaten and the old couple had retreated after wishing everyone good night, Maya found herself being confronted by Dennis and Ksenia. "What did you and Toni talk about?" they pressed her, moving their chairs in on her.

They wouldn't leave her alone, she understood. These past few days, Ksenia had jumped at every chance to speak to Toni about herself, using other people as facilitators. There was a Bulgarian screenwriter who spoke some Russian, plus Toni's housekeeper was from the Russian-speaking part of Ukraine, and Ksenia availed herself of their services along with Maya's. It was clear she was feeling jealous now, being under the impression that the great master had asked Maya where she saw herself as a filmmaker or something like that.

"He wanted to know what life in Russia is like."

"And?"

"I told him everything's fine. That Moscow's great and getting better."

"What the hell?" Ksenia and Dennis both stared at her, aghast, as if she'd just sprouted legs out of her head. Maya asked herself why she hadn't come up with something better to say to them, too. She could've made something up.

"What did you expect me to say? I don't want to bad-mouth my country in front of all these people."

"You understand there's a difference between a country and its regime, I assume?" Ksenia inquired, cocking her head.

Maya felt heat rise to her face. Who gave Ksenia the right to use this patronizing tone? "And I assume you would've told everyone about the horrors of the regime. How brave of you that would've been! Because I never once heard you speak out against it—back in Russia, I mean."

"You're not being fair," Dennis said, coming to his wife's defense. "You know she'd stop getting work if she did."

Most films produced in Russia were state-funded and had to obtain distribution permits from the Ministry of Culture. That was why people who wanted to continue working in the movie industry kept their mouths shut. At least that was the general assumption, but it could also be that this situation was grossly exaggerated or that people were self-censoring out of mostly groundless fear. People back home did a lot of things preventively, always expecting the worst to happen.

"I have a position, even if I can't be vocal about it," Ksenia said. "You, on the other hand, seem to take no interest in what's going on. Like it doesn't even matter to you."

"That's right, it doesn't. I'm not wasting my life worrying about things I can't change, like whatever the government does."

Maya was having difficulty breathing. Why did they expect her to involve herself in politics? For one thing, to form a rational opinion and take a stand, you had to study political science, history, and who knew what else; otherwise, it felt baseless. She hated it when people believed themselves to be experts in areas where they had no expertise whatsoever. And she had no desire to become more knowledgeable about this particular subject. What for? Wasn't she already busy enough trying to build a career in a field that wasn't favorable to women? All her life, she'd conformed to other people's notions of what she should be doing. Now, for the first time, she was doing something she actually loved—and these people were judging her for it?

Ksenia slowly shook her head from side to side. "You could maybe afford not to care a couple of years ago, but not now. Not after Crimea. Not with the war in Donbas going on for three years and everything else."

Maya suddenly remembered something like an altercation she'd had with Lena when they were both working for a celebrity magazine and Lena was her direct supervisor, maybe six or seven years ago. Their editor-in-chief had gone to visit Ramzan Kadyrov in his estate in Chechnya, and someone had to write a report from that trip (said editor never bothered to do these things herself) about the wonderful stables Ramzan had built and the lavish dinner he'd thrown in her honor. Lena adamantly refused, so their deputy editor asked Maya to write the piece. She did.

"What was the problem?" she asked Lena afterward. "Why didn't you want to do it?"

"Are you serious?" Lena rounded her eyes. "Kadyrov is a world-class terrorist. He murdered thousands of people and continues to kill and torture."

"That can't be true. He's the head of Chechnya."

"Don't you understand anything?" Lena gave her a withering look, as if to say she couldn't believe her ignorance. "He's convenient to Putin. He's a devoted vassal and can do anything he pleases as long as he's loyal."

Maya was skeptical. She thought that people like Lena were suffering from a hypervigilant type of thinking, their picture of the world skewed. She said as much, and Lena replied, "Just read the news for twenty minutes a day, will you? From independent media outlets, not state-controlled ones." And Maya did it for a few days but became convinced that these alternative reporters were laying it on thick on purpose.

Ksenia wasn't done yet. "You're supposed to be an intellectual—you're a film director," she said. "An intellectual cannot be apolitical."

"Not true," Maya said. "Look at Toni. All his life, he made movies about love and death and grief and friendship. The eternal things. He keeps clear of politics. Is he not an intellectual?"

Ksenia didn't have an immediate comeback to this, so Maya left her and Dennis to join a cluster of people at the other end of the table. The dinner crowd had broken up into groups of three or four and spread out, with some folks still sitting in their chairs and others standing under the trees or in the main alley next to a fountain, talking and laughing. The moon had come out, bathing everything in a ghostly silver light. Maya felt that the evening had been ruined and tried to distract herself by thinking about how beautiful all this would look on film—the garden, the dinner remains on the table, the guests, so different from each other and so unusual-looking. She asked a tall Swede for a cigarette. He lit it for her and watched her blow smoke. She wanted to give him a mysterious smile, but her lips were trembling and wouldn't cooperate.

The company she'd joined was discussing Japanese cinema. Since she didn't know anything about it apart from having watched a couple of Kurosawa's movies, she tried to listen and learn, but her mind kept drifting to her own work.

Until about ten years ago, film directing had been a male profession in Russia. Maya could name just three notable Soviet female directors. The most recognized among them was perhaps Kira Muratova, who had created her own film language that drew on human ugliness and cruelty. Her work wasn't universally understood; people called it absurdist, postmodern, and esoteric. But it had never been political. You wouldn't find an explicit message in Muratova's films even if you tried. *Ha!* Maya thought, continuing her mental dialogue with Ksenia. *What do you say to this?* She hoped to carve out a niche for herself as well. She just needed to resist the pressure from people who believed she had to fit their ideas of what a director should or shouldn't be.

CHAPTER 2

Two weeks later, waking up in her own bedroom, Maya reached for her phone and, among messages from her sister, an ex-coworker, and various businesses wanting to sell her their services, saw a text from Alex. Immediately, she was jolted into a state of high alert.

He'd texted, *I'm in Moscow. Meet you for breakfast?*

Maya got out of bed and, hiding behind the curtain, peered out onto the street. If he was ready to meet her for breakfast, he was likely somewhere near. He could be watching her windows right now. But she could see no one who looked remotely like Alex. The ten-lane Novoslobodskaya Street wasn't busy, this being a Saturday. The traffic was light, cars driving by languidly, while the pedestrians presented a picture of a lazy weekend in town—a young family with a stroller, an old lady with a bag on wheels, a group of teenagers, and two young women tottering in their high heels. But Maya's stomach lurched uncomfortably.

Where are you? she texted back.

The reply came so quickly it felt prewritten.

Not far. Kofepot in twenty minutes?

Maya swore and headed to the bathroom to get ready.

She and Alex went back a long way. They dated for a few months when they were both eighteen. She fell in love with him—or at least in what seemed like love at the time—and then one day he vanished without an explanation. When she got over him, he reappeared, expecting everything to be like before. He'd had to sort some things out, he said. It turned out that his Armenian parents had arranged a marriage for him years ago, when he was barely out of diapers, and this hadn't been a problem until he met Maya. When he realized he wanted to spend the rest of his life with her, he had to tell his fiancée, as well as two sets of parents, that the deal was off. Some horrible scenes followed: his mother even threatened suicide. But ultimately the business was taken care of, and now he and Maya were free to have a committed relationship.

Why he hadn't thought to clarify this to her before going off the radar for two months, she couldn't understand. She would have waited for him, no doubt. But after his abrupt absence, she had already moved on. Her feelings for him had petered out, and she was dating a guy from school, which she related to Alex in no uncertain terms. He flew into a rage, becoming loud and aggressive, nearly hitting her, demanding that she drop the other guy and start dating him again. Frightened to tears, Maya told him to never contact her.

The next day, Alex sent his apologies on a postcard attached to a bunch of roses. He continued to call her despite Maya repeatedly telling him that they would never be together again. She even had to ask her dad to talk to him, but still, Alex wouldn't quit. He started turning up in unexpected places, like parties he hadn't been invited to and parts of town she ventured into by chance, which meant he was following her. Even though he did nothing to harm her, Maya got more and more apprehensive, becoming convinced that Alex was disturbed, perhaps not completely sane. When she moved out of her parents' apartment, he quickly found out her new address and "bumped" into her as she was leaving her building. Then he "accidentally" found himself standing in line behind her at the supermarket, feigning surprise and making small talk. This went on for years.

When Maya moved in with her much older boyfriend, Alex accepted a job in Sweden. She thought she was free from him at last, that he'd finally lost hope, but his stalking of her only grew more creative. Perhaps it had nothing to do with hope now and was more like a perverse habit he had no intention of shaking off. She went on a press tour once with a group of journalists to a remote village in France. Except for her editor, not a living soul knew exactly where she was going, but Alex showed up at her hotel one morning, an unusually shaped leather case in his hands. It contained a trumpet, she learned. For the life of her, she couldn't figure out what that meant until it dawned on her that, in one of their previous conversations, she'd mentioned half jokingly that she was thinking about learning to play the instrument.

He sent her other presents, including concert tickets and extravagant bouquets, and to casual observers like her colleagues at the various magazines where she worked, his behavior seemed romantic. To her, it appeared creepy and menacing. Lena was the only person who agreed with her. "Why don't you put an end to this whole thing?" she kept asking. "Just stop answering his texts." But this wouldn't work, Maya knew, and going to the police would make no difference either. Law enforcement authorities famously told people to contact them only when they had something serious to report. To investigate a seemingly upstanding guy showering a woman with gifts—on the basis of what? The fact that he gave her the creeps? They'd laugh in her face. Maya felt safer pretending to be friends with Alex and keeping him close. This way, she reasoned, he was unlikely to try anything funny.

When she arrived at Kofepot, Alex was already there. Every time Maya saw him, he looked more and more European—broad smile, smart clothes, uninhibited gestures—and she wondered if she was reading too much into what she had always thought of as his unhealthy fixation on her. Could it be that he truly believed they were old friends now? They ordered coffee, and Maya asked him if he had any particular business in Moscow.

"Yeah, I'm on a business trip. We have a new Russian client, a big one, so I'll be coming here more often."

She wasn't overjoyed to hear this, naturally. Also, she couldn't remember exactly what line of business Alex was in, but asking him about that seemed gauche. He'd probably told her a million times.

"So, what's up with you?" he said. "How was Rimini?"

Maya nearly jumped. That feeling again, her insides churning. How the hell did he know? Was is possible that he'd tracked her down again?

But he was looking at her with innocent curiosity. Oh, right, she'd posted about being at Toni's house on Instagram.

"It was great. Honestly, these past two years were awesome. I'm a little sad the program's over."

"What are your plans now?"

Maya hesitated. Should she tell him? There was likely no harm in letting him know she was about to shoot her first feature. The internet would know about it pretty soon anyway.

So she gave him the story.

After her return from Italy, Maya received a text from producer Belov's assistant, saying that he liked her screenplay and wanted to see her. Maya whooped when she read it. He wasn't a household name—in fact, she'd never heard of him until one of her teachers mentioned that Belov owned a small production company that made medium-budget films, most of which were well-liked by critics, viewers, or sometimes both. Also, he wasn't an asshole, reportedly, which was rare in this business.

Maya didn't tell Alex, but she had spent more than an hour agonizing over what to wear, fishing things out of her closet, trying them on, and then taking them off. On the one hand, she felt the need to appear professional. But what did this mean? Most filmmakers she knew wore ratty sweatshirts or cardigans. On the other, she wanted to play up her femininity and the fact that she looked younger than her age—in her experience, this always made things go more smoothly. Men in positions of power weren't comfortable around women over thirty-five, struggling to see them as full human beings. Maya sometimes discussed this with Lena, who would fume and say things like "It's not going to get better, because these same men are running the country!" Lena often brought up the recent law decriminalizing domestic violence, which made it clear that, in the eyes of the lawmakers, women of all ages didn't deserve consideration. For her part, Maya had to figure out how to navigate the film industry, where middle-aged men occupied all the gatekeeping positions. If this meant she had to wear a clingy sweater and laugh in a silly way, fine. As long as they didn't ask for more.

Belov had an office in a handsome mansion off Chistoprudny Boulevard. His assistant, a twenty-something woman with a distracted air about her, glanced at Maya briefly and motioned for her to go through the door to her left.

Sitting behind an Ikea desk, Belov squinted against the light pouring through the window. Maya immediately liked his intelligent face and his overall appearance. He looked like he was into a healthy lifestyle rather than the drunken get-togethers that were standard in the industry, where connections meant everything. The common wisdom was that there was no better way to bond than to drink until you couldn't make sense and could barely move. Maya had been anxious about this for a while, since she wasn't a big drinker and couldn't stand talking to wasted people.

On Belov's desk, three iPhones were arranged in a neat row. One of them buzzed and started to travel sideways; he tapped it into stillness.

"So," he said after Maya had settled into the chair across from him. "Tell me about yourself. Your email said you're just graduating from VKSR."

In a few sentences she'd prepared beforehand, Maya told him about her background in linguistics and journalism and how she'd always dreamed of directing movies but had been too afraid to seriously consider filmmaking as a career—until she wasn't.

"What was so scary about it?"

"I guess the idea of competing with the greats. I mean, how sure of yourself do you have to be to think you've got something to say that Kubrick and Scorsese haven't already said?"

"And what made you change your mind?"

She shrugged. "I just woke up one day, opened VKSR's website, and filled out the application. I thought, let's see what happens."

It was true—she had no idea why she'd done that. But this was the dumbest, most uninspired answer, evidence of her having no originality whatsoever. She should've prepared a better one! Yet Belov, seemingly satisfied, went on to discuss her two student shorts, which he'd watched and found funny and strange. Then he brought up the draft she'd sent him.

To her own surprise, Maya had written a horror film. In her screenplay, the medics responsible for keeping Lenin's mummy in a stable condition come up with a revolutionary elixir. When applied to a living human, it turns out to have extraordinary rejuvenating and beautifying properties. But then those who use it metamorphose into murderous ghouls, and Lenin comes back to life as a monster intent on seizing control of Moscow. Two main characters—a disillusioned female doctor and a slacker guy she initially dislikes—become reluctant allies as they try to survive the ensuing chaos and combat the horde of creatures led by the monster.

"This is just great," Belov said. "It's an art-house horror, and how many of these are out there? I don't remember seeing any in the last few years. Also, it's funny and will be directed by a woman. The critics will go wild over this, I'm sure."

Maya struggled to keep her composure. She couldn't believe what she'd just heard. Her classmates had ridiculed the script, which was too lowbrow for their taste, and said she had to do better if she hoped to sign with a respectable producer. Like them, she was drawn to serious, high-stakes dramas that explored the complexities of the human condition; she'd made many attempts to write a screenplay in that vein. What she saw on the page, however, always felt disappointing. Was it possible that her mostly happy childhood and relatively uneventful life had made her unfit to write the kinds of stories she admired? Then, suddenly, the idea about the mummy occurred to her and seemed so much fun that she wrote the entire script in a week, chuckling to herself along the way.

Belov continued to talk. He thought Maya's characters were fully realized and had believable motivations. He also liked that suspense would be built mostly through storytelling, without relying too much on special effects, and that the movie therefore wouldn't be too expensive to produce.

"You know how many scripts I get that require building a humongous set from scratch?" he said. "The story takes place either two hundred years ago or in outer space. I mean, if you want to make your first movie, why are you willfully lowering your chances?"

Maya felt relief wash over her when Belov admitted he loved the script as it was. She had dreaded the possibility that—even if he liked the idea—he would ask her to rewrite the screenplay, perhaps multiple times, as most producers did. They talked a bit about casting, which they both agreed was crucial. There was nothing worse than actors being inauthentic in horror films, overplaying emotions and thereby cheapening everything. They touched on postproduction elements—color, sound, and graphics. Naturally, Maya wanted the film to be visually ambitious, though she was open to using low-cost techniques like unsettling camera angles. One thing they couldn't cut corners on, she said, was the zombie makeup. It had to be realistic, and would likely require some investment.

"Sure, sure," Belov mumbled, adding that he saw major festival potential in the project.

"Do you think we can get permits to film in the city center?" Maya asked. "This is a story about Moscow as much as anything else."

Belov said it wouldn't be a problem since he knew just the right person in the administration. Then he pressed his hands together.

"I think I'm ready to offer you a contract. How about we start shooting late August, early September? We can do the whole thing in five to six weeks. Otherwise we'd have to postpone until spring, and I don't see why we would want to do that."

Maya hadn't thought this was possible—landing a contract on her first try, especially after everything she'd heard from her peers, the very people who were supposed to be cheering her on. She felt like jumping for joy but had to remain professional.

"Sounds good," she replied with as much dignity as she could muster.

"This is huge!" Alex said when she recounted all this to him. "Unbelievable! Congrats! I'm so happy for you!" He bumped his coffee mug against hers.

Right away, he peppered her with businesslike questions about the production budget and such. Maya told him that Belov had offered her three million rubles for the shooting alone, with plans to discuss postproduction and marketing funds after filming wrapped up.

Three million was a decent amount, but it still meant Maya would have to scrimp and ask everyone to lower their usual fees. She would need to cut her own wages (she'd already set a laughably small weekly rate for herself) and find a way to do the same with equipment rental. This was the reality most directors who weren't superstars faced: endless compromise.

Stroking his shiny black beard, Alex said, "I have some cash lying around, you know. I can invest a little in your film. Pay for the catering, say."

Maya contemplated his suggestion. This wasn't uncommon—receiving additional funds from friends or anyone willing to contribute to a good cause. It appeared that he wanted to be involved in the production not for her sake but for his own, hoping to have a good time. Fine, she wasn't against it. The more normal their relationship became, the better, she thought.

"Thank you. That would be wonderful."

"Did I tell you I write music?" Alex beamed at her proudly. "I don't mean to brag, but I'm not bad. I can do the soundtrack, and it would be free of charge. If you don't like it, that would be fine, too. I'll send you some demos so you can think this over."

Maya was pleasantly surprised by these developments. She'd heard of this phenomenon: when you started a project people believed in, everyone began to coalesce around it, offering their services and asking nothing in return. It was as if creative work generated positive energy, inspiring generosity. Or maybe being part of something new and exciting was gratifying in itself.

"What's that?" Alex suddenly said in a tone that made Maya flinch.

He was peering at the inside of her arm, where several dark bruises were visible. She'd become so stoked talking about her news that she had pulled up the sleeves of her sweater without even realizing it.

Maya knew she had to tell him this was none of his business, but it was as if the words had gotten stuck inside her. After a few tense moments, during which he glowered at her, she said, "Oh, this? I was moving my furniture around."

He seemed unconvinced. What did he think those were, hickeys? This was such a gross violation of boundaries, asking her about her body in this way. She wanted to splash her leftover coffee in Alex's face and enjoy his expression afterward, but she did no such thing, saying instead that she had to go.

"I thought we'd spend the day together," he said. "It's Saturday."

Coldly, Maya replied, "I have stuff to do. I don't have days off anymore, now that I have a movie to make."

"Can I tag along?"

He was getting bolder, perhaps because she'd agreed to take money from him. But she could change her mind anytime.

"I'm going to the bathroom," she said. "Don't wait. I'll text you when I have details."

Scrolling through her Instagram feed, Maya lingered in the bathroom for a few minutes. Then, as she left the café, she paused by the entrance, pretending to decide which direction to go, but really scanning the area for Alex. Given that he had nothing better to do, he might try to follow her. She figured it would be smart to take the metro, where it was easier to disappear into the crowd. But as she descended the escalator and waited on the platform, she kept furtively looking around, her heart jumping every time she saw someone resembling him. He had a rather generic appearance: medium height, black hair, jeans, and a dark blue jacket. If she didn't want to lose her mind, she had to stop.

Maya had lied to Alex—today was going to be all fun, no work. First, she was meeting Lena for lunch, then a graduation party was scheduled for six in the evening. She would start working tomorrow. At home, two Moleskines waited for her, filled with notes she'd taken while watching the classics of the horror genre, along with some obscure but interesting slashers. Systematizing her scribbles and sifting through them for ideas would be no easy task.

Since they hadn't seen each other in a week and Maya wanted to announce her news in person, Lena didn't know anything yet. When the waiter had taken their order and retreated, Maya said in a faux-casual tone, "So, I signed with Belov. I'm starting to shoot at the end of summer."

"Oh my god!" Lena cried out. "Let's celebrate! Champagne!"

After they toasted to Maya's imminent success and she'd recounted her meeting with Belov, Lena asked, "Are you sure about him, though? Don't you want to hear what other producers might say? What if you land a deal with a big name, like Rodnyansky?"

Maya had already considered this and come to the conclusion that she didn't want to risk it. "A bird in the hand is worth two in the bush."

"Maybe you're right. I'm so happy for you! You're going after your dream. Do it for the both of us!"

Lena had a dream of her own—to be a fiction writer. She'd actually published a book some years ago but didn't have time to write anymore. She had to support two people on her own, since her son's father didn't think it necessary to either pay child support or be a part of his life in any other way.

"Did I tell you about the interview I did with Khlopovsky a few weeks ago?"

Khlopovsky was easily the most famous living Russian director. He'd successfully worked in Hollywood and was treated as an auteur even though he sometimes made high-grossing commercial movies. He was now in his late seventies and married for the eighth time.

"We spoke for an hour, and he seemed to like me," Lena said. "Afterward, he wanted to know more about me, so I told him I published a novel once and would devote my life to writing full-time if I could. And you know what he said?"

"What?"

"He looked me in the eye and went, 'Honey, why the hell are you wasting your life on this stupid shit?'"

"'Stupid shit' meaning doing celebrity interviews?"

"Yeah. Easy for him to say!" Lena said, suddenly seething with resentment. "His father wrote the Soviet anthem and sold millions of books, there's all this money and power in the family. I'm sure none of them know what it's like when you have a hungry child and no money until your next paycheck."

Maya felt bad for Lena. Literature famously paid very little; an average author's advance for a published book equaled anywhere from two to four restaurant dinners. But before she could offer any sympathy, Lena said, "I have my own piece of news to share."

"Do tell!"

"I had sex with Misha." Lena gave Maya a defiant look, as if she expected to be given a hard time and was prepared to defend herself. "I had him over at my house the other day."

"The baby, you mean?"

"He's so not a baby! He's two meters tall and a fully functioning adult. He has a day job and side gigs and rents a room. His parents live far away, so he's alone in the city."

"Not anymore, though. How was the sex?"

"Amazing!" Lena's expression became dreamy. "He smells like milk, and I mean *everywhere*."

Then she realized what she'd just said and put her hand over her mouth. They both burst out laughing.

"Gross!" Maya squealed. "Baby!"

"He's coming over again tonight."

"What does Ilya think about this? Have they met?" Ilya was Lena's son.

"Of course. He's totally cool about it."

In a couple of hours, after completing her ten thousand steps around Tverskoy district, Maya headed to the graduation party, which was actually a second one. The first had been a stuffy affair where everyone crowded around tables loaded with vodka and cured meats while their teachers reminisced about the past. It hadn't satisfied Maya's classmates; they felt it hadn't been celebratory enough. They wanted to show off their partners and have a blast gossiping and making general fools of themselves, so they rented a restaurant for tonight.

The place was nearly full when she arrived. Tables were packed with people she already knew and those she was seeing for the first time. There was Agatha, with her shock of red curls (the volume of her hair was staggering—it was the size of a heavy-duty washing machine) and her filthy rich husband. The husband wore a disgusted expression as he eyed the plates of food in front of him, perhaps wondering how he was supposed to ingest these low-class provisions, while Agatha kept getting up from her seat—to let people better appreciate her model-like body and her expensive outfit, Maya suspected. There was Stasik, whose latest short film Ksenia had found silly and lame, sitting beside a sour, big-nosed woman who had to be his wife. Dato, their classmate from Chechnya who exoticized the place in his student shorts, mining it for every last dreg of beauty and strangeness, had brought to this fête a man who looked almost exactly like him. Maya had conjectured that Dato was gay, but, to the best of her knowledge, he'd never come out to any of them.

"Hey, come sit with us!" Ksenia shouted, pointing to a seat directly across from her.

Maya took it, and then an extremely tall young person plopped down into the empty chair next to her. He looked fifteen or so, and Maya assumed he was someone's son.

"I'm Mark,'" he said and shoved his hand at her. His hair was long and wild, his eyes huge.

These bohemian kids were totally unselfconscious and treated adults as their equals. Which was fine, but Maya could never be like that, what with her Soviet upbringing. She couldn't bring herself to use the informal "you" when she addressed someone conspicuously older than herself, and most of those people resented her for drawing attention to their age in this way.

From across the table, Dennis remarked, "Mark's my partner," and Maya was momentarily confused as to what this might mean.

"We always work together," he clarified. "He's a cameraman, too."

Maya took a surreptitious look at Mark. Was she losing her eyesight? He still looked fifteen to her. Okay, maybe seventeen, if she squinted. Meanwhile, he poured her a glass of wine with a self-assured gesture of someone significantly older and touched his glass to hers. At least he wasn't drinking hard liquors. She had an impulse to tell him to eat some protein first.

In a few minutes, they struck up a conversation about the Dardenne brothers' hyperrealism.

"I'm not against their style," Mark said. "As a viewer, I get it. It's almost documentalistic, like they're shooting with a handheld camera. This makes everything more immediate, and you can't help believing what you see."

"It's like you're there with the characters."

"Exactly. But professionally, it doesn't appeal to me."

"Why not?"

"Because that's what I did in high school with my phone, you know? I want to create a more sophisticated, maybe even stylized picture. I'm interested in all kinds of unusual lighting techniques."

"Like what?"

"Like moving the colors into the cooler spectrum. Have you seen *Drive* with Ryan Gosling? When the camera is on him, the colors are cool, and when it's on his girlfriend, they are warm. It's really obvious when you know it. Or like in *The Godfather*, when you light actors from above so that the viewer can't see their eyes."

Maya studied Mark's face for a long moment. "What have you worked on? Anything I might've seen?"

"I did a small independent feature and two series. *Sparta* and *Exes*."

"Those are big! That's really impressive."

A bit later, Maya went to use the restroom. When she got out of the stall, there was Ksenia at the sink, fixing her lipstick.

"How did you like Mark?" she inquired.

"He's all right. Why do you ask?"

"If you ever want Dennis as your cameraman, he'll want Mark to be his first assistant."

Ksenia seemed to be certain that Maya would be hiring Dennis as her cinematographer.

"Then it won't matter if I like him or not. I'll need to know how good he is."

"He's still in school, but he's incredible. You'll see."

"How old is he, though? Over eighteen, I hope?"

"He's twenty-one. But I have to warn you—be careful."

"What do you mean?"

"He's married and has a daughter."

"What? At twenty-one?"

"He's technically twenty. His birthday is next month. And she's like three months old."

Maya shook her head. Lena had had her son at twenty, but that had been a long time ago. Nowadays people knew better than to have children so early—or so she thought. "How old is the wife?"

"Twenty, I think."

"You've met her?"

"Sure. The daughter is cute."

"Why should I be careful, though?" Maya asked, puzzled, as they were leaving the bathroom.

"He's somewhat of a womanizer." Ksenia grinned.

Maya had to roll her eyes. "This conversation is too absurd to continue."

Back at the table, Mark was devouring a steak. "So, what kind of movies do you want to make?" he asked.

"Original," Maya said. "Award winning."

He stopped chewing and blinked at her, his mouth open halfway.

"Kidding," she said. "I mean, I wouldn't mind critical acclaim and all that . . . You caught me off guard. I guess I want to make devastating intimate dramas."

"Is that what your screenplay is? The one you're sending out?"

He seemed to know a lot about her. "Well, no. It's a . . . horror movie."

Mark regarded her for a second, then his face broke into a wide grin. "Wow! I mean, wow! Are you serious now?"

They didn't get a chance to continue the conversation because someone began tapping a glass with a knife. It was Agatha, who announced, "Let's all share our professional news. It's okay if you have none! But every bit of news counts, even if it seems small. We're here to support each other."

Somehow it was obvious that she wanted to brag about the news that she had. Maya saw Ksenia pinch her mouth.

Dato was the first to go. He'd been approached to shoot a music video, he said, and he'd also secured funding for another short about

Chechnya. Everyone cheered. Stasik reported that he'd landed a gig in a writing room for a sitcom. Another guy, Vova, in what appeared to be a reluctant announcement, shared that he'd been hired as the first AD on the next Fyodor Bondarchuk blockbuster, the details of which he couldn't reveal as he'd signed an NDA. This was huge, and the crowd whooped. Then Agatha, visibly annoyed at having been upstaged, came out with the disclosure that she was doing her own feature with a ten-million budget.

"Who's producing?" Dato asked.

"I am," Agatha said.

They didn't have to ask where the money was coming from. Her husband sat next to her, looking pleased.

"You need an AD?" Dato said.

"I do. Hit me up tomorrow, we'll talk."

After a pause, during which several people declined to say anything because they had nothing to report, Ksenia told the group that she was meeting a few interested producers next week to talk about her screenplay. Maya knew that Ksenia was meeting no one because the script she'd been working on wasn't even finished. Then it was her own turn to share, so she told everyone about her meeting with Belov, adding that she was scheduled to start shooting in August or September.

This was exactly what each of them dreamed of—directing their own feature-length film, backed not by a wealthy spouse or a benevolent uncle but by industry professionals who had placed their trust in you, deeming you worthy of it. Maya's classmates went wild, jumping up from their seats, clinking glasses, toasting her, and shouting congratulations. Ksenia was the only one whose mood visibly darkened after this piece of news. Shortly thereafter, she left together with Dennis, citing a massive headache.

Mark stayed and, when Maya began to collect her things, asked her, "Where do you live? Are you getting a cab?"

"No, my place is a short walk from here."

"I'll walk with you. It's too late for you to be outside alone."

Maya chuckled. It was all she could do not to ask him if his parents were okay with him being outside at this hour, then remembered he was a parent himself.

They strolled down Tsvetnoy Boulevard, which was quite busy at midnight. People congregated around benches under the trees, drinking, laughing, and listening to music. Couples walked hand in hand, their dogs running around unleashed. Bikers and skaters maneuvered around pedestrians, while some policemen were scattered here and there. Suddenly, Maya's heart raced as she spotted Alex in the crowd. She inhaled sharply and peered ahead to confirm it was him, but he was gone.

Mark didn't notice anything. He was telling her about his studies at the GITR Film and Television School. A few of his teachers were good, he said, but mostly he felt he was wasting his time. He was learning more at the various jobs he worked and was thinking of dropping out. Also, because he was studying part-time—he had to support his family, after all—he didn't have a deferment from the army. So now he had to bribe the officers at his local draft board.

Still trying to catch her breath, Maya asked, "Don't you get an automatic deferment because of your baby?"

"No, it's only when your kid's disabled."

"Jeez. And how much is the bribe?"

"About four thousand bucks."

"What do you get for that?"

"Supposedly a permanent document that says I'm unfit for service."

"Maybe it's a good deal, then."

"I could go to Europe on this money and stay there three months if I'm frugal. Maybe even four."

They began coming up with different ways to stretch the sum in Europe. Then Maya told him about her time at Toni Morino's house and how amazing it had been. "I don't think anything like that will ever happen to me again."

He snorted. "I'm sure even better things will happen to you. You'll become famous, and people will be all over you. An oligarch will fall for you and set you up in a mansion in the south of France, where you'll drink wine and write. A bunch of writers and filmmakers will come and stay with you—who doesn't love free shit, right?—and you'll have these great conversations and come up with tons of ideas."

Maya laughed at this vision of her future, which she kind of liked, if she had to be totally honest. "Somehow I doubt that an oligarch will fall for me."

"Why the hell not? Look at Anna Morozova and Vera Saakayan. They hooked up with these moneybags, and they're not even good-looking. You are, though."

The vibe she was getting from Mark was definitely flirtatious. He kept touching her from time to time, ostensibly to steer her away from drunk people and hazardous curbs, and it wasn't unpleasant. In fact, she was attracted to him, she realized, but since he was married, nothing could happen between them.

When they got to her building, she asked if he would be okay getting home.

"What if I say no? Will you invite me over, then?"

"Haha. Have a good night!"

He planted a kiss on her cheek and left.

At home, Maya fell on her bed, too tired to undress or take off her makeup. She really had to stop doing this—after thirty-five, your skin didn't forgive you for negligence. One last time, she promised herself, pulling a throw over her legs. She closed her eyes, expecting to fall asleep at once, but didn't. She was too excited, blood thrumming in her body. Was she really on the cusp of starting an amazing career? In her head, bits of future reviews appeared: "tremendously accomplished, stunning debut," "burst onto the scene," "announced as a major new talent." Maya imagined herself wearing beautiful dresses, arriving at the red carpet of international festivals, flashes going off, crowds cheering. Then she was shooting her second movie, then her third. She was invited to work in Europe, making a film in Italian, then in French. And what about Hollywood? That was too much, perhaps. She met with her idols—Pedro Almodóvar, Gaspar Noé, Aki Kaurismäki—who were dazzled with her. As her consciousness flickered, dissolving into a dream sequence, Maya saw herself swimming in a pool with a view of Tuscan countryside—could this be the famous Khlopovsky villa?—the great Europeans circling her silently, Almodóvar in a crimson one-piece. Even in her dream, Maya was ashamed of being such a sucker for validation.

And then she was ripped from the fantasy space by a piercing sound. Her eyes wide open, she instantly felt as alert as if she hadn't been sleeping at all. Had someone just rung her doorbell? It was used so rarely she didn't remember the sound it made. Yet it couldn't have been anything else.

Maya was lying in bed, thinking about how unlikely it was that anyone would want to visit her unannounced in the middle of the night, when it rang again. It was her doorbell, and it resonated through the whole apartment. As it continued, she told herself she had to get up and look through the peephole. It was important to find out who was doing this, to make sure it was just some rando who'd had too much to drink and mistaken her apartment for someone else's. She willed herself to move but found that she couldn't, suddenly so sick with fear now that her body wouldn't obey her. Not even a finger would move. This was what people meant when they said that terror paralyzed you.

There was a pause in the ringing, and then it started again. Maya continued to lie stiffly, her skin perspiring. She watched the long shadows on the wall in front of her, cast by the bedside lamp she hadn't turned off for the night. They seemed to stretch longer and creep sideways, as if growing feelers. Her heart beat so loudly that it almost drowned out the ringing.

This was good, Maya desperately thought. Maybe she could use this in her movie.

CHAPTER 3

"Why aren't you eating?"

Even in Maya's earliest memories, her mother's face was always anxious and sad, but today, it looked more so. It seemed that, with age, people either became wiser and happier (as evidenced by Toni Morino) or grumpier and more suspicious of life and people in general (a much more frequent occurrence, at least in their latitudes). Her mother definitely fell into the latter category.

"I'm not hungry."

Maya couldn't bring herself to say that the food was too heavy. She'd spent her childhood eating this kind of stuff—beet salad with walnuts and mayonnaise, pork with fried onions, mashed potatoes with lots of butter—but now her stomach refused to cooperate when she did, and afterward she felt sluggish and achy for hours.

"Mom, she's too refined for your cuisine now," Polina said. "Haven't you noticed? It's all chicken breast and green salad for her."

Maya's sister could be counted on to say the most abrasive thing in any given situation. She'd always been disagreeable, but lately her disposition had worsened, likely due to the fact that she'd spent most of her adult life with a man who claimed he wasn't ready for a family, then left her for another woman and married. At forty-two, her chances of meeting another man were slim, considering her personality. Not that she wanted to meet anyone, it seemed. She went to her accountant job, came home, and watched TV together with Nini, her old chihuahua. Nini was the love of her life now.

"I'll have another helping!" their father announced cheerfully. "The food is so good, dear." He smiled at their mother.

Maya felt guilty. "Maybe I'll have something later. I had a big breakfast."

Her mother looked at her as if to say, *You knew you were coming for lunch.*

"Anyway, what's new with you?" their dad asked, the question directed at both of his daughters, presumably.

"Nini is too old to eat normal dog food now," Polina said. "Even the canned stuff. I have to buy special liquid meals for her, which are expensive."

"Oh my," their mother said. No one seemed to want to discuss this further.

"I have news," Maya volunteered. "I've signed a contract with a producer and will be shooting my first movie this fall."

For a second, everyone appeared stricken. Then Polina said, "Wow, cool! We have to drink to that!"

Normally, their parents didn't drink. Their mother said, apologetic, "I don't think we have anything."

"We can toast with lemonade, it's fine," Polina said, grabbing the bottle from the table and starting to pour.

After Maya divulged some details of the upcoming production, her mother said quietly, "So this means you won't be starting a family anytime soon."

It was their parents' ultimate dream to have grandchildren. They didn't much care if their daughters were productive members of society, if they accomplished great professional success or even just simple human happiness. What they wanted for them was to procreate, as if the absence of kids on Maya's and Polina's end somehow devalued their own efforts spent raising them. If their family line didn't continue, their parents' thinking probably went, there had been no point in their sacrifices and the hardships they'd overcome. Since they'd already given up on Polina in this respect, they kept pushing Maya into thinking about having children—the sooner, the better.

"To start a family, first you have to meet someone to start a family with," Maya mused darkly.

"Good luck with that," Polina said. "Your last train left a while ago."

The woman Polina's ex had left her for was twenty-five and had big boobs.

Maya couldn't blame her sister for being so jaded, not really. Her own love life to date had been just as pathetic as Polina's, if not more so. She'd spent a whole decade with a man twenty years her senior, being loyal to him, cooking him daily meals, being friends with his friends, and partaking in his stupid hobbies, like fishing and collecting unusual rocks. He was a supremely dull man who hadn't been all that nice to her, and she wasn't even sure she'd ever been in love with him. Could she have been so scared of life that she'd preferred staying with him just for the sake of being in a stable relationship that she knew wouldn't bring her any surprises, unpleasant or otherwise? And here she was now, fancying herself capable of saying something new and provocative to the world.

"What will your movie be about?" her dad asked, genuinely curious, as far as Maya could tell. She hesitated, unsure if she should keep going. Maybe it was better to switch the topic to something lighter, less charged with everyone's old grudges and unmet expectations.

To her family, Maya's decision to quit work and study directing—at midlife, no less—seemed utterly incomprehensible. They were practical, down-to-earth folks who saw artistic endeavors as frivolous and only suited to those with independent wealth and no obligations. Her parents had done their best to teach their daughters the merits of a secure, respectable job that let one steadily increase one's income and social standing. No number of symphonies, paintings, novels, or films—each offering solace and meaning—could convince them that the people who created such works deserved respect, perhaps even more than engineers, lawyers, or doctors. After many attempts to justify her choice, Maya had come to believe that there was no way to explain the necessity of art to people who didn't experience it as a necessity.

It was because of her parents' contempt for creative pursuits that they hadn't enrolled her in any extracurriculars as a kid, even though she'd begged them to let her try dancing, painting, or playing an instrument. They hadn't seen any value in that, hence Maya's childhood, which she remembered as filled with sticky nothingness—until that one lucky day when, around the age of ten, she discovered a way to escape. Her parents had several shelves full of books—in their milieu, these signaled a certain measure of success, much like a furniture set from Czechoslovakia did. She'd opened many of these volumes before, out of sheer desperation, but the sentences had been too dense for her to extract any meaning. This time, however, Maya found herself engrossed in the adventures of a man on a desert island, comprehending maybe sixty percent of what was written. But even that seemed like a miracle, and the more she read, the more she understood. After she'd finished every last tome on the shelves, she joined a local library, then moved on to a larger, more central branch, where they also screened rare films.

In all those years, she'd never seen her parents pick up a book.

How would she even begin to explain that she was making a horror movie? Their understanding of the genre likely didn't go beyond cheap jump scares and gore. On her way over, Maya had debated how to present her project and decided to describe it as a psychological thriller with a touch of mythology—true, in a way.

This was what she tried to convey now. As she spoke, she became aware of blank facial expressions all around, signaling that her words weren't being appreciated. Perhaps if she'd written something historical—like a script about WWII that focused on great human suffering and extraordinary, larger-than-life personalities—they would have been more impressed. The terrible thing was that she could totally see how, from their perspective, her story seemed to hold little value. Her parents were from another generation. Culturally, it was like they'd come from a place both isolated and stuck in time. Speaking with decreasing conviction, Maya eventually fell silent, her last sentence trailing off.

There was something resembling pity in her father's eyes when he said, "You think people will be interested in seeing this film?"

The conversation had to be steered away from her movie, quickly, to a topic they could all enjoy talking about. Nothing good could possibly come out from continuing this discussion. But, stung and unable to stop herself, Maya said, "Why wouldn't they? People love watching thrillers. And movies about characters struggling against a force that's bigger than them."

"If you say so."

"Also, people watch movies for reasons that have nothing to do with their subject matter. Aesthetic ones, for example."

"And you think that, in terms of aesthetics, you could deliver something . . . original?"

This somehow sucked all the strength from Maya. She wanted to yell that had they been more interested in the life of the mind or the beauty of things, she would've been much better equipped to make a work of art that was worth people's time—but she knew it was pointless.

Then, suddenly, a recollection floated to the surface of her consciousness. She remembered how, in her last year of high school, after becoming enamored with movies and spending months with a cinema club that was quite progressive for its time, she'd said to her father that she wanted to study film in college. Dad had replied that, in that case, she would have to move out and manage on her own, without any help from him. But if she chose to study something at least halfway practical, he said, he would continue to support her until she became an independent adult, fully capable of providing for herself. Maya's spirit was crushed.

"Why did you decide to become a director all of a sudden?" her mother was asking, obviously forgetting that they'd been through this a few times. "I imagine it's much harder to start out when you're not young anymore. There's less room for making mistakes."

Maya almost choked on the sip of lemonade she'd taken to calm her nerves. "Are you kidding me?"

"What?"

"I wanted to start out early! I was planning to apply to VGIK after high school, but Dad said I'd have to leave home and support myself if I did!"

Everyone appeared shocked by her words. Polina, her mouth open, let her fork freeze in midair, and a piece of meat plopped down onto her plate.

Their father ventured carefully, "Honey, I never said anything of the kind. How could I?"

Maya stared at him. "You did, and it hurt me. A lot. Not to mention that my life could've turned out differently."

He looked unconvinced. "Dear, you're mistaken. We didn't have the conversation you're describing."

"You're telling me I imagined it?"

"I have no idea. I just know what I did or didn't say."

Not only had he said it, but he'd also forgotten that he had, which probably meant that he'd said it casually, in passing, attributing little significance to their exchange. But to sixteen-year-old Maya, a timid and insecure soul, that conversation had marked the end of her aspirations.

"It's so unlike your father to give anyone an ultimatum," her mother offered. "I think you misinterpreted what he said. If he said anything, that is."

"Right. Stupid me."

"If you wanted to become a director so much," Polina piped up, "why didn't you go against Dad's wishes? That is, again, if we assume that conversation really took place."

"Because not everyone is so courageous that they can just take on the world without any support from their family. Some people need help. Most, actually."

"We always supported you, honey," Dad said, giving Maya an encouraging smile. "And we support you still."

He was referring to the money he'd given her over the past few months, when she was still in the program and had run out of savings.

Maya felt diminished all over again. Her parents believed themselves to be good, upstanding people who did everything right, and this idea of themselves was so entrenched it couldn't be challenged. Instead, they preferred to think of her as ungrateful and capable of coming up with all manner of lies about them.

Why was it that in the presence of her own family, she always felt that she wasn't enough, that she had to do better? In elementary school, Maya hadn't been a stellar student. She was disorganized and kept forgetting things. She didn't make her parents proud. They wanted her to be good at math and other sciences, but she hated those subjects. In retrospect, it wasn't that she wasn't bright—it was just that no one cared about what she liked or was interested in. At university, her parents weren't impressed that she'd become fluent in five languages and even started teaching some of them. And later, whatever other achievements came Maya's way always seemed unimportant. Maybe if her movie became a sensation, her family would finally take notice.

"What's that? You're doing it again?" her mother said, horrified. Following her gaze, Maya saw that on her left arm, bright-red spots were blooming. She must've pinched herself without realizing. She'd done this throughout childhood whenever things got too difficult or exciting, pinching herself to the point that she cried. Lately, she'd resumed the practice. Her cheeks burned as she wondered why she hadn't pinched her thighs instead.

"Show me!" Her mother reached out for a closer look, but Maya swatted her hand away and pulled her sleeves down. A physician, their mother didn't believe in treating her daughters for common colds, stomach flu, or any number of other ailments. As children, Maya and Polina had to suffer through them without assistance. "Just drink lots of tea," their mother would advise. Yet when it came to their appearance, she was always on guard, loathing the idea that their neighbors might think her daughters weren't well-adjusted.

Luckily, Maya was saved by her sister, oblivious to nearly everything that didn't directly concern her.

"You want to spend the night at my place?" she suggested. "Nini will be so excited to see you!"

"I have to work on starting a family," Maya said dryly. "Better spend my nights somewhere else."

Leaving her parents' house, she felt devastated. This was supposed to have been a celebratory occasion! These people were her family, and yet they were the only ones who couldn't share her joy and anticipation. She decided to avoid gatherings like this at all costs, at least for the next few months, as she needed all her psychological resources to make her movie.

Maya had started by interviewing people for the director of photography position. With the money she had at her disposal, she couldn't get any of the top guys. Those available and interested were competent mid-level professionals. However, she could see right away that each would be difficult to work with. At the first meeting, they already showed signs of not truly respecting her vision. She'd heard countless stories about cinematographers trying to hog the blanket on set and becoming confrontational over matters large and small. Also, men hated to be bossed around by a woman, so she would have to come up with ways of tricking them into compliance. But she didn't like the idea of spending her energy on this—she wanted to concentrate on the movie itself. She had to find someone who would be her true collaborator. In the end, Maya had no choice but to turn to Dennis.

For their three-way meeting with Belov, Dennis had brought along a lighting plan he'd come up with.

"In the first sequences, I want to use high keys for outside shots," he explained. "We're going to have a nice soft picture with minimal shadows. The mood I'm going for is cheery and positive. Nothing yet tells the viewer that scary things will happen."

"Excellent idea," Maya said, "but we'll have to use natural light as much as we can. We don't have the money for high keys."

He sighed. "Right. Okay. But my overarching idea is to start out with soft lights and, as the story progresses, to add contrast and hardness. The narrative will become more dramatic, and the picture will, too."

Belov nodded appreciatively. "Sounds like a plan. What do you think?"

"Love it," Maya said.

Dennis glowed and reached for his iPad. "I did some storyboarding, too."

Being agreeable was his most salient personality trait. He couldn't have been Ksenia's husband otherwise. But, as Maya had been warned, he wanted Mark to be his second cameraman. Despite having reservations, she said yes. And this turned out to be her first serious problem.

They'd been texting since that night Mark walked her home, and he'd been pressing her for a meeting under the pretext of discussing the film, just the two of them. Her best efforts aside, their texts were becoming flirtatious, and she kept thinking of Mark's face, his mouth in particular, and his large, gentle hands. She remembered how he held her by the elbow when they crossed streets. Agreeing to work with him wasn't a good idea, she knew. His presence would be distracting at best—and she didn't even want to consider the worst. But she could see no way out of this situation, now that she'd confirmed to Dennis that he could bring Mark in as his assistant. The only reasonable thing left to do was to tell this young Casanova that their relationship would stay strictly professional. Maya decided to have this conversation today. They were scheduled to go location scouting, and she just had to find a moment alone with him.

In less than an hour, the three of them met at Patriarch Ponds and began to go through different spots, rejecting some and selecting others. They liked the idea of zombies creeping up on well-dressed people sipping their expensive drinks in restaurants along Bronnaya and on nannies pushing toddlers around the pond in their deluxe strollers.

"How about doing a riff on Bulgakov?" Dennis suggested. "We could have a head bouncing off the asphalt right here."

"Great idea!" Maya felt a sudden pang of resentment. He was thinking like a director. She should've come up with this idea herself.

"How's this a riff on Bulgakov?" Mark said.

Maya and Dennis both stared at him. "Berlioz's head, at the beginning of *Master and Margarita*."

"Haven't read." Mark shrugged.

Maya and Dennis exchanged a look of disbelief.

"I guess people don't read anymore," Dennis said.

And Maya thought that she definitely wouldn't be hit on by someone who hadn't read *The Master and Margarita*. She'd read it for the first time when she was eleven, for chrissakes. Yet Mark kept looking at her in a way that was unprofessional and highly distracting. With the aim of turning him off, she had worn baggy pants and a ratty sweatshirt, but it wasn't working, apparently. She felt his near-constant gaze on her like a type of radiation that made her skin hot.

"Let's go to Kotelnicheskaya Embankment," Dennis proposed. "I have this spot in mind that'd be perfect for one of the final scenes. The sun will be setting, which is exactly when I want to shoot it, at sunset. The light will be in everyone's eyes, driving them crazy."

On the way over, he and Mark recounted to Maya some of the bizarre situations they'd had to deal with in their work. They had much more experience than her, given that so far she'd only made the two student shorts, which couldn't even be considered real productions. Then their conversation turned to casting. Maya wanted to try Nikita Brodsky for the male lead. He wasn't well-known—yet. The popular opinion among industry professionals was that he was bound to become famous in a few months. He had just finished filming a series for Channel One, the market leader. No one doubted the project would be a hit.

"By the time our movie comes out, he'll be a star," Dennis mused. "Which will be great for us. Or not."

"Why 'or not'?" Maya asked.

"He'll start getting big offers and won't want to compromise his career."

"And?"

"He'll become one of those people who keep quiet. He hasn't said anything about the Gogol Center raid, and he's been in several of Serebrennikov's productions."

"What are you talking about?" Maya said. "What raid?"

Both men looked at her, clearly shocked.

"Where do you live? In another galaxy?" The expression on Dennis's face was hard to read, but it resembled disgust.

Mark explained, "The Investigative Committee searched Gogol Center and Serebrennikov's apartment. So far, he's just a witness in an embezzlement case. But we all know that won't last."

Kirill Serebrennikov had directed a few movies—which Maya wasn't crazy about—but he was mainly known for creating the Gogol Center, an arts complex and cultural institution that had become a hub for progressive Russian theater. As Maya had no interest in theater, she hadn't seen any of his shows. She knew, however, that many young actors and directors idolized him and that he was a darling of the foreign press and European festivals.

"Why do you think every actor who's worked with him has to say something?" she asked Dennis.

Again, both men looked at her in a way she didn't like.

"Because this case is political. He's become too much for the system. He's too outspoken, too unpredictable, too free. They slapped together a case—not just to scare him, but to send a message to all of us who aren't okay with how this country is slowly sliding back into the Dark Ages."

"I think you're reading too much into this."

"I think you don't understand what's going on. Which is strange, but whatever."

Maya felt she was being shamed again for not being politically engaged. She hated this, along with all the mansplaining that came with it. If they valued freedom so much, why were they denying her the right not to involve herself in what held no interest for her?

On Kotelnicheskaya Embankment, they walked back and forth along the Moscow River, discussing the merits of shooting from various angles. The most obvious landmark, which begged to be included in the shot, was the high-rise—one of Stalin's famous Seven Sisters—but Mark was against it.

"Cheesy," he said. "Overused. A fresh take would be to stand right here and look at the other side, at the bridge and that yellow building next to it. By the way, what is it?"

"I think it's just a residential building," Maya said.

"On the one hand, I agree." Dennis appeared thoughtful. "I'm all for fresh takes, as you know. On the other, this high-rise is beautiful. I mean, it's stunning. How can we not use it?"

"If we shoot from the angle I have in mind," he went on, "we'll get that building with the sculptures and also part of the square. Look."

Dennis framed the shot on his iPhone and showed it to Maya, then to Mark. Marveling at the picture, she congratulated herself on picking him as her cinematographer. This was an unusual, if not odd, perspective on a place everyone knew so well that it had become a cliché. It would never have occurred to her to see it this way.

"I'll make a note of it," Mark consented. "I like that there's this steeple in the background. It interrupts the space in this disturbing way."

Mark had a Nikon with him, and when Dennis stepped away to take a phone call, he showed Maya a few pictures he had taken of her throughout the day. She hadn't even realized she was being photographed.

"Oh my god," she said. "These are exhibition-worthy!"

"Nah, I can do better."

But he probably knew how talented he was. He showed her other pictures, of people and places, and she took care not to stand too close while looking at his camera. She thought her attraction to him was palpable and was almost expecting Dennis to comment on it, but he didn't seem to notice.

"I gotta run off," he said in a few minutes. "I have to meet Ksenia for dinner. You taking the metro?"

"It's a beautiful day out," Maya said. "I'll walk."

"I'll walk with you," Mark said.

Her first impulse was to say she wanted to be alone, but then she saw that this might be a good time to talk to him. She hadn't yet had the chance to convey to Mark that any hopes he might harbor of charming her needed to be squashed, and that absolutely nothing could happen between them.

As they strolled side by side, however, she couldn't think of a way to bring this up. Maybe if he touched her? But he was keeping a polite distance. Suddenly, Maya experienced a surge of embarrassment. What if she was merely imagining his aura of male longing, a manifestation of her own pathetic fantasy fueled by hormones? It wasn't a secret that, to twenty-year-old men, women over thirty-five seemed ancient. To him, she was an old hag! He would surely think she was a basket case if she mentioned the possibility of their affair. He would laugh about it later with Dennis, exchanging meaningful glances and making jokes about her behind her back throughout the shoot.

As Mark began to describe the camera he dreamed about getting one day, Maya's mind wandered, strategizing for the evening ahead.

She'd been on edge all week, worrying about things and sleeping poorly. She kept waking up in the middle of the night, overcome by terror. No one rang her doorbell again, and Alex was back in Sweden, as evidenced by his Instagram. Clearly, her nervous system had been wrecked by watching over fifty horror movies in the past couple of months. What she needed now was some quiet time to herself. Maybe even meditation.

When they got to her building, Maya was looking forward to parting with Mark and having a long, luxurious bath. But, as she reached for the door handle, Mark said sheepishly, "Sorry, I really need to pee. Can I use your bathroom real quick? I promise I'll be out in like two minutes."

Maya let him into her apartment, and while he was in the bathroom, dropped her tote bag on the floor and kicked off her shoes. Her laptop was in the living room, so she went there to turn it on.

"I'm leaving," she heard him call out from the front hall.

The next thing she knew, Mark's mouth was over hers, his hands were underneath her sweatshirt, and then she was on the couch, where her pants came off. She heard herself groan even as she struggled to make sense of what was happening. He was inside her now, pushing, rocking. Her own flesh, hot and buzzing, felt so pleasurable that the back of her head crawled, sending currents all over her body. Her eyes burned, then tears streamed down her face.

She couldn't tell how long this went on for, and then she came, shuddering.

After the front door had closed behind Mark, Maya was left stunned. A fully functioning adult—a director, no less!—she had no idea how this encounter had come about. Had he tricked her into it? Had he been planning it all along? Or had she taken advantage of him, ensnarled him, using whatever charms she possessed without perhaps realizing it? For the life of her, Maya couldn't recall the moments leading up to her finding herself atop the couch, pantsless.

But she did remember how Mark felt inside her. She fell back down on the couch, brought her hand to her crotch, and climaxed again, knowing all the while that her profound moral ruination could not be accounted for and that she was unfit to be in society.

CHAPTER 4

Maya was just about to leave her apartment when things in her field of vision went blurry, and she sank to the floor in the front hall, clutching at the coat rack. She squeezed her eyes shut and sat like that for a minute or two, disoriented, struggling to breathe. This wasn't good—today was an important day.

Everything was moving way too fast. Over the past two weeks, she'd managed to bring on board a highly regarded set designer, a team of young but talented makeup artists, and a seasoned casting director. Three days ago, that same casting director called to tell her a famous actor liked her screenplay so much he was willing to play the lead's friend for the minimum pay. All these amazing people were now working for her, studying her script, doing research and prepping. It was really happening, her movie. And when this fact truly sank in, Maya was suddenly gripped by the fear that she wouldn't be able to live up to the expectations building around her.

With a screenplay like hers, it was so easy to make a crappy, clichéd picture that would become an object of ridicule. Why had she ever thought, even for a second, that she had enough talent to turn a horror flick into a piece of art? All her life, she'd been just another person, with nothing to distinguish her from the crowd. And to think that now, at thirty-six, she could create something remarkable on her first try—it was delusional. Her parents were right. If she'd been gifted, it would have manifested long ago, in one way or another.

Maya didn't want to make a movie anymore—not now, not ever. As this thought crossed her mind, her hand slid down to pinch the inside of her thigh, hard. The surge of adrenaline shocked her into a state of alertness, if not composure. Whatever she thought about herself didn't matter. There was no going back now. She had to continue what she'd begun and find a way to make a decent film.

She stood up and looked at herself in the mirror. Her expression was wild, and she felt an unnerving sensation that she was peering at a stranger—a thin, ghostly pale woman with raven hair and very dark eyes. Who was she? Maya couldn't reconcile this image with her sense of self and tried saying, "Maya Kotova, film director." Still, she wasn't convinced.

She had no time for this; she was already late and needed to leave at once.

Halfway down the stairs, she suddenly froze, pivoted, and scrambled back up, scalded by the realization that she hadn't locked her apartment door. People in a state like hers burned down their apartments, neglecting to turn off their irons or stoves. Back inside, Maya methodically checked every appliance, ensuring each one was switched off. Then she carefully turned the key in the lock. Placing her hand on the handle, she jerked it. It felt secure. She tried to step away but felt compelled to check again. And again. And again.

An hour later, Maya arrived at the rented studio, where her team had already set up a camera and a table with refreshments. They were auditioning actresses for the lead role. In the days prior, Maya had reviewed nearly fifty self-tapes and picked out the ten actresses she liked best, most of whom were now sitting in the hall. Ksenia was scheduled to make an appearance later. She had been under the impression that she would get the part without having to try out for it, just as Dennis had assumed the cinematographer job was his, only to be told that Belov insisted on taped auditions, reserving the right to approve principal actors. Which was actually true.

"How are you feeling?" Olya, the casting director, asked. She was in her early fifties, a veteran professional, and her presence felt comforting.

"Honestly? A little out of my depth."

This was such an understatement that Maya blushed. She knew she had to project authority, but she just couldn't get ahold of herself.

"It's fine. It's your first movie!" Olya squeezed her arm. "You'll be great." Then she smiled mysteriously. "You ready for the name reveal? The actor I told you about is . . . Andrey Krasov!"

Maya gasped. "No way!"

Krasov was a celebrity, known for doing both commercial projects and offbeat indie films. His name in the credits meant automatic news coverage and viewers flocking to theaters. True, there was an aura of scandal about him—he was reportedly prone to quarreling with people he didn't like and had a reputation for being an eccentric—but this made him all the more appealing to his audience.

"He asked to come in and read today, after we're done," Olya continued. "Do you mind? He's leaving town, and he really wants to meet you."

"Of course I don't mind," Maya said. "Oh, wait! You sure he doesn't think he'll be the lead?"

"He knows he's a character actor, trust me. He's been in this business long enough."

While Olya attended to last-minute chores, Maya settled in the director's chair and took a selfie. She posted it on Instagram with the caption *Ready for first day of auditions* and immediately got three likes. Since it became known that she was shooting her feature debut, she'd gotten a bunch of new followers on all platforms. People she hadn't heard from for years had started reaching out to her with suggestions to meet up and grab a bite or see a show or just talk on the phone and catch up. "Mark my words," Lena had told her. "When the movie comes out, everyone will be your best friend all of a sudden. Especially the people who wouldn't deign to look your way when you were a nobody."

"I'll always have only one best friend," Maya replied. "And you know who that is."

"Don't forget to thank me in your Oscar speech, then!" Lena laughed.

For today, Maya had chosen a scene that allowed the actresses to showcase both their dramatic acting chops and their ability to portray believable terror. She knew it was tricky, as the world-famous Russian dramatic school wasn't particularly well suited to horror movies. A sense of measure and proportion had to be employed alongside everything else. According to the script, the two main characters met in a hospital—she was an emergency-room doctor he'd come to see for his partially chewed-up arm—and ended up running away from the ghouls and locking themselves in the storage room. Waiting out the invasion, they struck up a sort of existential conversation and chatted until a zombie appeared, armed with a neurosurgeon's cranial drill.

The first contender entered the room and sat down in the designated chair.

The sense of power that washed over Maya then was overwhelming. She'd never experienced anything like it. Sitting in this high chair and watching the actress hoping to be selected by her, Maya felt her lungs expand and her back straighten, as if she were being filled by a new person.

"Please introduce yourself," the new Maya said.

"My name is Victoria. I'm thirty-two."

The actress had a pretty, albeit anxious face, and was thin enough that this might be unhealthy. They spoke briefly about her experience and professional history, after which Maya suggested she read the scene she'd prepared.

Victoria took a few breaths and fixed her incredulous gaze on Olya, who was reading for the male lead. "How old are you, anyway? Twenty-nine? And you're still taking odd jobs, crashing at friends' houses, partying? How long are you going to do this for?"

"I don't know. I don't have a plan."

"I see so many guys like you. Wasting their best years with no plan, no idea what they even want to do with their life." Victoria shook her head disapprovingly.

"You sound like my mom."

"I'm sure she's heartbroken watching your life choices."

"I get it, you're a doctor. You have to be this way. But doesn't it ever occur to you that there's no one correct way to live? That people are different?"

"What's that?"

"What?"

"That sound."

Victoria's face transformed into a mask of terror, her eyes huge, her lips trembling. "Look! It's moving!" She grasped her head with both hands and started wailing.

This was so bad it was hilarious, and Maya had to keep herself from laughing.

"Let's try again from the beginning," she suggested. "But perform it simply, there's no need to overplay. Don't think of this as supernatural material. Take it seriously, commit to the scene. If you need to, forget that there's a zombie—just think of something scary happening. Not someone rising from the dead, but someone dying."

"Okay," Victoria said, pinching her lips.

She went again but didn't apply any of Maya's feedback. She was also visibly nervous. Once the scene was over, Maya asked her, "Are you okay? You can take five minutes, if you'd like, and try one more time."

"I'm fine," the actress said almost rudely.

It was hard to imagine that her self-tape had been one of the best. Maya remembered her being relaxed and seductive. "Then we'll do a cold read of another scene, if you don't mind."

This was common practice, yet Victoria's indignant expression telegraphed that she did mind. She grabbed the paper from Olya, scanned the lines, and started to read, still in her chair. She wasn't using the space or her body, trying to do all the work entirely with her face and voice.

"I'm sorry," Maya interrupted her. "Could you try a different approach? This film has some drama and comedy elements. The tone is lighter and more fun than a straightforward horror."

Victoria made another attempt, without much success. Maya thanked her and told her they would get back to her.

The next candidate was on her feet at once, walking about the room, picking up objects as she delivered her lines and putting them back down. Her acting was too theatrical, evoking memories of the shows Maya had watched as a child. All those people onstage talking in loud, unnatural voices, wearing over-the-top costumes, making exaggerated gestures. Even then, she'd found them ridiculous.

"Sorry, could you tone it down a bit?" Maya appealed to the actress. "Try to be more subtle. Less is more, you know? Play the realities of the moment, don't think of what's coming next."

The actress squeezed her head between her hands, shook it from side to side, and emerged from this exercise with a subdued expression on her face. She proceeded to perform the scene in a less vigorous manner, as if she'd dialed down every one of her mannerisms by a factor of two. But it was still too much.

Watching her and taking notes, Maya became conscious of that same sensation again. This was the best job in the world. Had she known what it was like, she would have applied to VGIK all those years ago, risking her father's wrath. She felt giddy, her fingers tingling. She was intoxicated by the feeling of being in charge, of everyone else in the room hanging on her words and deferring to her judgment. This was what it meant to be fully alive—to be intensely present in every moment.

Two hours later, no one appeared to be a good fit. Yet Maya didn't lose heart, her hopes set on the candidate scheduled to read second to last. She'd watched her self-tape several times last night and decided that this was her leading lady. In the video, the actress's face was remarkably expressive. Her voice was deep and rich; her features stark and refined.

The actress slid into the chair opposite Maya's. "My name is Vera. I apologize, I didn't have time to learn the lines."

Something was off about her. She took a crumpled paper out of her purse, straightened it out, and read, "How old are you, anyway? Twenty-nine? And you're still taking odd jobs, crashing at friends' houses, partying? How long are you going to do this for?"

It became clear that Vera was high on something. Her pupils were dilated, and she kept swallowing and laughing, as if it were a tic. Olya looked at her with a gaze full of pity.

A drug problem was a big no, of course. If an actress came to audition in this state, she couldn't be counted on to appear on the set at the designated time and do her job. Maya cut the interview short and thanked Vera, who immediately asked, "Did I do well? When's the first day of shooting?"

Olya led her out and came back, sighing. "Unbelievable!"

"Tell me about it." Maya paced the room. "Here I was, worrying I wouldn't be able to make a choice because everyone would be so good. And what do we do now? Another round of casting?"

"We have one more to go. Ksenia's outside in the hall."

Ksenia had asked to go last, clearly thinking of her competitors as an opening act for her. Maya didn't like the idea of making Ksenia her leading lady, if only because she'd seen too much of her over the past two years and filmed her in two of her shorts. She wanted to work with a fresh face. But doing an additional round of casting and auditions would delay the shooting, increasing the probability of it then being derailed by bad weather or something else. And who knew what that might lead to? Perhaps everything would have to be postponed until spring. She was loath to risk this.

"Fine, ask her to come in."

Ksenia carried herself like a queen. She greeted everyone present and introduced herself with a few sentences about her acting experience. Then she started reading from memory, and, almost instantly, Maya surrendered to the inevitable. Ksenia was good. No, she was very good. Her character was charismatic and annoying at the same time. She'd found just the right tone for the scene and had managed to convey change not only in the situation, but also in her character. It was obvious that she'd put some effort into developing the role. Knowing that Belov would be watching the tape, she worked with the camera like the professional that she was. When Maya asked her to do a cold read, she aced that scene, too.

"This is really impressive," Maya finally said.

She knew she had to say more, utter some words that didn't come naturally to her. A regular person would be fine with this kind of praise, but Ksenia wasn't a regular person. Her ego was tender and the size of a hot-air balloon. Together with Lena, Maya had gone to see Ksenia perform at one of the smaller experimental theaters. Afterward, they waited for her in a café nearby, and Maya had to coach Lena on how to best compliment Ksenia on her acting. "Try saying something excessive, bordering on the outrageous. You'll feel silly, but to her, it'll be perfect!" Lena then tried her best, but it wasn't enough. The next day, Ksenia complained to Maya, "This friend of yours. Does she even understand theater? She was so cold."

Now, Maya attempted to be more effusive. "You were ravishing!"

Ksenia was still peering at her, expecting more.

"Out of this world!" Maya glanced at Olya, who joined her at once.

"Yes, totally! This might be the best acting I've seen in . . . weeks."

Ksenia looked peeved, as though she thought she was underappreciated but had to resign herself to the situation where people didn't have the breadth of mind and soul to fully recognize her greatness.

Luckily, there came a thundering knock on the door, which promptly swung open. In came Andrey Krasov, a huge grin across his face. "Ta-da!" he said. "Coffee and croissants for everyone!"

A wonderful aroma spread through the room as he headed toward the refreshments table, two large boxes in his hands. Ksenia, who was in his way, spread her arms as if to hug him, but her gesture came out tentative and hard to interpret, so Krasov just nodded at her without stopping. Having placed his provisions onto the table, he went straight to Maya. "You must be the director. Honored to meet you!"

He was looking at her with the intensity of someone whose life's dream to make her acquaintance had finally come true. Maya's face flushed painfully. This was a high-profile actor, a real star, and he was honored to meet her?

Krasov enveloped her hand with both of his. "I called my agent the second I finished reading your script. I said to her, I have to be in this movie! It's going to be up to you, of course, but I hope you'll like me."

He giggled, and Maya wondered how he knew she was the director.

"I'm sure I will. So pleased to have you. And I appreciate what you said about my screenplay!"

Krasov stood in the middle of the room. "I'm ready if you are!"

"What about the . . . coffee?" Maya mumbled stupidly. Overwhelmed with this whirlwind of a man, she'd lost the sense of what she had to do and why.

"Uno momento!" Krasov went back to the table, unpacked the boxes, and presented her with a glistening pastry and a lidded cup. Out of the corner of her eye, Maya saw Ksenia take a croissant and park herself on a folding chair. She hadn't asked if she could stay, but Maya didn't feel like challenging her just now.

Krasov had picked a scene where his character, a friend of the male protagonist, is meeting him after an extended absence—and then zombies descend on them. Right away, Maya could see why he was famous. Not because he'd done certain people favors, but because his talent was so expansive it seemed almost too much for one actor. His character came to life with his own little quirks and gestures. Addressing Olya, who was reading for the male lead, as "old chap," he kept interrupting her and darting every which way as if unable to contain his energy. This character was adjacent to Krasov himself, yet a fully realized human being.

"What do you think?" he asked Maya when the scene ended. "I can also make him funkier, like so."

He started from the beginning, transforming into a different person. This guy was a deadbeat who leeched onto people, duping them with his goofiness. Krasov's play was spellbinding. Maya laughed, forgetting her half-eaten croissant, then asked him to read another scene just so she could watch him some more. Again, he was funny and utterly believable.

"Guess what? The part's yours," she said at last, and he rushed to enclose her in a hug.

"I'm leaving town tomorrow, but in September, I'll be at your disposal."

"Great! We'll reach out to your agent about the schedule."

Krasov went around the room, shaking hands with everyone. "You look familiar," he said to Ksenia. "You're an actress?"

"I'm the female lead," she said regally.

"Cool! I'll see you around, then."

Maya was irked by Ksenia's statement. What nerve! She had no way of knowing how good the other actresses had been, and Belov hadn't yet seen the tapes. But Maya let it go, having no energy for a confrontation. After discussing the details of other auditions with Olya—they needed to find the male lead and fill the other supporting roles—Maya opened the Yandex Taxi app and ordered a car.

As she made her way to dinner with Lena, her euphoria dwindled to nothing. She craved her friend's reassuring presence now. Lena was the best—or maybe the only—person to help her make sense of everything that was happening.

In a secluded restaurant booth, away from other customers, Maya told Lena about the auditions and how impressed she was by Krasov.

"Can't wait to meet him. I'm so excited!" Lena said. "I can already see the billboards and your pictures in the event pages. Did Belov say anything about taking the film to festivals?"

"He mentioned it. He said almost no one in Russia does horror movies. And a horror made by a Russian woman—who ever heard of such a thing? According to him, they'll be fighting over it."

"That's exactly what I told you, remember? You'll have to get me some invites. I'm one of the actors now!"

Lena would have a part with some lines, Maya had decided. Since she was trying to stretch the budget, she welcomed anyone who could participate for free. Most of the background actors would be friends of friends and acquaintances. Lena had agreed to be eaten by zombies.

"We'll be partying in Cannes and Venice!" she said dreamily. "Maybe even Sundance? I'd love to go there. Never been."

Over mains, Lena started telling her about Misha, her twenty-something lover. First serious tensions had appeared between them. He wanted to party, experiment with illegal substances, and do all those wild things young people dream about doing when they leave their parents' home for the first time. And Lena was a working mother who preferred quiet dinners and going to bed before midnight.

"Our interests don't overlap at all," she said. "We can't have a relationship. The only thing we have in common is sex."

"But you said you didn't want a relationship with him."

"I'm starting to. I can't help it."

"Shit. Don't get attached to him!"

"I found and reread that article you reminded me of."

"Which one?"

"The one that said that when you start sleeping with someone, your body produces oxytocin, which makes you fall in love with that person. It's all biology. So basically, the author argues, don't sleep with people you don't plan to fall in love with."

"You better break up with him, then. The sooner, the better." Maya was now thinking about how the article might pertain to her own situation.

"It may be too late already," Lena sighed.

Trying to sound casual, Maya began, "Mm, remember this Mark guy I told you about?"

"Which Mark guy?"

"The twenty-one-year-old."

"Oh, right. The one Ksenia warned you about. What about him?"

"He'll be my second cameraman. And I . . ."

Feeling supremely stupid, Maya couldn't bring herself to say that they'd had sex. But there was no need, as it turned out. A look of incredulity flashed across Lena's face, after which she burst into an unstoppable fit of laughter. Maya had to wait it out, passing the time with sips of water and finishing the bread she had no appetite for.

"Sorry!" Lena finally said, blotting her eyes with a napkin. "I'm not laughing at you, I promise. I'm laughing at the joke the universe played on you. First you go all righteous on me for wanting to sleep with a child—your term—and then you go ahead and sleep with an even younger one! Who has a child of his own! Who's now your employee!"

Maya, too, could see the irony in this development. If she believed in some sort of higher being or cosmic intelligence, she'd think she was being punished for hubris in a clever and very specific way.

"Sorry for being holier-than-thou. I'm an idiot."

Lena waved her off. "We're all so incredibly dumb, you know? I think I'll get to seventy and be none the wiser."

There was another important topic Maya had been meaning to bring up.

"I need your advice on the professional front," she said when they were done discussing the Mark conundrum.

Lena put her silverware down and prepared to listen.

"So at first, I had a pretty good idea of what kind of movie I wanted to make. But then pressure started building up, I had so many things to think about all at once, and I kinda lost what I thought was my concept. It just disintegrated somehow, and now I have nothing to hold on to. I'm afraid I'll end up making a piece of schlock."

In fact, Maya had many ideas as to what her film should be like—it was just that she couldn't unify them in a coherent vision. She didn't know what her voice was, and she tried telling herself that it was fine, that you couldn't be expected to have a fully formed voice until you actually made something. Yet she felt more lost than she'd anticipated.

"I'm sure nothing of the sort will happen," Lena said with authority. "I know you, and I know you'll make a great movie. But I get what you're feeling. I'm here for you."

Maya felt better, if not totally reassured. She trusted her best friend, who was always fiercely honest.

"Can you remember what your idea was at first?" Lena asked.

"I thought I'd make a kind of a hybrid picture—part horror, part drama with some humor in it."

"And what's wrong with that? Sounds awesome. I'd run to the theater to see this movie."

She wouldn't run to the theater, Maya knew, if someone else made this film. This wasn't Lena's habitual fare at all. In fact, Argento's *Suspiria* might be the only horror movie she'd seen recently. They'd watched it together, as part of Maya's research, and it was more an art film than a horror one.

"It just started to seem uninspired, like I'm not trying hard enough. Shouldn't I be reaching for more, aesthetically?"

Lena considered her words.

"I'm just a layperson, of course, and maybe what I'll suggest is too on the nose, but what if you picked a color—green, for instance—and made everything different shades of green? Including the zombies! If you manage to pull this off, it can look very stylish."

Green was Lena's favorite color. She was wearing a green blouse right now. And she was probably thinking of *Suspiria*, which had a lot of red in it.

"Also, you could try going for a slightly heightened reality," she continued. "Even in realistic scenes, where your characters are just going about their business. I'm thinking of a subtle eerie quality. This would disorient your viewers without them even noticing."

Maya nodded, and Lena went on. "There would be exaggeration, but so small you wouldn't necessarily pick up on it. You want to create your own singular world and make it unsettling."

Lena had used the word "subtle"—this was key. It was important to err on the side of good taste. Maya didn't want to become one of those young and supposedly hot directors whose films were nothing more than pretentious ego trips, whose every shot screamed, "Look at how smart and original I am!" She'd seen tons of movies like this, full of gimmicks that didn't serve the story. Admittedly, there were some over-the-top artists out there who were brilliant, and what distinguished them from the show-offs and the wannabes was their measure of talent. Which was something you couldn't break down into easily grasped categories. And you couldn't ever be sure that you yourself possessed talent, Maya thought. You had to depend on other people to tell you.

Lena asked the waiter for more bread, and Maya said, "There's something else I'm struggling with. What I want to say with this film."

"What do you want to say with it?"

"I don't know, that there's evil in the world. That human nature is fragile. That in each of us, there's a potential for malevolence. That we have to actively fight our darkest impulses . . . But this is all so trivial! Talk about done before."

"It's not trivial if it's said in a very specific and original way."

Everything seemed to be coming back to the notion of originality.

At home later that night, Maya took an extremely quick shower. She never used to think of herself as particularly impressionable, but showers and baths had been ruined for her by *Psycho* and *A Nightmare on Elm Street*—temporarily, she hoped. As it stood now, she had to put on cheerful, energetic music in order to get herself under the showerhead, and still she was careful not to turn her back to it. Then she got into bed with her laptop.

She still felt untethered. What she'd thought of as her staggering good luck—Belov signing her straight out of the program—was proving to be not so great after all, actually putting her at a disadvantage. She'd written this script because it seemed easy and fun, not aiming for any sort of profundity. And now, she was scrambling to inject it with meaning and develop her own visual language on short notice. If she'd had more time to prepare, she could've polished her screenplay, aiming for deeper, truer emotions, getting rid of clichés—which, she was certain, had found their way into the text. She could've given more thought to every element of the film, planning out every shot, finding unusual angles and adding unexpected details. Lena's suggestions weren't bad, but little tricks like those couldn't just be forced onto a script. Maya's professors always said that the use of unconventional devices had to grow out of your material. If you imposed them on the narrative, they would stick out like something extraneous, and even the most unsophisticated viewer would pick up on that. You had to know what you wanted to say with your innovations of form. You had to know what you wanted to say *period*.

She needed to talk to someone capable of unexpected insight. Someone deeply knowledgeable about both the commercial and creative aspects of filmmaking. Someone wise, with tons of experience.

Suddenly, the realization hit her, making her gasp. She'd wasted a once-in-a-lifetime opportunity!

Why hadn't she spoken about her screenplay with Toni Morino?

It was already finished by the time she arrived at his house, and she could have quickly translated it and given it to him to look at. But she was so busy enjoying herself there that the thought never even occurred to her. With a horrible sinking feeling, Maya pictured Toni's kind face and the careful way he had of looking at you. He was a generous person—perhaps when you've accomplished everything you've ever dreamed of, it was only natural to be generous—and he would've happily given her advice. To each of his guests, Toni devoted an hour of his undivided attention. During her hour, she asked him about his creative process. He tried to steer the conversation toward her own work, but at the time, it seemed inconsequential to her and not worth his time.

What a moron! Maya was ready to start tearing her hair out. It was inconceivable, her own stupidity and shyness, or whatever it was that had made her behave that way. One of her teachers had said that to be a filmmaker, you had to become shameless, otherwise you'd never be able to get anything done. He was right, Maya understood now. What could she still do with the little time she had? Maybe she could get inspired by some of her colleagues' ideas, if not outright steal them. She considered the movies she'd been meaning to see and settled on *The Babadook* by Jennifer Kent, which she'd heard a lot about. There weren't any zombies in it, but it was praised for its fresh take on the horror genre.

Maya got comfortable in bed and started watching the film, her laptop resting on her stomach. Ten minutes in, she regretted her decision: the movie was jarringly spooky, and it was already past midnight, which added to its effect. She'd also turned off the overhead lights, leaving only a tiny lamp on her bedside table. Yet rather than hitting the pause button and resuming at some other time, she continued to watch, through an inertia she couldn't explain. Soon, a sickening dread enveloped her.

Wasn't this exactly what makers of horror movies were after—their viewers shaking and whimpering, wishing for this exquisite torture to stop but unable to look away? Well done, Jennifer and team. Maya continued to watch for another twenty minutes or so, her heartbeat throbbing in her temples. And then, out of the corner of her eye, she saw it—the entity, the Babadook—creeping up the wall in her own room, darker than the darkness around it.

Her piercing shriek echoed in her head where it was stuck. She knew it was only her mind playing tricks on her, but her terror became so great, it didn't seem possible to survive it. And so, Maya slapped her laptop shut and did what the woman in the movie had done—pulled the blanket over her face.

CHAPTER 5

"There's something about this shot I don't like," Maya said, "but I can't quite put my finger on it." Flanked by Dennis and Mark, she was leaning over a playback monitor the size of a small MacBook. "I wish this thing was bigger," she added.

This was their seventh day of filming, and it was not going according to plan. Since the beginning, the production had been plagued by chaos. Maya had wanted to shoot all the outside scenes first, while it was still sunny, but the rains had set in earlier than expected. Overhauling the whole schedule had proved impossible, given that so many people were involved and the rental equipment had been already paid for, so they had to film under overcast sky, using high-key lighting and going over the budget. Then Krasov's availability changed because of a new contract, and they had to do some additional reshuffling. New challenges kept presenting themselves nearly every hour; the crew was on edge; people couldn't help barking at each other. Maya told herself she had to project serenity but, finding it unsustainable, had to give it up.

Despite all this, she was loving the process. Her hope that once she started shooting things would sort themselves out and a unifying vision for her movie would appear of its own accord didn't pan out. But it almost didn't matter now.

She'd heard that people became addicted to making movies. Once you got a taste of this world, of its excitement and sense of purpose and the camaraderie you shared with everyone on the set, it sucked you in so completely you wouldn't even consider leaving. This was what people meant when they spoke about the special movie magic, and they got hooked on it, craving it, wanting to experience it over and over, even if all they kept getting were shitty jobs that paid next to nothing. The exhilaration she felt made her move and think quickly, transforming her into someone she didn't recognize—capable, productive, assertive. She couldn't get enough of it.

Today they were filming an office sequence in one of the Moscow City skyscrapers. The view from the windows was breathtaking, and Maya decided to use it. She wanted to shoot the first scene in one take. It began in the kitchenette, where Lena and Alex, playing the central character's colleagues, were gossiping about him. The camera slowly pushed in on them, then pulled back and panned to Nikita Brodsky—the lead—who suddenly walked in through the door, creating some awkwardness before he retreated to the open space where he occupied a small desk, the camera following him. There, he glanced out the window, with the camera positioned behind his shoulder, framing the glorious city panorama. The camera then zoomed in on his phone, where a message popped up.

"You don't like the whole thing? Or just parts of it?" Dennis asked.

The take they'd just done was preliminary, and they could still fix things—if only Maya could articulate how it didn't correspond to the picture she had in her head.

"The whole thing, but the last part in particular. We need to go slower when he goes into the corridor and then the office. Also, the shot's way too cramped there, we need more breathing space."

“What about the kitchenette?”

“Let’s try a different angle? Start closer to the floor, as if we’re sneaking in on them from below.”

Mark separated from their group to relay instructions to the Steadicam operator, a fortyish man with a windblown face who resembled a bodybuilder, presumably from all the exercise he got carrying the heavy camera and its gear strapped to his torso.

They started filming again, but Lena messed up her lines right away.

“So sorry,” she said. “I’m really nervous.”

“It’s fine, you’re not a professional actress. Just try to concentrate. Also, this thing you did, licking your lips—”

“Sorry about that, too.”

“No need to be!” Maya said. “I liked it, it worked. Can you do it again?”

The camera rolled, and Lena addressed Alex, who was holding a cup in his hands and spinning a spoon inside it. “Don’t you think his comportment is haughty? He’s projecting this sense that he’s too good to be talking to people, to be having these random conversations like we’re having now.” She licked her lips.

Silent, Alex spun his spoon faster. Nikita entered as Lena announced with great feeling, “The other day, he looked at me in that way he has and said, out of nowhere, ‘There’s nothing like listening to Brahms when it’s raining.’ What a prick!”

After the take was done, Maya called a break and watched the playback. The scene still looked nothing like what she had visualized, making her wonder if it was because she had little experience or if some other external factors had come into play, like their small budget.

For the most part, those who weren’t one of the three principal actors wore their own outfits on camera. As an editor at a fashion magazine, Lena had access to designer garments, and now she had on a silk yellow blouse with a bow over the nape of her neck and a tight pencil skirt. With her sharp blond bob, she was stunning. But Alex, in a plaid shirt and a burgundy cardigan, looked like the dull office manager that he was. The only thing off-kilter about him was that he was clearly seething with rage, which, Maya decided, was great for the scene.

She could sense the reason behind his emotional state. Between takes, he kept watching her with jealous eyes. He seemed to have understood by way of some preternatural intuition that something was going on between her and Mark, despite their efforts to keep their affair a secret. Fortunately, Alex was leaving for Sweden tomorrow, and Maya was really looking forward to his departure.

Their next scene depicted zombies invading the building, with Lena and Alex falling victim to their attack while Nikita attempted to fend them off. Maya had spent weeks discussing the precise nature of these creatures and what they were supposed to look like with her cameramen, the artistic director, and the makeup people. It was important that the ghouls didn't come off as looking silly and cheap on screen, but there was also no possibility of prepping every actor for hours at a time. After much deliberation, they'd settled on a human-adjacent look: bluish skin tones, subtle broken blood vessels, and distinctly red eyes. Close-ups would feature actors wearing colored lenses, while postproduction could adjust the eye color for other scenes.

Before Maya could say "Action!" they had to go through several rounds of rehearsals. Lena was doing a fine job dying ("I've been preparing for a week!" she said. "I watched videos on YouTube and learned from the best, haha"), but Alex was like a mannequin, utterly unbelievable. For the hundredth time, Maya regretted that she'd let him participate. Finally, more than an hour later, they started filming as the ghouls—three of them, to keep the costs down—rushed into the office, overturning furniture and roaring. Nikita snatched a souvenir machete from the wall and began swinging. Fake blood flowed, but not extensively.

After they wrapped for the day, Maya was giving pointers to Sanya, her first AD, when she noticed Mark lingering nearby, probably hoping to go home with her. But this wouldn't do, at least not tonight. Alex was also hanging around with no apparent pretext, and she knew he would follow them. There was no way to convey this to Mark without the possibility of Alex noticing. If she sent Mark a text now, he would reveal himself by the confusion that would appear on his face upon receipt and his reflexive glance at her. And if she spoke to him, Alex could read their body language. Consequently, the three of them kept circling each other, trying to find things to do, until Alex came up to Maya and proposed a dinner. "I know it's late," he said. "But I'm leaving tomorrow. And I really want to talk to you."

Seeing no other way out of this situation, she accepted. Mark left at once, his face set in a glower. She would explain to him later that Alex was an old friend, Maya thought, then suddenly became furious. Mark was married, for crying out loud! She didn't owe him an explanation. She was a single woman without obligations who could do as she pleased, accepting dinner invitations—and more—from anyone she liked.

But mostly, she was angry at herself, for falling into a pattern of being in a relationship with Mark. She was supposed to do the complete opposite—break it off at the earliest opportunity. They had no future together, so their affair couldn't be justified even if his early marriage had been ill-advised and he would split from his wife in a few years anyway. Maya hated what she was discovering about herself by means of this entanglement with a guy almost half her age. She'd never had the ambition of being a saintly figure with not a blemish on her reputation, but she was used to seeing herself as someone possessing at least common decency. And now she didn't know what to think.

Alex took her to an expensive restaurant, which was nearly empty at this late hour. He always paid for her meals when they went out together, so she didn't bother offering to split the check anymore. She was more exhausted than hungry and ordered a fish soup with some warm bread on the side.

He spoke about the shoot and how he'd enjoyed watching her direct people on the set. "I'm honestly floored by how competent you are and how determined to make sure every little thing fits your vision. It's like only you know what it's supposed to be, and you make everyone bend to your will. It's mind-blowing."

Maya didn't tell him how far this was from the truth. After a whole day of speaking to the actors, the operators, the sound crew, and everyone else, she didn't have the energy to form coherent sentences. Alex seemed happy to do all the talking, though. He rambled on some more about the things he'd noticed, like the fact that some members of her team were better than others at doing their job. Then he abruptly asked, catching her off guard, "Are you sleeping with Mark?"

"What?" Maya nearly choked on a piece of boiled potato. "What gave you this preposterous idea?"

Alex studied her face, his own expression inscrutable. He appeared to believe that he had a certain claim to her, though how he rationalized it to himself she had no clue. More likely, it wasn't a rational thing at all. In any case, the best strategy was to deny everything and steer the conversation away from this topic. Yet Maya suddenly felt so incensed that she raised her voice. "Who gave you the right to ask me these kinds of questions? Are you my mother?"

She waved at the waiter and demanded the check, which prompted Alex to apologize. "Sorry if I overstepped here. You're totally right,

I'm just . . ." He trailed off, looking sheepish, and shoved his credit card at the waiter before the guy had a chance to place the bill on the table.

Maya ordered a taxi, refusing Alex's offer to pay for it. In the car, she pressed her hands to her eyelids, feeling deathly tired. Here she was, thirty-six years old, only now realizing that she'd let a needy ex-boyfriend cling to her for most of her adult life, all because she'd mistaken him for someone dangerous. He was just a pathetic hanger-on, it was obvious now. Add to this the fact that she'd wasted ten years of that same life—her best years!—on another man, who hadn't been good to her and had contributed nothing to her growth as a person. If anything, he had impeded her intellectual development by dragging her on those countless fishing and hiking trips and doing at-home karaoke.

Because of an illegally parked car the taxi couldn't reach the entrance of her apartment block, so she had to cross the huge courtyard formed by four residential buildings on foot. The lighting was dim, and she felt uneasy. As she approached her entrance, a tall figure detached itself from the wall, its face in the shadows. Instantly, her pulse quickened, and a wave of dizziness washed over her.

Then she realized it was Mark. "What the fuck! You scared the shit out of me."

"Sorry. I didn't mean to."

"Have you been here this whole time? It's late."

Maya didn't have the heart to tell him to go away, so he followed her into the building and then up the stairs. The moment they were inside her apartment, his hands were all over her and they were kissing. Then he carried her into the bedroom, where he dropped her on the bed and took off his sweatshirt in one swift motion.

It was absurd how quickly Maya forgot about getting at least a few hours of sleep or all those other things she kept worrying about.

She was consumed by pure sensation, her mind emptied of thoughts. There was just her blood pumping and waves of pleasure rolling through her body. She couldn't tell how much time was elapsing, or whether it was elapsing at all. One thing she was certain of—she had never experienced this feeling before; she had never felt so fully present in her own body as she did now. Mark was moving inside her, yet she didn't perceive him as Mark, or even as another human being she needed to acknowledge. As she climaxed, an unfamiliar noise, reminiscent of a cow or some other large animal bellowing, escaped her throat.

They took off their remaining clothes and climbed under the blanket. Breathing into Mark's shoulder, Maya debated if she should tell him how he made her feel. She used to be unable to grasp why so many people she knew seemed obsessed with sex. To her, it had always felt like nothing special—an enjoyable but rather awkward affair that often left her wondering what her partner thought of her. But this was huge! Now she understood what all the buzz was about. Admitting all this to Mark would be totally embarrassing, though. He was barely out of his teens, and what would he think of her, a grown woman, if she confessed that this was the first time she'd had real sex?

Mark pulled her closer, making it clear that he wasn't leaving anytime soon. This was none of her business, but Maya asked anyway, "Where does your wife think you're spending the night?"

"I told her I'd crash at Dennis's."

"Do you ever do that?"

"Sure."

Was she the latest addition to Mark's collection of conquests? The idea revolted her, though only for a moment, quickly replaced by jealousy toward his other hypothetical women. She told herself she should be thinking not about them but about his wife, the poor kid stuck at home with a baby. Yet this failed to elicit any reaction from her brain, which was swimming in endorphins.

They had sex again in the morning, then Maya rushed to the bathroom, seeing that she was running late. Mark left while she was still in the shower—they'd agreed that they mustn't be seen together off the set. Without as much as a sip of coffee, she left her apartment, hoping to go over her notes for today on the metro. Her mind refused to focus on work, however. She could think only about Mark. People stared at her as she smiled stupidly from ear to ear, powerless to stop it.

Today's set was a spacious apartment whose owners, Maya was told, had departed for a vacation in Italy. "Nice pad," she said to herself, just as she had a few days ago while looking at the photos her art director had taken of the mint-green walls and the elegant furniture. Mark was in the kitchen with Dennis, filling up on coffee and pastries. Maya greeted both of them, pretending she hadn't seen Mark less than an hour ago, and poured a cup for herself. She was biting into a cheese danish when Sanya—a bright twenty-six-year-old obsessed with keeping everything in order—found her.

"Nikita is rehearsing in the nursery," Sanya reported. "And Ksenia . . . She's not happy with her outfit and is making a fuss."

"What about it makes her not happy, do you have an idea?"

"She doesn't like the color."

Maya strode into the main bedroom, where the wardrobe assistant stood before Ksenia with a forlorn expression on her face. "Good morning! Oh god, this color looks gorgeous on you!"

Ksenia gave her a suspicious look. "Really?"

"Absolutely amazing! It makes you look like Isabella Rossellini in *Blue Velvet*."

Maya didn't know why she'd said that. Ksenia, with her small features and dark-blond hair, looked nothing like Isabella Rossellini, with or without the blue jumpsuit she was wearing. Sinking so low, lying to someone's face—not just someone, but a friend! But Maya had to do everything in her power to avoid conflicts over trivial matters, especially if they concerned Ksenia. Ever since she was little, Maya had been taught to avoid confrontations, but Ksenia seemed to thrive on fights, seeking them out and using them to advance her goals.

Which she didn't fail to demonstrate once the shoot began. They were slated to film several scenes involving the two protagonists and the male character's best friend. The trio convened at the friend's place to figure out a way to defeat the ghouls, perhaps by getting to Lenin, who, they already understood, was their leader. Since Krasov was late, Maya rearranged the shooting order to film a dialogue between the protagonists that was meant to take place when the friend stepped out of the room. This conversation provided a moment of levity amid all the fight and chase scenes. Nikita and Ksenia were sitting on the couch, both of them projecting the tension their characters felt in the wild zombie-apocalypse situation.

"This almost feels like the old life," Ksenia said, in character. "It's so quiet."

"We could even pretend we're on a date." Nikita, handsome, with a mop of dark hair, gave her a smile.

"Let's do it!"

"What?"

"Pretend we're on a date."

"Okay."

"Ask me something."

Nikita got lost in thought for a moment. "Where do you see yourself in ten years?"

"I said a date, not a job interview!"

"It's what I could think of off the top of my head."

"Fine." Ksenia shot him a devious look. "I see myself heading a state-of-the-art emergency medicine clinic. But I also have time to travel around the world and read. You?"

Nikita shrugged. "I don't know. Maybe I've built a company that makes robots. Or else I've become an expert in zymurgy."

"What's that?"

"I'm not sure. Something to do with wine."

Ksenia made a face that made everyone burst out laughing when Maya said "Cut!"

After two takes, Ksenia announced to Maya that she wanted to try doing the scene differently.

"Differently how?"

"We could be having this conversation while sort of cruising around the room. I feel there's space to do something interesting here by using movement."

Nikita appeared aghast at the suggestion, perhaps not wanting to suddenly begin improvising, or possibly shocked that Ksenia would interfere with the director's work in this manner. Maya pondered various ways to react. She already felt like an impostor, and now Ksenia was challenging her in front of the crew, implying that what she'd come up with wasn't good enough. What was Ksenia's problem, anyway?

Softly but firmly, Maya said, "There's already too much movement in other scenes."

"If you cruise around the room, that's one or two additional camera setups," Mark piped up. "We don't have time for that."

Ksenia ignored him and continued addressing Maya. "The best directors give actors freedom. It's always a good idea to listen to people's suggestions."

"I appreciate your suggestion, but it won't work with what I'm trying to do here. Let's roll."

Ksenia's mouth became a straight line. From that moment on, she began sabotaging the takes by making her character sound either too bitchy or too detached, and yet her game was subtle enough that it was impossible to call her out on it. Maya couldn't believe what was happening, fuming inwardly while giving directions, saying try this or that. This was unacceptable conduct, and they were halfway through the film! If Ksenia had tried something like this in the beginning, Maya could've spoken to Belov about finding another female lead, but now she was stuck. Mark seemed to be the only other person perceptive enough to notice what was going on, as evidenced by the looks of commiseration he cast at Maya from time to time.

After a while, it seemed pointless to continue filming the scene, so Maya said, "We're done," hoping she could figure something out in the editing stage.

She heard applause erupt behind her.

It was Krasov, smiling so widely he appeared unhinged. "This was great!" he said. "Sorry I'm late! I was at the protest today, and there was hell there, complete chaos, I couldn't get out in time. Cops closed the streets around the courthouse."

Maya had forgotten about his lateness, her mind occupied by Ksenia's disruptive behavior. "What courthouse?" she said, more out of politeness than genuine interest.

"Basmanny. It placed Serebrennikov under house arrest? What a circus!"

Serebrennikov again. Maya tried to recall who she'd spoken to about him but couldn't retrieve the memory.

With Krasov there, the mood on the set lightened at once. He showered Ksenia with attention, and, clearly flattered, she appeared to set aside her dustup with Maya. He kept telling stories and making jokes—some of them at his own expense—and laughed at them so unselfconsciously that everyone was charmed. Even Mark, who Maya could sense disliked him, gradually warmed up to him.

In the next scene, the three characters sat at the dinner table, snacks in front of them, along with sheets of paper and a map of the city.

"I've been working at the hospital lab these past few nights," Ksenia said. "And I think I might be on to something."

"Like what?" This was Krasov.

"Like a possible antidote."

"Seriously?" Both actors gaped at her.

"But we need to do some testing. Which means we need to capture a ghoul, tie it down, and douse it with the solution."

"Sounds like a plan," Nikita said. "But it's easier said than done."

"How about we find a dart gun and shoot it with a tranquilizer," Krasov suggested, "like they do with large animals?"

"That might work," Nikita agreed, and looked at Ksenia expectantly.

After a couple of takes, Maya announced a break and went to use the bathroom. There, she looked at herself in the mirror and was surprised to see that, despite having gotten very little sleep, she looked radiant. Was this because she was excited to be filming or because of Mark? She felt his presence on the set as if he were connected to her with wires that thrummed with charged particles. Whenever he came closer, he sent a current of them through her body.

This was bad. This couldn't possibly end well. But she was helpless against it.

Leaving the bathroom, Maya found herself ambushed. "Can I talk to you?" said Krasov, a happy, earnest expression on his face.

They went to a corner where they wouldn't be disturbed.

"I love your script!" he started. "Literally every sentence of it. I just wanted to ask if you'd be open to a suggestion."

"Of course," Maya said. "What do you have in mind?"

She saw Mark in the distance. He made a heart with his hands, making sure no one else saw it.

"What if we tweak a couple of lines? In the next scene, instead of discussing movies, the characters could talk about plays. Then my character can mention seeing *A Midsummer Night's Dream*."

When she replied with an uncomprehending stare, Krasov added, "It's our chance to do something important."

"I'm afraid I don't follow."

He seemed baffled. "It's Serebrennikov's show. The prosecution claims he took state money to produce it but never actually staged it. Which is a blatant lie, of course. I've seen it with my own eyes."

Since Maya stayed silent, Krasov pressed on. "This would make our movie immediately relevant. Elevate it by grounding it in today's political reality."

Maya was startled by the implication that her film needed elevating. Hadn't he just said that he loved the script, every sentence of it?

"I'm afraid I'll have to say no," she said. "It's my deliberate choice to stay out of politics."

Krasov's face fell, but he managed, "You certainly have a right to your position."

"Also, they are discussing zombie films, not just any old movies. Their conversation moves the plot."

But he was already walking away so quickly as if he were afraid she would infect him with her position.

What the hell? She was getting tired of people making her feel like shit just because she didn't share their righteous indignation. Would Krasov, too, behave like a petulant child now? She'd heard stories about him; his eccentricity apparently bordered on volatility. Some people circulated unsavory rumors regarding his possible sex addiction. There was also his much-publicized divorce and child custody battle.

But the rest of the shoot proceeded without incident. For the last two scenes, they dimmed the lighting. A disco ball threw streaks of red, yellow, and blue onto the walls and the furniture. The trio of characters, having emptied two bottles of wine, let loose before the next day's mission, dancing to the beats of electro swing.

The actors improvised. Ksenia did a sexy routine, sliding up to Nikita and teasing him, before kicking off her shoes and breaking into a Charleston. Then Krasov took hold of her and spun her around while Nikita watched. After this, the two men had a dance-off, coming up with all sorts of crazy moves that had the crew in stitches. Finally, as Ksenia and Krasov fell on the couch, seemingly exhausted, Nikita performed a solo dance at Maya's suggestion. Advancing toward the camera and looking directly at it, he moved slightly off rhythm. He flailed his long arms like tentacles and something wild appeared in his eyes, suggesting an unknown depth to the man he was playing.

This was exactly what his character needed, and Maya made a mental note to tell Nikita how brilliant he was when they were out of everyone else's earshot.

After the final take, she said, "And we're done for today! Great job, everyone!"

The crew erupted into applause, then started moving around, laughing and talking, producing a near-deafening noise. The actors' performances seemed to have electrified everyone. Krasov, pumped on adrenaline, darted this way and that, gesturing wildly, initiating conversations with people only to drop them a moment later. Maya wanted to take him aside and say something heartfelt to him, rectifying the impression she'd made earlier. But before she could do this, he put his hands to his mouth to form a megaphone and trumpeted, "Too-roo-rooo! I have an announcement! Let's all go to Pushkin for dinner! Everyone's invited, my treat!"

People whistled and whooped. Ksenia shot Dennis an amused look as if to say *How much money does this dude make?* and Mark asked Maya, "You going?"

Dennis, thinking the question had been directed at him, grinned. "Hell yeah! A free meal at Pushkin? Count me in!"

More than anything now, Maya wanted to go home with Mark, but she couldn't miss out on this opportunity to hang out with everyone. Also, her absence would be conspicuous and get people talking. She glanced at Mark, trying to impart this notion to him telepathically. Perhaps they could both go for an hour and then leave without drawing attention to themselves.

At the restaurant, their party was escorted to a private room with a single long table. There were only twelve of them, as not every crew member had been able to join. From the way Krasov spoke to the maître d' and the waiters, it was clear he was a regular. Maya studied the dark wood paneling, the lamps with velvety shades, and the bookshelves full of tattered volumes, probably fake. This wasn't her first time here—she'd been to Pushkin before, for interviews with celebrities—but she'd never ordered anything aside from tea. She was scanning the menu for the most reasonably priced item when Krasov announced, "I'll order for the table, if everyone's okay with it." To the waiter, he proceeded to list a dizzying number of dishes: salads, veal and chicken cutlets, pickled mushrooms, cured fish, various pies, even rooster combs in cream. Nikita, giggling quietly so as not to distract him, made a video of Krasov placing the order while the waiter's expression became progressively sweeter and somehow haughtier.

Mark had seated himself on the same side as Maya, but far enough away that for her to see him, she'd have to lean so far forward her face would end up in her plate. When food started arriving, Krasov launched into a story of his traversing the Gobi Desert by motorcycle. Dennis kept interrupting, inquiring after the practicalities. Didn't the wheels get stuck in the sand? How deep was it? How many people were there with him?

Krasov patiently answered his questions and continued, "So, we're in Mongolia, near the Chinese border. We stop for the night, set up our tents. We were told it was safe, no issues. Anyway, we didn't see anyone for miles. Then, in the dead of night, we wake up to this noise—it's like an army invaded! My pal, who's got a gun, just starts firing out of reflex and ends up shooting me in the arm!"

Krasov pulled up his shirt sleeve, revealing his bullet scar. "Honestly, I don't know how he didn't kill us both. It was pitch dark. And it turned out it wasn't even people! When we got out of the tent, we saw these huge, hairy cows—probably just curious. They wanted to be friends with us."

"When was this?" Ksenia asked.

"When I was eighteen."

She stared at him for a moment. "Seriously? When I was eighteen, I could barely afford to eat anything decent, let alone travel. Maybe that's why having all this food around now is so hard." She fished a single rooster comb out of a cast iron pan and bit into it. "This is tasty."

"So what was it like, being you at eighteen?" Krasov egged her on. "Tell us."

She looked at him defiantly. "I worked as a stripper."

Someone said, "Wow." A trace of bewilderment passed across Krasov's face.

"It was exhausting work," Ksenia went on. "Imagine dirty old men not just ogling you but always wanting more. When they order a private dance, they know they aren't allowed to touch you but they don't care. They try putting their crusty fingers inside you, they squeeze your breasts, hurting you. They want to hurt and humiliate you. And you're just a hungry kid. You left your unhappy home in the middle of nowhere and came all the way to the capital to become an actress."

Ksenia's face took on a vulnerable, defenseless expression as she spoke, but all Maya saw was a performance. It was an obvious attempt to manipulate her audience: Ksenia simply couldn't bear not being the center of attention, even for a few minutes.

"Once, I had a huge amount of money on me—twenty thousand rubles. Five went to my landlord, another five for a month's worth of food, and ten was for clothes. I never had nice things, I basically wore rags. So I went shopping, thinking about jeans, a dress, and I really wanted a trench coat to feel classy. Mass market brands felt like luxury to me! I went from store to store, trying things on, debating, going back again. I wanted to spend my money wisely."

Ksenia chuckled and took a bite of another rooster comb. *Nicely done*, Maya thought, watching others' rapt faces. A pregnant pause.

"And then I saw the most beautiful white leather jacket. It was the most exquisite piece of clothing ever, something out of this world. I went in and touched it, and it felt like baby skin under my fingers. The salespeople tried to kick me out, seeing how poor I was. The jacket cost exactly twenty thousand rubles, which I had on me right then. I was under a spell, so I bought it and wore it over my T-shirt that was practically falling apart. After that, I got myself a chocolate ice cream and sat on the curb, eating it and crying. Because it was the happiest I ever felt in my entire life."

Maya nearly clapped. Who knew if this story was even true, but Ksenia had done a great job telling it. The others sat perfectly still, as if under a spell themselves, until Krasov shouted, "Let's drink to happiness! And to getting through tough times!" The party mood bounced back as glasses were raised and clinked.

People started sharing stories from when they were eighteen. Nikita recounted an infatuation that drove him to steal a chicken, which he clutched to his chest as he fled from the furious owner. He ended up having to jump from a bridge, and the poor bird expired in his arms, presumably from terror. Meanwhile, Maya was trying to think of a story to share for Mark's benefit, something they could laugh about later. She leaned forward, pretending to reach for some blinis but really to steal a glance at him—only to find his seat empty. He must've slipped out while she wasn't looking.

Trying to sound casual, she asked Sanya, sitting next to her, "Mark didn't leave, did he?"

"Oh, he had to go home. It's tough when you have a baby, I guess." Sanya made a tragic face, then shrugged, as if to suggest her incomprehension of the notion that some people voluntarily chose to have babies.

And just like that, the conversation stopped being interesting, and the wine took on a bitter aftertaste. Maya didn't want to be here anymore. She had to wait, however, ensuring that her departure didn't appear connected to Mark's. For a few minutes, she remained seated, careful not to let her mouth curl downward, then gathered her tote and went up to Krasov to thank him.

"Let's talk soon!" he exclaimed, all smiles. "I have an idea for a screenplay. We should collaborate!"

Maya promised to stay in touch and headed outside, where she found Ksenia smoking by the restaurant's entrance. No matter how much she wanted to avoid a confrontation, she couldn't pass up this opportunity to speak to her in private.

"I wanted to talk to you about what happened today. What you did was unacceptable," she said politely but firmly. "I don't want it to happen again."

"What did I do?" Ksenia opened her eyes wide, faking innocence.

"You know perfectly well what you did. I won't tolerate it. When you shoot your own movie, you can do whatever you want. But this is my movie, and you will do as I say."

Ksenia eyed her with what seemed like contempt, which prompted Maya to add, "I can't replace you at this stage, but I can find a way to cut your part down if you refuse to follow instructions."

Maya instantly regretted her last comment, noticing a change in Ksenia's expression that portended, if not the end, a serious shift in their friendship. But it was too late—she couldn't take back what she'd said. For a few moments, she stood beside Ksenia as they both watched people in the middle of Tverskoy Boulevard enjoying their late-night stroll. A limousine went by, with two young women sticking out almost halfway through its sunroof, filming themselves on their phones, their hair flying.

Letting out a cloud of smoke, Ksenia swiveled sharply to look at Maya. "Mark's wife found out about you two. You should've been more careful."

Shocked, Maya tried to make sense of her words and couldn't. How was this even possible? Both she and Mark had taken great care not to reveal themselves. He'd sworn he hadn't told a living soul about their affair, and they made sure to delete all their texts.

"The minute I saw you talking to him that first time, I knew you'd get involved," Ksenia went on with a smirk. "I tried to warn you!"

"You did," Maya said. "Thanks. I have to go now."

As she walked away, she couldn't help but obsess over what Ksenia had said, weighing the possibilities. The wife couldn't have discovered their secret unless someone had told her—that much was clear. But how could that someone have found out? There were only two options: either they had been deliberately spied on, or Mark had told Dennis despite promising her he wouldn't.

Maya's phone binged, and she hastily reached into her bag, hoping it was a text from Mark. Instead, it was a message from Belov.

He usually watched the dailies, or at least pretended to, and sent her some encouraging comments when he felt like it. But this time, his message was anything but positive. He pointed out that they were only halfway through the shoot and she'd already used up most of the budget. He wanted her to fire several people and ended with *Let's discuss this first thing tomorrow.*

Suddenly, it all became too much. A headache that had been slowly brewing flashed between Maya's temples, blinding her for a moment, then continued to pound like someone's steady arm delivering blows. A great weight seemed to settle on her, making her feel small and helpless. Even taking another step felt daunting. How was she supposed to handle all of this at once? Maya wanted to talk to Lena, but it was nearly midnight. Lena got up early for work and must have been asleep by now.

Maya forced herself to move in the direction of her home. She, too, needed to get a good night's sleep. Then, with a rested brain, she would be better equipped to tackle the problems she was now up against. The most important thing was finishing her movie, even if it meant letting some crew members go. She would lower her own wages or even forgo them entirely. She didn't need much: she could survive on coffee and cheese.

Lena had said once (and she'd heard this from her therapist), "Things will work out in the end. Or at the very least, it will become clear that they won't." To Lena, this pragmatic perspective on life seemed somehow comforting.

Maya was turning these two sentences in her mind, trying to decide if they formed a profound or a meaningless statement, when she entered her building's lobby. She walked over to the rows of mailboxes and opened her own—not because she was expecting anything, but because she needed to perform small actions that made her feel in control of her life. As she climbed the stairs, she sifted through the mail, which was mostly just advertising booklets and leaflets. Then, amid the clutter, she spotted an envelope with no return address or stamp. Her name was printed on it in all caps, and the whole thing looked so deliberately unlike regular mail that it clearly aimed to attract attention.

Maya opened it, and her heart leaped into her throat. The message, made from letters cut out of magazines and newspapers, read: *You're going to regret what you did, bitch. Just wait and see.*

CHAPTER 6

By the time the final day of shooting arrived, Maya's nerves were completely shot. She'd had to fire four people. Mark was acting as if she were just another director he was working with, having abruptly stopped all one-on-one communication with her. Ksenia, though highly professional on set, ignored Maya when the camera stopped rolling. Dennis seemed to have taken his wife's side, becoming distant and cold. The production kept being plagued by money and scheduling issues, which Maya would never have been able to sort out without Sanya, her one true partner. It was amazing how competent and patient she was, despite her young age.

Maya herself wasn't. She was having panic attacks almost every day now.

She managed to forget the menacing letter for the most part. When Lena had first seen it, she screamed in terror, just like a character in a thriller. Whoever it was who had crafted the letter, this was the reaction they were going for. Maya couldn't help laughing, and Lena said, indignant, "You really think this is funny?"

"I didn't until you screamed. Sorry! It was a nervous laugh."

"We have to go to the police with this!"

"They won't do anything. But they'll be amused—we'll make their day."

"At least we can make them put this on record."

"So that when I'm killed, they'll have a lead?"

Lena didn't have a comeback for that. "You have an idea of what they're referring to? What did you do that you're going to regret?"

"Could it be my affair with Mark?"

"I doubt it," Lena said. "That doesn't seem like something a twenty-year-old mother would do. This has to be someone connected to filmmaking. It's from a movie, right?"

"From hundreds of movies, literally. *Seven. Zodiac. Copycat.* Just off the top of my head. It's a cliché. Overused."

Lena gave up on the idea of going to the police but insisted that Maya move in with her for the time being. So now, Maya slept on Lena's couch. She felt safe with two other people in the apartment, even though the arrangement wasn't ideal. It didn't help her get more rest; her sleep was becoming progressively worse, and she was consuming copious amounts of tranquilizers, unbeknownst to Lena. During the day, Maya moved through the world as if underwater, sounds and other stimuli muffled. She spent most nights in a trance-like state that wasn't exactly sleep. For the night before the last day of shooting, Lena—worried endlessly about Maya—gifted her a stay at the Ritz-Carlton. She had a voucher from the hotel management, a gesture for a project they had collaborated on.

It was late in the evening when Maya took the elevator to the tenth floor and found herself in an improbably opulent suite with windows overlooking the Kremlin. She'd never stayed in a room like this before, not even during her magazine career, when press trips around the world often involved five-star accommodations. Too tired after the shoot, she hadn't thought to pick up food on her way here and was now ravenous. Luckily, there was a surprise for her on the table—a tiny bottle of champagne and a charcuterie board under a metal cloche, elegant like everything else. Maya drew herself a bath and carried this improvised meal into the bathroom with her. Afterward, she settled into the most comfortable bed of her life and set an alarm, expecting to sleep for eight hours straight.

Yet her mind continued to race, too agitated and filled with anticipation. People kept telling her she was on the brink of something great. Belov, his assistants, most of her crew. Her favorite professor, whom she'd invited to the set. Lena, of course, who claimed that Maya's childhood traumas prevented her from seeing the extent of her own talent. Followers on Instagram, who had seen the snippets of video Maya posted. Even Ksenia had remarked once, clearly in spite of herself, that she'd changed her mind about Maya's script and now thought it was clever.

Maya didn't know if she believed them, often switching between two opposing states: a euphoric one, where what she'd written felt like, if not the epitome of genius, an unusual and inventive narrative; and another, a dark and horrifying one, in which it appeared glaringly stupid and devoid of meaning. The world didn't need another mediocre piece of art—or, even worse, something that fell short of being considered art. Fear paralyzed her whenever she contemplated the possibility that her film would both flop at the box office and be destroyed by critics.

She would find out her fate soon enough. After a few weeks of editing and two months of postproduction, they would be ready to submit the film to festivals. Today was October 5. It was unrealistic to think they would make Berlin, Belov had told her, but they should be ready for Cannes, whose submission deadline was in early March, and Venice, with its late April deadline. He had abruptly stopped nagging her about going over budget. He seemed happy with what she was doing and had even gifted her a new iPhone a few days ago, claiming it was for her birthday. Her birthday had been in June, she reminded him. "It's a late present," he chuckled.

Maya stayed in bed, fully awake, for what felt like two hours, then got up and stood next to the window, peering outside. The Kremlin and the Historical Museum next to it looked like gingerbread houses out of some fairy tale. The stars atop the spires glowed deep red against the dark sky. Soon, it started snowing, and the cars whizzing by along Mokhovaya Street began to slow down. Huge fuzzy snowflakes hovered in front of her face on the other side of the glass.

Around six in the morning, she realized she wouldn't get even a moment of shut-eye. She felt dizzy as she stepped into a hot shower, hoping it would revive her. It didn't. She made her way to the restaurant downstairs, where she was presented with a complimentary breakfast so luxurious it made her eyes hurt. She took a few photos for Lena's sake and cut into her blinis with caviar. They were supposed to be delicious, but Maya felt nothing; her taste buds seemed to have atrophied overnight.

Her eyes bugging out and her head buzzing, she arrived on set earlier than expected. It was only a fifteen-minute walk from the hotel. They were filming at the Saltykov-Chertkov Estate, a lavish eighteenth-century manor house located near the Lubyanka metro station that Belov had managed to secure for a good price until midnight. Sanya was already there, running around and issuing commands over the walkie-talkie.

People kept trickling in. Soon, Ksenia and Nikita were at the makeup station, and Dennis was propped behind the camera alongside Mark. A new actor, made up to resemble Lenin on steroids, paraded through the ballrooms with a coffee cup in hand, making anyone who saw him crack up. Maya took a selfie with him under the pretext of promoting her movie on social media, but really because she liked how he looked.

They were several hours into filming when Belov appeared and stood behind Maya. Nikita and Ksenia had been chasing the zombie Lenin all day. Now, in one of the more baroque ballrooms, they finally overwhelmed him, pinning him under a pile of gilded ottomans upholstered in velvet—cheap replicas made specifically for this sequence that still looked authentic on camera. The actors, made to appear as if they'd already sustained some damage from all the running and fighting, seemed genuinely exhausted yet were having a lot of fun.

"Get him, get him!" Ksenia shrieked, in character.

Nikita lunged atop the furniture, pressing his weight down. Lenin squirmed and wheezed beneath the ottomans. Fortunately, they'd rehearsed this scene a few times, and Maya was reasonably certain that the actor was still okay, not crushed to the point of needing medical assistance.

"Where's the antidote? Put it on him!" Nikita yelled.

Ksenia reached into the tote bag she had with her and fished out a spray bottle. Lenin immediately became more active, writhing so energetically that Nikita nearly fell over, having to hold on for dear life, or at least pretending to. Ksenia rushed toward Lenin but slipped and fell dramatically before quickly crawling the rest of the way on her knees, spraying him in the face. General mayhem ensued as Nikita collapsed to the floor, followed by the crash of furniture. Behind Maya's back, Belov roared with laughter and slapped his thigh.

When, more than an hour later, they were finally done, Maya was brought to the center of the room and took a bow as everyone applauded her. The ovation lasted nearly a minute, and it was hard for her not to discern in it a specter of future triumphs. Images of herself standing on the stage of the Palais des Festivals flashed through her mind, even as she tried to swat them away. Trying to fully enjoy the present moment, she stole a glance at Mark, who hadn't said a word to her all day, and caught him looking at her with a tense yet somehow affectionate expression. He was right, of course. If she wasn't strong-willed enough to keep away from him, he had to be the one to do it.

Ksenia, Maya noticed, had only pretended to clap along with everyone else. She didn't even try to conceal her jealousy, looking extremely cross at not being the brightest star in the room.

In the next room, a buffet had already been set up with hot and cold dishes. When, on cue, members of the crew began moving toward the tables, a commotion at the entrance announced someone's arrival. Alex emerged from the hallway, holding a bouquet of what must have been a hundred red roses and an enormous stuffed giraffe. Belov raised his eyebrows, amused, while Maya heard Mark burst out laughing somewhere behind her.

"What is he doing here?" she groaned, talking to no one in particular.

Sanya whispered next to her, "He kept texting me, so I invited him. I didn't know I wasn't supposed to, sorry."

Maya had no choice but to say it was fine. She made Alex retreat back into the hall and leave his gifts there, out of view. She hoped someone would take them. Had he wanted to make a spectacle or was he just a ridiculous human being? She couldn't tell. He seemed happy and breathless. He didn't look like someone who could've sent that vicious letter to her.

"I'm so glad I made it!" he said. "I had a meeting this morning, so I had to race to the airport the moment it ended."

"You didn't have to," she told him, regretting, all over again, her decision to involve him in this project. What had she been thinking? She'd given him yet another avenue by which to attach himself to her, of her own free will.

"I wouldn't miss this for anything!" Alex was grinning ear to ear. "Also, I'm done with the first draft of the music. Can we meet tomorrow and listen to it?"

Luckily, she didn't have time to reply. Belov clinked on his glass, calling for attention. He launched into a long toast, congratulating everyone on the completion of the shoot and promising the film a stunning trajectory. He was careful not to toast the movie itself, as this was considered a bad omen and cinema people studiously avoided drinking to the success of a movie before its release. Then crew members took turns saying how much this job had meant to them and sharing their experiences of working with Maya. They thanked her for creating a fun and supportive atmosphere on the set, eventually moving her to tears.

Sanya, who had also started crying, hugged her and said she was by far the best boss she'd ever had. "If you ever want me to join you on another project, just whistle. I'll drop everything and run to you."

Maya told her she'd hire her again at the first chance she got. Meanwhile, she was watching Mark out of the corner of her eye. A beer in one hand and a breadstick in the other, he was talking to a pretty makeup artist, seemingly engrossed in the conversation. He used the breadstick as a conducting baton to stress certain points.

Suddenly emerging next to Maya, Ksenia nearly shoved Sanya aside. "I finally finished my screenplay!" she announced. "Can't wait to hear your thoughts!"

They hadn't spoken much since their falling out. Maya mumbled a half-hearted congratulations, which Ksenia took as a sign that she had secured Maya's agreement. Ksenia immediately opened her mail app on her phone and dispatched the email. "Now you have it. I know you'll be busy with editing and all, but I'd appreciate it if you could take a look in the next week or two."

Maya could only admire her gall.

The next moment, Ksenia was after Belov, clearly hoping to get him interested in her script, too. She began trailing him like a pilot fish while he followed Lena around the room, refilling her glass and offering her various snacks. Lena looked smashing in one of her dresses from work, a scarlet number decorated with balls of white gauze at the front, but Ksenia appeared determined to stamp out their nascent courtship. *You could film this*, Maya thought, watching.

"Where's Krasov?" Alex asked, pretending that he'd just stumbled upon her in the chaos of the party. "Is he coming?"

"He's filming in Thailand."

"Filming what?"

"Some comedy by Sarik Karapetyan."

"Who's that?"

Sanya came to Maya's aid. "You've lived in Europe for too long! He makes these asinine, cringey comedies that make your blood curdle."

"Why did Krasov agree to work with him?"

"Money." Sanya shrugged and gently led Maya away.

"Thanks," Maya whispered.

"Actually, I wanted to tell you something," Sanya said when they found themselves alone, partially concealed by a potted palm. "Krasov . . ." She lowered her eyes and pinched her mouth.

"What? Tell me!"

"I had to block him because he kept sending me dick pics and wouldn't stop."

Maya gasped, and Sanya hurried to say, "I've done nothing to make him think that he could. Didn't flirt with him or anything like that. I can show you our chats. And the pictures."

"God, no! I don't want to see them." Maya had to come up with something to say. "Thank you for telling me! Let's talk about this tomorrow, after a good night's sleep. I'm exhausted and a little out of it. Be sure to text me first thing in the morning."

Eventually, Lena and Belov left—independently of each other, alas—and the party became louder. It somehow seemed more crowded, too. Maya felt deathly tired after the sleepless night and the whole day of work. She ordered a taxi and made a beeline for the bathroom.

As she was trying to close its door, a tall person inserted themselves into the opening and quietly locked them both inside. She was so startled it took her a second to understand who it was. Mark was standing next to her, his eyes boring into her face, and then they lunged at each other and started kissing. She felt him unzip her jeans and lean her against the sink. His smell was intoxicating. Touching him felt so natural, as though they hadn't been apart this whole time, weren't meant to have been. Happy, suddenly drunk, Maya laughed while he pushed inside her. When they both came, clutching at each other, they knocked over a soap dispenser.

Someone banged on the door.

"Coming out!" Maya yelled.

Cracking open the door, she saw Alex, his face very pale. She was too high on endorphins to register the change in him since she'd last seen him, or to wonder why he, out of all the people here, had the most pressing urge. He let her pass without giving her an indication that he recognized her, after which a great deal more than a soap dispenser crashed onto the bathroom floor behind her.

Before she had a chance to reverse and reenter, some other people rushed inside. Thuds and moans were coming from the bathroom now. When Maya managed to get back in, the space was packed, and she had to crouch and peer from underneath someone's elbow to witness Mark twisting on the floor while Alex hit him with a fist.

Finally, other men pulled them apart, and Dennis hoisted Mark atop the toilet bowl. The lower part of Mark's face and the front of his shirt were covered in blood.

Handing his friend a wad of bunched-up paper towels, Dennis said, "He broke his nose! What was that about?"

For a while, Maya was unable to comprehend what had just happened. She stood pressed to the wall, taking in the scene: people doing sensible, practical things like running water from the tap, asking Mark questions, discussing between themselves the implications of his answers. After a few minutes, she slung back out into the main room, where the meaning of the event coalesced into solid form and collapsed onto her.

She found Alex half hiding under the potted palm where she'd previously stood with Sanya, his eyes darting around and his jaw muscles flexing like a B movie villain's. Getting near him, Maya hissed, "Get the fuck out!"

She let her voice become screechy and awful. "Don't you dare contact me or any of these people ever again! You hear me? Get lost, now!"

CHAPTER 7

Emerging from a viscous, hazy, excruciating dream—she had been running away from someone or something—Maya reached for the clock on her nightstand. It said eleven twenty a.m. Her bedroom was dark, filled with air that seemed thick with murk. November was the worst month, had always been. Even in the best of times, you had to consolidate all your strength and sheer will to get through it, dulling your senses to its gloom. It made the harrowing nature of the human condition so apparent you had no choice but to self-medicate.

An empty blister pack was lying next to the clock. Maya turned to her stomach, burying her face in the pillow, but it was hard to breathe that way, so she twisted her head to the side. Where was her phone? She groped for it, found it under the blanket, and looked at it with one eye. Eight new messages, none from Mark.

She'd texted him before going to bed, having imbibed an impressive quantity of Italian white. This was one of her several texts to him that had gone unanswered. From Dennis, she knew that his nose was healing fine, but she wanted to hear this from Mark himself. Considering what had transpired, it was clear they couldn't see each other anymore, yet she craved any kind of contact with him, even if it was letters on a screen or just an emoji.

After many attempts to convince herself otherwise, Maya had had to admit she was in love. In addition to being miserable, it was also inexplicable. How was it possible, she asked herself, that this very young person, with whom she had almost nothing in common, had suddenly become so important to her that her every waking minute was consumed by thoughts of him? She tried to determine what it was about Mark that made her feel this way, in the hopes of somehow hacking it and making it go away, but had come up with naught. Perhaps it was simply her animal self reacting to his smell, which was, in turn, just her genes expressing themselves—or something to that effect. Maya resisted this notion, however. Being reduced like that, to a physical body helplessly drawn to another body? No, she didn't want to believe that she was governed purely by primitive impulses. There had to be something nonrandom about their mutual attraction.

Her phone vibrated under the pillow, and she reached for it, immediately flooded with shame. He never called. People his age didn't make phone calls.

"I haven't seen you in almost three months!" her mother said. "Why isn't your video on? I want to see your face."

"Well, I don't want you to see my face," Maya said. "I don't feel good."

"Are you sick?"

"No. It's just, you know. Have you looked out the window? It's November."

Maya hadn't visited her parents since before she started shooting. She realized now that she would postpone it even further.

"Are you guys okay? Do you need anything?" she asked, praying that they didn't.

"We're fine. Your sister, though! She's been more difficult than usual lately. You should talk to her. She comes over and makes us throw stuff away. Nice things! It's maddening."

Maya's parents had become hoarders, and she knew that Polina had been trying to make them conform to a certain standard of living by ruthlessly cleaning out their apartment from time to time. Maya didn't have patience for that. Also, who cared? They could live the way they liked. And she emphatically didn't want to talk to her sister, who was going to ramble on about her ex and her dog and how everyone was plotting against her at work, while all Maya wanted to talk about was Mark and her movie.

After hanging up, she got out of bed and stumbled into the bathroom, whereupon she glanced at herself in the mirror and, in addition to hideous eye bags, discovered several gray hairs that she could swear hadn't been there yesterday. Her hair, black and lush and shiny, had been her most trusted asset—until now. Well, what did she expect, at thirty-six? This was the universe reminding her that she shouldn't be losing her wits over someone who'd just stopped being a teenager.

Her whole body ached. Not because of old age, Maya suspected, but because of what her life had become. She was taking too many pills, without which she couldn't sleep anymore, concealing this fact from everyone, including Lena. Thankfully, no more anonymous letters had arrived. Still, some days she felt she was descending into depression. It was hard for her to do anything productive, and she didn't want to see anyone except Mark, yet he was maintaining radio silence.

Maya turned on the coffee maker and cobbled together a breakfast out of an egg and leftover hummus. There was also some cheese in the fridge, which was fine to eat, she decided, if she cut the moldy parts off.

Settling at the table, she took two ibuprofens and washed them down with a large gulp of coffee. In her journalism days, she'd once written about a scientific discovery that emotional pain could be lessened by common pain relievers. Until now, she hadn't had a chance to test this finding. The immediate result was that the pills made her feel worse, having somehow gotten stuck in the middle of her esophagus.

She ate some cheese, hoping that it would push the pills downward, and opened the editing software on her laptop.

Before doing anything, she tried to picture her film as a coherent whole. She needed to focus on what she wanted to say to her viewers and how she planned to say it. It was all on her now—there was no one left to help, guide, or even bounce ideas off. Last week, Belov had abruptly fired the editor she had just started working with. According to industry insiders, that guy could turn even mediocre material into a masterpiece, and she was devastated by the decision, the reasons for which Belov hadn't bothered to explain, mumbling something vague about finding someone better. When this would happen, he was unable to say. Maya felt she couldn't afford to just hang around—the festivals weren't going to wait—and had resolved to compile a rough edit herself, thereby saving some precious time.

She had already completed the first two sequences and was pleased with the outcome, confident that she'd found the right tone and rhythm. Next, she needed to establish a sense of development and an arc for each character, without being too on the nose about it. It was grueling work—watching nearly identical takes over and over, painstakingly choosing between them, then going back and starting over after noticing something she'd missed the first time. One take might be stronger in terms of acting, another in terms of lighting, overall mood, or the precision of details. This was about constant compromise, like everything in the art of film. After an hour of this back-and-forth, Maya would finally settle on a particular take, only to realize that it worked less well with the rest of the sequence than other options.

The only way to avoid being weighed down by this was to view it as part of her learning process. She took copious notes, jotting down ideas on how the scenes could have been sharpened, to be used during the filming of her next movie. Even so, each small failure distressed her, leaving her a little sadder and less sure of herself. She didn't even want to think about how she would tackle the horror and action sequences alone—things she had absolutely no experience in.

Maya powered through until everything blurred in her mind and her eyes stung. Then she turned off airplane mode on her phone and read the texts that had arrived while she was working. Two were from journalists requesting interviews. She already had a Q&A and photo session scheduled for the magazine where Lena worked, and agreeing now would mean two more. Lately, the media had been very much into celebrating women making progress in traditionally male-dominated professions. "It also helps that you're attractive," Lena had quipped. "And that you look younger than your actual age."

None of the texts were from Belov. Was it her, or had their exchanges grown awkward? Every time she had to text him now, she felt like a supplicant he'd rather not be reminded of. Maya reviewed their recent message history, looking for evidence of this, but nothing in it confirmed her suspicion. Maybe it was all in her head. She texted him again about the colorist Dennis had recommended, trying not to sound annoying. This conversation had been going on for a while, and she didn't understand why Belov was stalling. Often, a colorist started working on the footage while the film was still being shot, yet they hadn't secured one almost two months after wrapping.

Then, in a different thread, she texted him about the sound-mix guy and the composer, both of whom were crucial for a horror movie. After the fracas at the wrap party, Alex had sent her the music he'd written, and she'd listened to it out of curiosity. It wasn't bad. It was good, actually, but she obviously couldn't use it. Informing him that she would be stopping all contact with him, she had blocked his number. He continued to text her from different numbers, however, so she had to tell him that Belov was considering filing a police report. That had finally silenced him.

Hungry and exhausted, Maya was reaching for the fridge when a text from Lena arrived.

Can you come over, please? I really need help, it said.

Jesus, what happened?

I'll tell you when you come.

This was very much unlike Lena, and Maya grew concerned. She quickly changed into jeans, which were just slightly more presentable than her house sweatpants, and hurried to the metro.

Thirty or so minutes later, she was perched on a low and surprisingly comfortable stool in Lena's living room. Its walls were painted deep green; the mismatched furniture, some of it from the thirties and forties, reminded Maya of New York apartments in Woody Allen movies. A huge stained-oak shelving unit was filled with books, old and new, and a few framed engravings were placed tastefully here and there. They looked ancient but had actually been created by an emerging artist. Several contemporary objects, like a splotchy painting and a marble-top coffee table, blended perfectly with the rest of the decor. One of the light fixtures was just a bulb on a stick, while another was a vintage chandelier with droplet-shaped crystals. Maya absolutely loved this space. She had a fleeting thought about filming something here.

Lena, extremely pale and seemingly thinner than the last time Maya saw her, was lying supine on a couch.

"Misha's high school friend came to Moscow for a few days," she said in a tragic voice.

"Ah, so this is about Misha! I should've known."

On her way here, Maya had gone over various possibilities of what might have happened and landed at a terrible diagnosis, either Lena's or her son's. Ilya was in his room now, engrossed in his favorite first-person shooter game. Upon arrival, Maya had stuck her head in there to say hi and observed him to be healthy and happy. Lena, on the other hand, appeared quite ill, but it was coming to light now that this was due to yet another instance of her twentysomething lover failing to be an attentive and trustworthy partner (a huge surprise here!). Maya was more than a little irritated with Lena, which didn't make sense, given that Maya herself was consumed by her ill-considered and mostly nonexistent affair. Maybe this was precisely the reason why.

"This friend of his is a girl," Lena was saying, "and she's spending two nights in his room, because that's all he has, a room. I asked him if he's going to sleep on the floor, letting her take the bed. And you know what he said?" Lena's face revealed the profound depth of suffering a human was capable of.

"Tell me."

"That they'll be sleeping in the same bed! He said it like it was no big deal. And when I freaked out, he called me crazy. Because, according to him, people don't have sex just because they happen to sleep in the same bed."

"You trust him?"

"I don't trust this friend of his. After he and I spoke, I collapsed right here on this couch. I thought I was having a heart attack!"

Maya held Lena's hand. "Yikes, you're hot!"

"It's like I'm eighteen again," Lena sighed. "I forgot what hormones can do to you. I'm sick of myself. Will you see if there's any wine in the fridge?"

From the kitchen, Maya carried over a bottle of wine along with some crackers and olives, then settled on the couch next to Lena, who had managed to bring herself to a sitting position. "Back to

Black" played through the speakers, adding to the dark mood slowly filling the room.

Clinking her glass against Maya's, Lena asked, "Anything from Mark?"

Maya shook her head no. Then one of their phones dinged, and they both lunged toward the coffee table, nearly knocking over the bottle.

"It's from my bank," Lena said sheepishly, and they burst out laughing.

"We're pathetic! Let's hide our phones and try talking about something other than our stupid love lives," Maya suggested.

"Tell me what's new with the movie. Can't wait to see myself on the big screen!"

Maya explained that she was attempting a rough cut on her own while Belov looked for an editor that suited him, and she had the impression that he wasn't as excited about her project as he had been earlier.

"Are you sure you're not reading too much into this? He could be busy, that's all."

"Could be. But it used to be that he was always wanting something from me, and now I'm the one always wanting something from him. And he's become hard to reach. He doesn't reply to my messages for days."

"I think you should start writing something new. I don't mean put this film on the back burner. Just, you know, when you have an hour, think about your next script and write some ideas down. Then start developing characters, et cetera. It's always good not to put everything you've got into this one thing. Life's long. You'll make many films."

Maya found this idea odd. Of course she was pouring all her efforts into this movie. How else could she ensure that it would be the best it could be? It had to be her breakout feature. She didn't have much time—she wasn't twenty. If she failed now, people might not give her another chance. In fact, she was certain they wouldn't. And the journalists, who were so keen on interviewing her right now? What about her professors, who expected her to create a piece of art that would push boundaries and be talked about? Her parents would be disappointed, confirmed in their beliefs about her worthlessness and folly. Maya felt her hands and feet go cold at the mere thought of this prospect.

"I'm thinking of leaving," Lena suddenly said, startling Maya out of her ruminations.

"What? What are you talking about?"

"You know, packing everything up, selling the apartment, and moving to the States."

As Maya tried to make sense of Lena's words, she cast her eyes around the room again. Everything in here was so particular to her friend's sensibilities. Lena wouldn't be able to take all these things with her. So she would just sell this place to someone? Someone she didn't know? The idea seemed gross to Maya, even somehow immoral. It violated something inside her, some deeply held values she couldn't articulate.

She looked over at Lena's face again, hoping to find in it an explanation of how this might be possible. Lena's parents lived in America. Years ago, she'd graduated from a university in New York. But so what? Instead of staying there, she'd chosen to come back to Russia. Maya herself had once spent a year in Spain, studying Spanish and making a lot of friends, but that didn't mean she would consider moving there all of a sudden.

"But why?" she asked. "Why now?"

"Everything's getting worse, almost by the day."

Maya didn't say anything, still trying to fit inside her head the idea of her best friend wanting to abandon her.

"In a way, I envy you," Lena continued, "in that you don't seem to be noticing what's going on. And you're not alone, by any means. I've had this conversation countless times with different people, who almost invariably ask me, 'What is it you don't like? It's great.' We'd be sitting in a chic eatery on Bolshaya Dmitrovka, eating langoustine and avocado mousse, surrounded by stylish people. It's easy to ignore a whole chunk of reality, because it seems to have nothing to do with you when you move from one place like that to another. But I can't ignore it, even if I haven't been personally thrown in jail or tortured."

"You want to be able to say what you think without repercussions, is that it?" Maya ventured.

"It's not even that. Maybe I'm weak or thin-skinned, but I feel terrified. Like, all the time. I know anything can happen to me because there's no basic human decency left, no respect for human life. This trickles down from the top of the system to its very bottom."

All Maya felt now was an intense ache constricting her chest. Just a few minutes ago, the two of them had been laughing at their preposterous involvement with inappropriate men, and Amy Winehouse was singing in the background, and life seemed full of promise despite minor setbacks. But now, she was staring something dark and incomprehensible in the face, something that was going to engulf her, leaving her powerless even to squeak in protest. Just to say something, she asked, "What would you do in the States?"

Lena shrugged. "Find a job and build some kind of a life for myself."

"What type of job?"

"No idea. An office job pushing papers? I'm obviously not going to be a chief editor like I am here, but it's fine, you know." Lena sighed and brushed her hair away from her face. "Ilya will be eighteen in three years. I can't let him be drafted and sent off to die in one of Putin's wars."

Maya wasn't totally oblivious, no matter what people thought of her. It was true that she mostly pretended it away. It was just something she had to deal with, she thought—a harsh environment not unlike the one her parents had navigated during Soviet times. They had managed to live their lives, having accepted the rules of the game, and had come out mostly unscathed. Her country was being run by crooks who engaged in behavior typical of crooks. Weren't most governments made up of crooks, though? In any case, Maya didn't want to spend her time worrying about things she had no control over.

Lena brought over some mortadella and nuts from the kitchen and topped off their glasses.

"It's not just about the army," she said, sitting back down. "I worry about Ilyusha so much it becomes debilitating. He takes a bus and then walks twenty minutes to school every day, and then goes back the same way. Any day, he might get picked on by thugs or troubled teens or the police, and then—I don't even want to think about what might happen then. There's a profound lawlessness here, as if this is some primitive medieval state, and it makes my skin crawl."

"You're serious, aren't you?"

"I've already started the visa application process."

"So you're not just thinking about leaving!" Maya cried out. "You're actually leaving!" Her nose tingled, announcing the imminent arrival of tears.

"Shh, come here." Lena pulled her close and enveloped her in an embrace. "Everything will be okay. You'll come visit me. Who knows? Maybe you'll even want to stay."

CHAPTER 8

It was still dark when Maya left her apartment, the air outside inky and prickling with cold. As she maneuvered through the snowdrifts surrounding her building, she tried to come to terms with the fact that Ksenia had signed with Kelianov—one of the biggest producers in the country, a household name—and was now shooting her first feature. He'd given her twice as much money as Maya had received from Belov, according to a trade publication. Maya told herself that this wasn't a competition and that a bigger budget didn't necessarily reflect greater artistry, as evidenced by the staggering amounts of money often poured into atrocious films. Speaking of which, the bus stop booth Maya was passing bore a poster advertising *Matilda*, cinematic drivel filled with tired clichés, stock characters, and moronic dialogue masquerading as a high-minded historical drama about the love affair between Tsar Nicholas II and ballerina Matilda Kschessinskaya. It had become a laughingstock among film professionals, despite boasting a budget of twenty-five million dollars, one of the biggest in the history of Russian film.

Swallowing her pride, Maya had reached out to Ksenia, knowing that Mark would be working with her. She longed to see him, and visiting the set seemed to be the only way. But Ksenia, never one to be subtle, had first taken her on a shopping outing. Three days ago, they met at the Okhotny Ryad mall. Ksenia wanted to get a couple of nice dresses—just to have in her closet, she said. She was clearly preparing for the various events surrounding her premiere, flaunting the direction her professional life had taken.

"I hope I'll be able to shop at GUM soon," Ksenia said, taking a clingy white affair trimmed with ostrich feathers and a few other things to the dressing room.

GUM was just a few hundred meters away, flanking the Red Square. It housed luxury boutiques and was more of a tourist trap than a real department store.

After Ksenia selected and paid for two red carpet–appropriate outfits (or what she considered as such), they grabbed a couple of salads from the food court and sat down to eat. Ksenia, maintaining the pretense that they were still friends, divulged the details of her and Kelianov's initial encounter.

"First, I met this woman, Lia. She's been in the industry for twenty years and knows everyone. By the way"—Ksenia pointed her fork at Maya's face almost as if she were trying to poke her eye out—"you should try and get friendly with people like her. I mean, you're set for now, but who knows? So, I took her to dinner a few times, listened to her rant about how everything's fucked up and how all men are assholes. Then she took me to this party, where she introduced me to Kelianov."

Ksenia peered at her mix of lettuces, studded here and there with chunks of unnaturally yellow cheese. "This is disgusting. We should've gone to GUM at least for lunch." She pushed the plastic container away from herself. "Anyway. I was like, I'm such a fan, I love all your movies—and by the way, I have a screenplay I just finished."

Maya could picture the scene: Ksenia standing opposite the formidable producer, using all her acting skills to charm him, smiling seductively and making her voice deep and velvety. Maya could never do this, not in a million years. Not just the seduction part—everything. If someone introduced her to Kelianov, she'd be terrified of coming off as needing something from him and would likely make a fool of herself by telling a stupid joke or saying "thank you" instead of "nice to meet you." Which she'd actually done on a number of occasions.

Not that being modest and decorous was any good; it had helped Maya exactly never. It felt more like a handicap.

"What did Kelianov say?"

"Something along the lines of 'very interesting.' I made him give me his mobile number and his personal email, then I sent him the script and followed up like five times. He didn't have a chance! He *had* to read it because he knew I wouldn't leave him alone." Ksenia grinned widely. "And then he called me and said, 'This is good.'"

After they parted ways, Maya went home and opened Ksenia's screenplay, which had been sitting in her inbox for weeks. It wasn't very good, but it wasn't bad either, based as it was on Ksenia's experience of working as a stripper in a small town and then moving to Moscow to become an actress. Plotwise, it wasn't very original, but Maya could see how people might be drawn to the narrative of a young protagonist overcoming adversity and making it in the big city. Perhaps Ksenia would find a way to elevate the mundane elements and turn them into artistic discoveries.

Who was she kidding, though? Ksenia cared about only one thing—becoming famous. There was a character in the script that Maya was sure Ksenia had written for herself: a thirty-year-old, sultry, wisecracking waitress who befriends the protagonist and helps her settle in the capital. This project was a vehicle for her acting skills.

Presently, in the early morning cold, Maya was heading toward Belorusskaya, where Ksenia was supposed to start filming in half an hour. She'd been happy to invite Maya since she needed spectators, eager to luxuriate in her own success. Dennis was her cinematographer, as expected, and Mark was his second.

Along First Tverskaya-Yamskaya Street, nothing was open yet, and pedestrians were few and far between. Maya spotted a delivery man in a green uniform some distance ahead, carrying a huge insulated bag on his back. The level of service in Moscow was unparalleled. You could get anything delivered 24/7, not just food. A hairdresser could make a house call in the middle of the night if you so desired; ditto for a doctor or any other specialist. Maya noticed how she kept coming up with arguments meant to prove to her imaginary opponent that living here was superior to living in other places. The opponent was Lena, of course. If only Maya could convince her to stay!

In her head, someone said, continuing this one-way conversation, "And what about the metro, huh?" From countless movies, she was familiar with the New York City subway—old, horrible, rodent-ridden, and covered with rust and piss. In contrast, the spotlessly clean Moscow stations, decorated with marble, mosaics, and crystal chandeliers, resembled ballrooms in Versailles more than transportation terminals. Every single foreigner she'd taken underground had been left speechless. The trains came every three minutes, no matter what, and never broke down.

As Maya passed the delivery guy, she stole a glance at him. He looked about thirty and underslept. Talking into his earpiece, he said, "You know how hard it is to find yourself in this life, right? Everything's just conniving to make you go off course." She gave him a smile, surprised by this insight at eight in the morning.

Finally, she arrived at the set—a nightclub with moderately cheesy decor that would surely look good on camera, with deep violet walls, gilded moldings, and boudoir-style lampshades. Film people were scurrying back and forth across the hall and rushing into the main space, which had a small stage in the center and café tables with couches instead of chairs arranged around it. Exotic dancers sat on the edge of the stage, absorbed in their phones, their legs dangling. Seeing no one she knew, Maya slowly made her way to the refreshments table at the far end of the room.

There, Mark was pouring coffee from a jug. They hadn't seen each other since her wrap party more than two months ago. He looked good; his nose seemed to have healed well.

"Hey," he said. "What's up?"

But before she could reply, he walked away.

Stupefied by this reception, Maya stood frozen before the table, not taking anything from it. It wasn't as if she had expected him to lock her in an embrace and declare he couldn't live without her. Okay, maybe some part of her had clung to that hope. But what she definitely hadn't expected was for him to treat her like a stranger.

A couple of minutes later, Maya followed Mark and found Ksenia and Dennis by the camera, arguing. They gave her half-hearted nods without pausing their fight over the angle for the close-up. Ksenia insisted it had to be dramatic, while Dennis wanted something more intimate. It was possibly the first time Maya had seen Dennis resist his wife on anything, but predictably, Ksenia won. She seemed completely in her element, presiding over the set as if she'd been doing this for years. Her back was straight, and she radiated calm, regal confidence.

Her lead actress was a stunningly beautiful young woman who looked no older than eighteen. Tall and thin, she had an intense presence. Maya instantly realized Ksenia had hit the jackpot with her casting choice—the film was bound to succeed if only because of the lead. The actress's face, with its fluid, ever-changing expressions, was mesmerizing, and her hair was so thick and long it moved through space as if it had a life of its own. One could just watch the hair. Onstage, the actress pretended to dance without actually making any real moves, rubbing the pole suggestively and circling around it. Maya guessed that she didn't know how to pole dance and that a professional double would be used for the dance sequences.

After the close-up, a sequence with a male guest was shot, followed by another with the club's manager. At twelve thirty, a lunch break was announced. Ksenia's first AD, a young woman Maya liked immediately, encouraged her to help herself to the food since they had plenty.

She put some salad and dumplings on a plate and stepped aside, distancing herself from the crowd. Not wanting to seem pathetic, she abandoned the idea of approaching Mark to start a conversation. Alone, she ate her lunch at one of the club's guest tables—until she saw Mark walking toward her, and her heart began to race.

He approached and plopped down on the couch across from her, regarding her calmly. Maya couldn't tell whether he was even glad to see her; his expression was inscrutable. She, on the other hand, was barely keeping it together. Blood rushed to her head and made a thrumming noise inside it.

"Hey," he said again. "What's up? What's new with the movie?"

This was clearly just small talk. Maya had updated Dennis on her film, and he must've relayed most of that information to Mark.

"Nothing much," she said. "Belov is acting weird, but I'm on it."

Mark nodded as if he already knew this.

"What's new with you?" she asked in turn.

He shrugged. "Just hustling, like always."

Then his face suddenly lit up, and he added, "I started volunteering for FBK, doing some camera work for them."

FBK, the Anti-Corruption Foundation founded by opposition politician Alexey Navalny, dug up dirt on corrupt government officials and pushed for more transparency through extensive investigative work and public campaigns. It made sense, Maya thought, that Mark would get involved with them. She'd heard they actively sought to engage younger generations.

"You want me to recommend you?" Mark said now. "They need people. It's your chance to do something worthwhile."

The implication that she wasn't doing anything worthwhile struck Maya as presumptuous, though she wondered if she was overanalyzing his words.

"Mm, I can't," she said, scrambling for an excuse. "I need a paid gig. I'm broke."

The shame hit her instantly—why did she have to unload her problems on him?—but Mark didn't seem to notice her last remark.

"Hey, how about coming to the protest on December 24? There's going to be a huge rally on Sakharova—against the rigged elections. It's the anniversary of Bolotnaya. I was too young to go back in 2011 when it all happened, but I'm definitely going this time. I'm trying to get everyone I know to come."

While he spoke, visibly excited, Maya hesitated. The idea of spending hours alongside Mark—marching, shouting slogans, maybe grabbing drinks afterward—was tempting. Wasn't that why she'd come today, to find some way to keep seeing him? But this wasn't what she'd imagined at all. She couldn't jeopardize her movie by joining a protest where she might get arrested and face real charges, even jail time. Her film was everything, and she couldn't afford to give Belov any reason to freeze the project.

Mark was watching her, waiting, and she knew she had to say something.

"My position hasn't changed," she said without conviction. "It's my conscious choice to stay out of politics."

His expression instantly shifted to something between pity and contempt, a look she'd never seen from him before.

"I get it, you want to be safe," he said. "But the thing is, as an artist, you can't ever be safe. You can go unnoticed if you're, I don't know, a stripper. But once you put yourself out there, they'll see you. And you'll have to pick a side."

Because Maya remained silent, taken aback by this tirade, he added, "It's because of people like you, complacent and self-involved, that our country is where it's at."

Mark shook his head, signaling his grave disappointment, then stood up and walked away before she could find the words to respond.

This interaction left Maya feeling so crushed that she walked off the set without saying goodbye to Ksenia or anyone else. As she made her way back to Belorusskaya, she began to seethe with anger.

Why did Mark think he could lecture her from a position of moral superiority? He was obviously too young to grasp that there was no black and white, that people had to make complicated choices influenced by various, sometimes binding circumstances. She also couldn't wrap her head around how he acted as if they didn't share a history and had never acknowledged that it had meant something to him. He looked at her like she was just another acquaintance he needed to recruit for his organization. Was that why he had approached her in the first place? To persuade her to come to the protest? And when he realized she wouldn't, he immediately lost interest and insulted her by calling her self-involved.

Maya's cheeks burned as she replayed their dialogue in her mind.

Pumped with adrenaline, she couldn't decide whether to head home or settle into a coffee shop with her laptop. By the metro station, she passed a kiosk selling press and spotted the latest issue of *OK!* in the window—the one with her first interview and photo session. Excitement surged through her, momentarily drowning out the Mark situation. She bought a copy and ducked into a nearby café, eager to take it all in.

She ordered a flat white and opened the magazine. Her photos looked fine, though somewhat heavily photoshopped. As she scanned the interview, she noticed several points that could've been expressed better—much better. All things considered, though, this was something to be proud of.

Unfortunately, Maya's excitement was tainted by her encounter with Mark. Her, self-involved! She still couldn't get over it. Of course, every creative person was somewhat self-absorbed, but come on—just look at Ksenia, who cared about nothing that didn't directly concern her and would stop at nothing to get what she wanted. It was so unfair. Where was the old Mark, kind and soft-spoken and reasonable? He'd clearly been radicalized by his new role.

This was it, she had to forget him. Just cast him out of her mind entirely. It was for the best—she would finally stop fantasizing about him. The whole story of her involvement with him had been absurd to begin with.

Maya turned on her laptop. In her inbox, there were several emails from other media outlets that wanted to write about her and her movie. Her first impulse was to say yes to all, but she stopped herself and marked them as unread, to be revisited later. She wasn't sure it was wise to publicize her project with no definite timeline for its completion. There was still no editor attached, and Belov hadn't replied to her last three texts, despite having mentioned in a prior message that he'd seen the rough cut she'd sent him and wanted to discuss it.

She looked out the window and saw a woman in an expensive coat hurrying by, a large paper bag that appeared to hold presents in her hand. A guy in overalls was decorating the storefront across the street with festive lights. Then something dawned on Maya. She glanced at the date in the corner of her screen—it was already December 15! Every year, all professional life stopped around this time as everyone prepared for and celebrated the biggest holiday of the year. No progress would be made on her film until the third week of January, if not later.

Checking the Cannes festival website, Maya confirmed that the deadline to submit feature films was still March 1. She stared at the date, and her vision clouded as she realized that her film wasn't going to Cannes. There simply wasn't enough time. She pressed her eyes shut. A few moments later, a voice beside her asked, "Are you okay?" She nodded vigorously, and the person shuffled away. At this point, it was more or less certain that her film wouldn't make it to Cannes—unless a miracle happened. Unless Belov texted her today to say that he'd found an editor, hired a postproduction team, a sound guy, and a composer. But he wouldn't, of course, because what did he care? Her movie was the single most important thing in her life, while he had many others.

"Here." The barista, who she hadn't noticed approaching, placed a cup on her table. The milk foam had a heart on it sprinkled with something pink. "On the house."

Maya thanked him. Did she look so pathetic that strangers felt sorry for her? This could never happen to Ksenia. Yet Maya couldn't quite figure out what she was doing wrong.

Lena believed she wasn't assertive enough.

"Let me call Belov!" she said when they'd spoken last night. "Seriously. Give me his number. I'll say that I'm the chief editor at *Glamour* and that we're waiting for your film. Why is he treating you like this?"

"Maybe you should've accepted his advances," Maya joked. "Then you would've been in a position to push him."

What would Ksenia do if she ever found herself in this situation? Would she find his home address, arrive unannounced, and not leave until he took action? Suddenly energized, Maya dialed Belov, but he didn't pick up. Right. If he'd wanted to contact her, he would have. He was clearly avoiding her.

Having received only a wage—a very low one that she had set herself—while filming, Maya was now out of money. She could always count on Lena for some freelance writing assignments, but that wasn't nearly enough to live on. She'd heard that Agatha, her ex-classmate, was shooting. Her husband had a shitload of money, so maybe they could offer her a position. Maya texted Agatha, then opened a website where film job listings were often posted. There was a vacancy at Mosfilm, one of the biggest studios, for a script scout. The description sounded great: reading scripts all day and presenting short reports to the studio director. Many people would want this job, so she needed to find someone who could recommend her for it. Maya emailed one of her professors, knowing he was friendly with the Mosfilm director.

Her phone dinged. It was a text from an unknown number.

How about I join you for coffee? We really need to talk.

This could only be Alex. Instantly, Maya felt that sticky sensation of being watched and had to resist the urge to frantically glance around. If he was spying on her, he probably had the sense to have hidden himself, so there was no point in looking.

Her heart now beat in her ears, muffling the music. She opened Instagram, but there was no recent activity on Alex's account. His latest post was a picture of him looking important against an office background, from a week ago. There were no indications that he had traveled to Moscow. To calm herself, Maya started watching people's stories and saw that Sanya had tagged a place nearby. But maybe this was from yesterday.

Are you near Belorusskaya? Maya texted her. *Want to hang out?*

Sanya's story turned out to be a day old, but within half an hour, she appeared in the doorway and sat down across from Maya, clearly happy to see her.

They chatted about this and that. Maya was dreading the question everyone kept asking—how the film was coming along—but Sanya, as if sensing her unease, didn't go there. Instead, she told Maya about the guy she'd begun dating, then described the new gig she'd found. She was working as the first AD for Gosha Tychinkin.

"Our schedule is all over the place," she said. "Like we're not shooting now because he had to go to Japan for I have no idea what, but something very prestigious, no doubt. So we're on a minivacation and will resume filming next week, when he comes back."

Maya had seen two of Tychinkin's films. The first one was so bad she couldn't believe her eyes, so she had to see it again, with someone else, to make sure she wasn't hallucinating. She watched his second movie out of curiosity, hoping he'd learned something, but it turned out to be just as atrocious, if not worse. She was certain that anyone plucked off the street would've made a better movie, even a cat. Yet Tychinkin, who had to be around thirty now, was continuing to enjoy his reputation as one of the most gifted young directors. How this was possible, Maya had absolutely no clue.

She asked Sanya what kind of movie Gosha was making this time.

"It's a comedy he wrote. Basically, it's a retelling of *Blast from the Past*, though he claims he hasn't seen it."

"Is the script any good?"

Sanya shook her head. "You might wonder why I'm doing this. I'd say the money is good. Very good."

"If you hear about other jobs like this, let me know."

They shared a laugh, then Maya asked what it was like working with Tychinkin.

"You have to swear you won't tell anyone what I said!"

"Of course."

"He's so in love with himself he puts to shame even the most egomaniacal narcissists out there. And I've seen a lot of them in this business."

Sanya's cheeks flushed with pleasure. Everyone loved nothing more than shit-talking, at least everyone Maya knew. Sanya described the way Tychinkin spoke, savoring the sounds his own voice was making, and how he peered into every mirror he happened upon, an expression of rapture spreading across his features ("I expect him to orgasm every time, I can't help it!" Sanya giggled). How he didn't seem to hear what anyone else was saying unless they were saying something worshipping about him. How he approached each new person with the obvious intention of figuring out what they could do for him. If he judged them as useless, they ceased to exist to him. Also, he only dated women who were incredibly beautiful and wildly accomplished.

"His current girlfriend came to the set. She was like two meters tall, dressed in Chanel head to toe. She's the CEO of some tech company. What she's doing with him, I can't wrap my mind around! A woman like her can have anyone."

They were having such a blast gossiping that Maya forgot about her own troubles for a while.

"I'm absolutely entranced with the guy," Sanya concluded. "Like I can't get enough of him. I keep wondering, does he completely lack self-awareness? Does it never occur to him that people laugh at him behind his back? So many questions and no answers."

"You make him sound fun." Maya wiped a tear from her eye. "Though I'm sure he's awful."

"Speaking of . . ." Sanya suddenly pinched her lips as if to prevent the words she was about to say from escaping her mouth. "What do you think about Krasov?"

"Why do I have to think about him?"

"You haven't heard?"

It suddenly became obvious to Maya that this was what Sanya had wanted to talk about from the beginning, and that she'd been waiting all this time to bring it up. "I guess not."

"Oh boy." Sanya's expression became pained. "I don't want to be the one telling you. Maybe google it later?"

"Now you have to tell me! You already brought it up."

"I guess I did." Sanya puffed in frustration. "A video has been leaked."

"Okay. What's in it?"

"It's gross. I'd rather not tell you."

"Seriously!" Maya exclaimed. "Just tell me."

"He's fucking a dog." Sanya jumped up from her seat. "I'll get a sandwich. You want anything? My treat."

Maya waved her off. Fucking a dog?! Idiotically, she wondered what kind of dog, then caught herself. It didn't seem that this could be real. It was clearly some sort of practical joke. While working on the rough cut, she had been struck all over again by how immensely talented Krasov was. In every shot, he was several things at once, the complexity of his character shining through. He elevated her movie, making every funny moment profound and vice versa. But sex with a dog?

Sanya came back with two sandwiches. She'd been flirting with the barista.

"What are your thoughts on this?" she asked cautiously.

"I have to make sure it's real first. But if it is—is there a way to cut him, you think?"

"What, from the video?"

"No, the movie."

"You mean reshoot all the scenes he's in?"

"You're right. Undoable."

They didn't revisit the topic while eating the sandwiches and later walking to the metro. At home, Maya found the video online and pressed play. She only watched the first few seconds of it, but that was enough for her to confirm it was Krasov indeed, with a dog. A big, scary-looking dog. The clip was all over the internet. Apparently, they'd even shown bits of it on Channel One during primetime. Every tabloid she could think of was screaming about it, calling Krasov "a pervert," "a degenerate," and "a depraved miscreant corrupted by the West."

Afterward, she lay in bed, staring at the opposite wall, trying to gauge what Krasov's sickening escapade could mean for her movie.

A number of outcomes were possible. People's reputations survived even the most abhorrent scandals, and by the time her film was released, the incident might already be forgotten, swallowed up by the news cycle. It would only be fair—so many people had worked on the movie, and why should they suffer for one actor's depravity? She, for one, didn't deserve to be robbed of what now constituted the meaning of her life just because she'd hired Krasov in good faith.

But the country was getting more conservative, which meant taking away rights from marginalized groups, policing women's choices, and treating anything seen as deviant—whether it was actually offensive or just a little weird—like a threat. Interested parties jumped at every chance to ridicule, scorn, and ostracize those who'd misstepped, intentionally or not. And Krasov, with his unfiltered personality, was often a magnet for outrage. On the other hand, he was popular, almost universally adored by his audience. She'd heard he had fans in very high places.

It was nearly impossible to predict the fallout, Maya concluded. Still, she couldn't say that her expectations about this were good.

CHAPTER 9

In the summer of 1998, Lena's parents sealed off their Moscow apartment and boarded a plane to New York, taking Lena, who had just graduated high school, and her younger brother with them. This was right after the Russian government devalued the ruble, triggering a widespread economic recession. Maya remembered the crisis, though her impressions had been somewhat clouded by turning seventeen that summer and feeling overwhelmed by her expanding sense of self and the world around her. Still, she recalled her parents' desperation as they struggled to put food on the table. Their family survived by foraging for mushrooms and growing potatoes on their tiny lot of land, which they were later forced to sell.

Lena's story was one of someone much luckier. Maya learned it when they were both twenty-four and met at the editorial office of a celebrity weekly. By then, Lena was a divorced single mom and Maya's boss, but that didn't prevent them from forming a close friendship almost instantly. Lena had managed to remain what Maya considered a normal person, unaffected by the obsessions of young mothers that rendered them unfit for social contact. She just had more problems than most people her age, but being extremely high-functioning, she made it seem easy—building a career in glossy magazines while navigating single parenthood, with the child's father missing from the picture. Or maybe she'd had to learn to be this way, it occurred to Maya much later. Without any relatives in Moscow, Lena could only rely on the services of people she paid.

Almost right away, Maya started going to Lena's apartment after work, sometimes spending the night. They could talk for hours—about relationships, writing, travel, family, and their dreams. They often discussed Lena's decision to return to Russia, which seemed inexplicable to Maya at the time. By her own admission, Lena's life in America had been amazing. Her father was employed by a large corporation, earning a generous salary with benefits for the whole family. Lena studied journalism at NYU, had many friends, and went to parties, theater shows, clubs, and museums. Then, around the time of her graduation, she gave birth to Ilya, delivering him at a New York City hospital. It made sense for them to live with her parents, who had by then bought a house in New Jersey, at least until Lena found a job and a day care for little Ilyusha. She could've easily found employment, what with her graduating at the top of her class. She could've been working for the *New York Times* or the *New Yorker* right now! That's what Maya kept thinking. But Lena had collected her things, strapped her five-months-old son to her chest, and returned to Moscow.

She claimed that this wasn't a decision she had to agonize over or even think about much. She just knew she belonged in Russia. This might have had something to do with her desire to help build a modern democratic society in her home country—back in 2003, this goal didn't seem unrealistic or foolish to her. She was also in love with Moscow and missed it painfully.

And now Lena was bitter and scared and moving back to the States. She hadn't sold the apartment yet, but she wanted Ilya to start the next school year in New Jersey, so she'd already bought one-way tickets for both of them.

Maya, meanwhile, was experiencing a profound, disorienting sense of loss. She was coming to the realization that this friendship was the defining relationship of her life. She loved her parents and sister, of course, but didn't want to be around them much. They were so different from her, unable to understand or accept who she was. As for the man she had spent a decade with, she was now certain there had been no real connection there. But soon, she wouldn't even be able to call Lena in a moment of desperation because there would be an eight-hour time difference between them.

This was unbearable.

The script Maya had just skimmed was somewhat different from the other thirty or so she'd read over the past several weeks. Like most of them, it was written with a clear objective to appeal to the preferences now dominating the industry. It followed a Soviet officer during WWII as he struggled with personal drama, got wounded in combat, recovered in a makeshift hospital, then triumphantly returned to the front line to help the Red Army defeat the Nazis in a decisive battle. She must've read at least five nearly identical scripts, but this one stood out by displaying some humanity and a sense of humor. Its dialogues weren't too wooden—she even chuckled a couple of times at the funny lines—and a few details were truly original, like the protagonist's girlfriend having only one eye since childhood and working in a lab that studied silkworms. When Leningrad, where she lived, was besieged and there was no food left, she ate the worms one by one, crying with her single eye.

Though Maya couldn't tell if the writer was being serious or meant this more as a joke, she forwarded the script to her boss with the subject line *A maybe—Great Patriotic War—Ivanov for the lead?*

Alexander Ivanov, an ex-classmate of Ksenia from GITIS, was now seemingly in every movie that came out. Maya was getting sick of seeing his smug face on posters all over the city, but he drove people to the theaters, so producers kept hiring him, intent on wringing cash out of him while this lasted.

Sending the email felt slightly transgressive. Her boss was Arseny Vitalyevich Gazarov, the all-powerful director of the Mosfilm studio. Founded in the 1920s, it was one of the largest in Europe and owned by the state. Gazarov, once considered an auteur for his edgy and innovative films—Maya loved his movie from twenty years ago, about a young guy drifting from one meaningless job to another and becoming disillusioned with life—had evolved into a classic apparatchik, conservative in his tastes and politics. Would he yell at her for sending him this script? She had no idea. He was prone to unexpected outbursts, but, aside from having to endure his occasional rants about the general stupidity of everyone who wasn't him, Maya's present appointment could be considered quite cushy.

She'd secured the job through a professor who'd gone to school with Gazarov. Her role was simple: read screenplays, from the slush pile or agents, and report anything promising to Gazarov. No one monitored her, and she had a small office with a window overlooking a tree-filled yard. She had a budget for books (which could be adapted into films) or lunch with industry contacts who might connect her with talented writers. Her salary wasn't bad either. Friends were amazed by how good she had it.

An hour later, her landline buzzed and blinked.

"Come," Gazarov said flatly when she picked up.

She went across the hall to his office, which was huge and filled with light. Various awards and expensive presents from adoring fans, like a bronze sculpture depicting him in a weird reclining position, crowded the floor and wall-to-wall shelves. Gazarov, overweight, beads of sweat covering his forehead, his glasses reflecting light so that she couldn't see his eyes, sat behind his massive mahogany desk. Maya lowered herself into the chair on the other side of it.

"Not bad, huh?" he said. "People crave stories like this. Simple and straightforward."

She wasn't sure if he really believed this or just followed the party line. Over the past few years, a lot of money had been poured into films touting their country's achievements. Often, it was the supposed triumphs of the USSR, which had somehow become synonymous with Russia.

"Actually, I thought it could stand to be more nuanced," Maya said.

"Maybe. Depends on what you mean. But first, we have to get rid of the worms."

"What's wrong with the worms?"

"They're gross." He made a face. "This has to be a serious, thought-provoking film that inspires the viewers. You should start taking notes."

Maya pulled out her phone and wrote down *get rid of the worms.*

"The girlfriend shouldn't be in Leningrad. Move her to some other place. Saratov, I don't know."

"Why?"

"Better not mention the siege in the present climate." Gazarov looked at her as if to say, *Don't you understand anything?*

She'd started to become aware of certain things lately, though she was far from understanding them. Like, what good could possibly come out of rewriting history and presenting it as a series of heroic victories? Nothing would be learned from it then. The siege of Leningrad, which lasted more than two years and resulted in the loss of 1.5 million lives, had recently become a contentious topic. You weren't supposed to mention the widespread cases of cannibalism or other horrifying events, especially to suggest they could have been prevented. A TV channel's license had been revoked after one of its presenters asked the viewers if they thought the Soviet leadership should've surrendered the city in order to save the lives of its citizens.

Saratov instead of Leningrad, Maya typed. She looked up at Gazarov again, who started pulling on the hair sprouting from his ear.

"Then there's this German officer, who's almost lovely. Why's he so kind and intelligent, I want to ask, like you want him to marry your daughter? He's the enemy, he should be a hateful scum."

"An antagonist should have some redeeming qualities," Maya countered. "That's the ABCs of screenwriting."

"This will be a mass product, not an art-house film."

"So you want to develop this, is that what I'm getting?"

"I don't know yet. Bring the writer in, let's talk."

She was about to get up and go when Gazarov said, "One other thing."

"Yes?"

He pouted. "You know my son Renat, the youngest?"

Maya vaguely recalled a youth who appeared to be high on something, dressed expensively and with considerable taste. "I think I've met him once."

"He's about to graduate from VGIK. He's been working on this, this—I don't really know what he's been working on. Can you look at it and maybe coach him on what needs to be done, how things work, et cetera?"

"Of course."

"Thank you. He'll come see you this week."

Back at her desk, Maya scanned the icons on her screen, studiously avoiding the one she should actually be focusing on. She then opened the notes app on her phone with the intention of transferring Gazarov's notes to her computer but somehow ended up on Instagram. And, lo and behold, there were photos from Ksenia's wrap party.

Maya had been invited but had chosen not to go. Her excuse had been that her stomach was acting up again. Studying the pictures now—of Ksenia, drunk and laughing; of Mark and Dennis, mock-fighting; of Ksenia's lead actress, a balloon in her hands, smiling beatifically—Maya was gripped by a dark feeling. It took her a few moments to recognize it as jealousy. She was jealous of Ksenia because she knew everything would be great with Ksenia's movie. It would promptly go to postproduction and would be ready on schedule. It would make Venice. The lead actress would become a star, and Ksenia would get loads of money for her next project. Nothing like what had befallen Maya could happen to Ksenia, ever.

Two weeks ago, Maya had finally managed to schedule a meeting with Belov. She had no idea what she would say to him, except that she was prepared to do whatever it took to finish her film. She'd agree to any editor or sound guy he suggested. She'd even cut Krasov altogether, if reshooting some scenes was an option. She was open to any changes, her own directorial vision notwithstanding. At this point, she was desperate, having spent months agonizing over the missing piece that would make everything fall into place. Walking into Belov's office, Maya resolved to wrestle a final, solid answer from him, even if it was "forget about the movie." Knowing he didn't want to release it would be easier than clinging to hope.

"What are you talking about?" he said, visibly baffled. "Of course I want to release it. I just can't figure out how, at the moment."

"Is this about Krasov?"

"Krasov, yes. He's blacklisted. Maybe this whole hullabaloo will die down in a couple of months and we can talk about this again. Still, we'd have to keep everything relatively quiet. No high-profile premiere or huge marketing campaign."

Maya felt a stabbing pain in her stomach. She had to place her hands over it.

"We can't cut him completely," Belov mused, "but we could reduce his screen time to a minimum."

"Can I start working on this? I need an editor."

"Give me some time. I'll get back to you in a few days."

He hadn't, of course. Maya had already understood that festivals were out of the question if he didn't want to attract attention to the film. A quiet release was still better than no release, she figured, but, for some reason, even a quiet release didn't seem a possibility anymore. Despite what Belov had said to her face, she'd gotten the impression that, in his mind, he'd already scrapped the project.

Presently, she was fantasizing about her next movie, which would have to be her breakout. Maybe she would look back on this experience later and see how everything had been for the best. She could write something truly great now. She had so much time and space—she could write for hours every day if she was so inclined, and Gazarov wouldn't even notice. If anything, her closeness to him was an asset; she could show him the finished draft, and perhaps he might want to develop it. Ksenia would definitely make the most out of this situation.

Maya forced herself to open the file she had avoided looking at earlier. It held the beginning of her next project, three pages in total. This was all she'd been able to write in weeks. She stared at the lines for a while, hoping that her brain would latch on to one of them and continue spewing out other lines, which would shape themselves into a story. But, like many times before, it failed to do so. Her mental processes responsible for writing original material seemed to have been paralyzed by what had transpired over the last few months. She felt like climbing under the desk and shriveling up there.

An hour and a half later, after squeezing out of herself and then deleting several lines, Maya shut off her computer and put her coat on. Dato, her ex-classmate, had texted to ask if she'd be up for meeting him, and she saw no reason not to, since no one cared when she came or went.

Maya took a bus to Kiyevskaya, then walked across Borodinskiy Bridge, regretting her decision at once. As befitted the beginning of February, it was bitterly cold. Freezing wind made her lips go numb and her eyes water, so she couldn't see the sweeping panoramas opening up on both sides of the river. She was half dead when she arrived at the café Dato was waiting for her at.

He didn't rise to hug her, being her standing height while sitting.

"You look amazing!" he said as she took off her outer garments. He was, of course, lying shamelessly; she'd lost weight and appeared haggard.

"Congrats on the new job!" Dato went on. "I'm so jealous of you."

People assumed that Maya's connection to Gazarov gave her an advantage when it came to her future projects. They failed to realize that her greatest obstacle was herself, not necessarily a lack of access to powerful men.

"There's nothing to be jealous of. I sit around all day reading terrible screenplays."

After they'd placed their orders and exchanged small talk, Maya asked Dato about the news he hadn't wanted to share over text. He assumed a significant expression.

"Remember the short film I worked on the last few months?" He paused, puffing out his cheeks, then blurted out, "I'm going to Berlin with it! I'm in the official program!"

Maya experienced this revelation as a blow to her solar plexus. She gulped down the glass of water in front of her.

"I'm so happy for you!" she croaked. "Congrats!" It occurred to her that she had to become a better actress if she wanted people to continue being friendly with her.

But Dato didn't notice anything, radiating excitement. "It's the chance of a lifetime, I know it, and I'm going to use it for whatever it's worth. I'll grab onto whoever expresses a shred of interest and won't let go. I'll be like a tick boring into their flesh. My flight is in less than a week, and I don't intend to come back."

"No!" Maya couldn't help exclaiming. "Not you, too!"

"What do you mean? Who else is leaving?"

"My best friend Lena is emigrating to the States. You've met her."

"Well, I don't know why she's doing it, but I have to get out. Did you read about this guy Ahmet, who was kidnapped in St. Pete in October, in broad daylight, and taken back to Chechnya? No one's heard from him since. He's probably not alive anymore."

"Why was he kidnapped? What did he do?"

Dato gave her a look. "He didn't do anything. He was gay. That's a dishonor for the family. His own brothers probably killed him."

This was the first time, to Maya's knowledge, that Dato admitted being gay, albeit indirectly. While she tried to digest what he'd just said, he added, "I want to bring a queer lens to stories, and I can't do it here. Even if I somehow find the money, my films will never get distribution certificates."

Working at Mosfilm, Maya was learning more and more about how these permits from the Ministry of Culture were issued—or, quite often, denied. By law, every movie had to get one in order to be released. Lately, a lot of skillful projects had been refused distribution, years of people's work and millions of rubles going to waste. Even Gazarov couldn't always make sense of this. According to him, random people sat on the ministry committees ("Where do they get these guys from? I've never even heard their last names!"), jumping at the slightest thing that, in their opinion, might offend moviegoers, like a man wearing women's clothing on-screen or some other hints at LGBTQ, or excessive violence, or characters breaking the law. No one knew what else they might find objectionable. There seemed to be no logic or consistency to their decisions; a film featuring graphic murder scenes might receive a permit without issue, while another, far less violent, would be denied.

"Have you talked to Agatha?" Dato said. "She finished her movie—I was her first AD. She applied for the certificate right away because she wanted it to be released on her birthday. And she didn't get it! They said her film promoted Western values, whatever that's supposed to mean. Her husband, Murat, had to make a generous donation to certain people, if you know what I mean."

"Did it help? Did she get the certificate?"

"She did. But she almost had a nervous breakdown."

Next, they discussed Ksenia's film and how it couldn't be too provocative for the same reason, which would be challenging since it was about a stripper. Kelianov was a huge name, of course, and it was hard to imagine one of his movies being denied distribution. Still, they agreed that the business was so volatile that anything could happen.

Inevitably, Dato asked Maya about how her own project was coming along, and she had to tell him.

"I'm so stupid!" she said after relaying the gist of the situation. "Why didn't I realize that Krasov was unstable? I should've asked around. People have been talking about him for a long time. Apparently, he's a sex maniac."

"That's not what you should've worried about."

"What do you mean?"

"This whole thing isn't about the dog."

"I don't get it. What are you trying to say?"

"It's about him being actively against the regime. He signed a letter against the annexation of Crimea in 2014 and did many other things since then. They had to get rid of him. Maybe they even set him up."

"Like how? Brought the dog to him, hoping for the best?"

"I don't know, but they definitely leaked the video."

"Why him, though?" Maya couldn't comprehend this new information. "There are other people who are against the regime."

"He's eccentric and unpredictable. Others can be bought off."

As Maya walked home from the metro later, she got the feeling that she was being followed. This time, however, it felt different from all those other moments of vague paranoia. There was nothing frightening about it now. She simply knew, matter-of-factly, that someone was there.

The base of her neck prickling—from focused concentration rather than fear—Maya continued her walk. After a few minutes, she paused by a bakery window, pretending to look at the pastries on display. She then slowly turned to see a man some distance away, observing her. He was unremarkable: neither tall nor short, dressed in a black puffer jacket, a black knitted hat, and dark pants. He just stood there, watching her, giving the impression that he didn't care whether she noticed him.

Maya resumed her journey home. A short while later, she stopped in the middle of the street and turned around. There he was again, the same distance away, standing and looking at her like before. He had been matching her pace precisely. Since it was getting dark, she couldn't really see his face but somehow knew that his expression was impassive, maybe bored.

She repeated this several times, contemplating whether she should confront him. But would that accomplish anything? He wouldn't tell her who he was. If he were willing to reveal his identity, he would have approached her and introduced himself. Maya also considered if she should go somewhere else for the night, perhaps to Lena's, but she didn't want to involve Lena in this, whatever it was. It was possible that Alex had hired a private detective to spy on her while he was in Sweden and unable to do it himself. In fact, this seemed to be the most likely explanation.

Maya turned around one last time as she reached the entrance to her building. The guy was still there, now standing under a tree, calmly peering at her.

All she could do was lock her front door and place a chair against it so that it would crash to the floor if anyone tried to sneak in. She would deal with this tomorrow, she thought; she needed to get some sleep.

The next morning, Maya was jolted awake by someone banging on her front door. Glancing at the clock, she saw it was only five a.m. Groggily, she shuffled to the front hall and looked through the peephole. An old lady stood there, a ring of white hair around her anxious face.

"What is it?" Maya said through the door.

"I'm your downstairs neighbor," the old lady replied in a high-pitched voice, straining to be heard. "My ceiling is leaking! The water is coming from your apartment."

"It can't be. Everything's turned off in here."

"No, it's definitely coming from your apartment! Let me in."

Feeling woozy from the pills she'd taken, Maya figured it would be easier to just open the door and let the old lady see for herself. She unlocked the door, but no old lady emerged through it. Instead, chaos erupted. Policemen in bulletproof vests, armed with semiautomatic rifles and wearing black balaclavas, flooded her front hall and spilled into the rest of her apartment, creating an overwhelming racket. Moments later, Maya found herself lying face down on the floor, her hands cuffed behind her back.

"This is a search operation," a voice said above her. "Here's the warrant."

A piece of paper was shoved into her face. She couldn't read what was written on it because it was held too close, and one of her eyes was pressed into the floor.

"Okay," she said. Her brain didn't seem to be working as it should.

Thankfully, she was soon propped in a chair next to the kitchen table, her hands free. The masked policemen—there had to be around six of them—were ransacking her apartment, pulling items out of drawers and closets and tossing them onto the floor.

A thirtyish man took a seat across from Maya, placing some papers and a pen in front of him. He wore an officer's uniform, though it didn't appear to be a police uniform, as far as she could tell. Stunned to the point where she couldn't find the words to ask him what was going on, she simply stared at his face. He had wispy reddish hair, almost no eyebrows, small, nearly translucent eyes, and a large, glistening nose. The overall effect was jarring, suggesting not years of study and self-discipline but a life spent on cheap beer, watching TV, and teaching swear words to a pet parrot.

The man gave her a long, intense look, then cleared his throat and said in a businesslike tone, "I'm Major Yunusov, a chief investigator at the Investigative Committee. As I mentioned, we're conducting a search of your apartment. Once we're finished, I'll be taking you in for questioning."

"Taking me . . . where?" Maya asked, her voice sounding hoarse and deep. She wouldn't recognize it on a recording.

"To the office of the Investigative Committee."

She studied him some more, again seized by muteness. Major Yunusov was playing with his pen, twirling it between two fingers. There was a large mole on his thumb.

"And what is this . . . in connection with?"

This line had likely come to Maya from one of the movies she'd seen. Her brain felt frozen, unable to produce anything original. The presence of men in the next room, rummaging through her belongings and making loud cracking noises, left her feeling physically violated.

"You'll find out soon enough. Please be patient." Major Yunusov didn't sound confrontational or irritated. It was just another day on the job for him.

One of the masked policemen searching her apartment brought Maya's laptop and iPhone over, placing both on the table. Yunusov opened the laptop and hit a few keys before activating her phone, which prompted him for the password.

"I need you to give me the passwords to your computer and phone," he said.

Maya had no idea if she had the right to refuse him access to her devices. From his tone, however, she sensed that this was something he couldn't demand from her. She shook her head no.

"Fine. I'll make a note of this in the protocol."

"Mmm . . . I need to speak to a lawyer," Maya said. Another helpful line from a movie, no doubt.

"Do you have one?"

"No."

"You're welcome to find yourself a lawyer after we're done with the questioning. Otherwise, the state will provide you with one, free of charge."

Two hours stretched on interminably before Maya was handed a search protocol to read and sign. Written in chicken scratch, it was impossible to decipher, so she had to ask Yunusov to explain what it said. Two young men in civilian clothes, who seemed to have appeared out of nowhere and were introduced as witnesses, signed the document alongside her.

Yunusov informed her that they were confiscating her phone, computer, and several notebooks filled with notes she had taken while working on her movie. This had to be connected to Krasov,

Maya thought, which meant that the situation would be sorted out soon. Their relationship had been strictly professional and they'd never discussed dogs or politics—except for that one time when she'd mentioned that she stayed away from politics. Maybe she wouldn't even need a lawyer.

Then Yunusov told her to get dressed, and Maya noticed that she was still wearing her old bathrobe with a pattern of oranges.

"Take a few things with you, just in case," he suggested.

"What kind of things?"

He looked at her as if she were dense. "Underwear, a toothbrush, some personal hygiene products." He yawned, his eyes tearing up. "A book, to pass the time."

This was when fear finally caught up with Maya. Major Yunusov was implying that he could put her in jail—tonight. Her throat tightened as she realized that this sudden raid could be the beginning of something much more ominous. Panicking, she began searching for her backpack, but for a few minutes, she just bummed around the apartment ineffectually, unable to find her belongings in their usual spots. Finally, she had to ask the policemen if they had seen the backpack and eventually spotted it under a pile of clothes on the floor.

In addition to the things Major Yunusov had mentioned, Maya had packed two bottles of water into her backpack, along with some soft bread rings and apples, which she was now munching on. She was being transported like a criminal, in a police van with security grilles on the windows. It was freezing inside and smelled like piss. There were no seat belts, and she slid off the slippery plastic seat whenever the car took a turn. She hoped she wouldn't end up on the floor, which was unbelievably filthy.

On the way to wherever they were taking her, Maya's thoughts raced chaotically, jumping from one topic to another in no particular order. Why had they used the old lady to get her to open the door? Who was she? Maya didn't recall ever seeing her before. Did they have a staff of old ladies, to employ in raids like this one? She'd be curious to know how much they were paid. What if this was her next movie? There was a script in this, she could tell. Who was that man who had followed her yesterday? Had he been following her to ensure she'd gotten to her apartment, so that they could raid it? Had Krasov done something else that she wasn't aware of? Could he have been arrested?

Without her phone, cut off from the world, Maya felt helpless and utterly alone. There was no way to contact anyone she knew or to google how she was supposed to behave during questioning or what her rights were. The prospect of spending the night in a cell, perhaps even with dangerous people, didn't frighten her as much as the thought of being apart from technology. She should have at least taken a notebook and a pencil with her—or, better yet, her old Dictaphone. That way she could've kept notes.

Through the window bars, Maya saw that the van had turned onto Arbat Street. Within a couple of minutes, it reached its destination. A section of a tall metal fence slid open, and after passing the checkpoint, the vehicle drove into the courtyard of a nondescript four-story building with an entrance topped by a cheap tin awning.

Two armed policemen escorted her inside. On the plaque near the entrance, she had glimpsed the inscription *Main Department of the Investigative Committee for the Investigation of Especially Important Cases* and briefly wondered if these people were for real, expending their resources on her. The idea that she could be an especially important case struck her as preposterous.

Inside, the building looked just as uninspired: walls painted a dull yellow, plastic moldings, and laminated doors. Portraits of uniformed officers, their faces severe, lined the walls. Maya suspected this was similar to the displays they had in high school, where photos of the top students were showcased for everyone to admire.

She was led into a stuffy room furnished with a single chair and a harsh halogen light fixture and told to wait. An impossible sleepiness overtook her, and she briefly considered lying down on the floor but ultimately thought better of it, unnerved by the camera protruding from the ceiling in the corner. The chair was stiff and uncomfortable, so she stood by the window, leaning on the sill. Outside, two baby-faced policemen with automatic guns slung across their backs were smoking cigarettes and laughing, puffs of smoke and vapor escaping their mouths.

Finally, after an hour or two (Maya had lost track of time), she was taken to another room farther down the corridor. Yunusov was already there, accompanied by a woman whose flesh was spilling out of her uniform—a white shirt with shoulder boards and a blue skirt so voluminous that Maya could have used it as a tent. Her lips curling into a grimace of contempt, the woman introduced herself as Colonel Troitskaya. Maya removed a scrunchie from her wrist and gathered her hair into a messy bun atop her head. Maybe if she made herself look like a wack job, they would realize she wasn't worth their time and just let her go.

In that room with the single chair, as she wondered what kind of questions she would be asked, she remembered an actor telling her once at a dinner party that a police investigator had taken acting lessons from him. The officer wanted to improve his skills to conduct interrogations more effectively. He'd revealed that they had entire textbooks on manipulation techniques and had been taught to draft outlines for future interrogations, mixing various tactics for the best result. That's why they'd come for her at five in the morning, Maya understood—it was one of their tricks. Sleep deprivation, they reasoned, would impair her ability to think strategically and generally lower her brain function.

"I won't answer any questions until you explain why you brought me here," she said presently. It took everything she had to sound calm. Her chair was wobbly, as if on purpose, to further destabilize her.

Yunusov and Troitskaya exchanged a look.

"Fine," he said. "You're being investigated for potential violations of Article 280 of the Criminal Code."

Since he didn't elaborate, Maya had to ask, "Which is? I can't say that I'm familiar with the Criminal Code."

"Article 280 establishes liability for making public calls to engage in extremist activities."

Maya felt something close to relief then. Nothing she'd ever said could be interpreted as promoting extremism in any shape or form. Moreover, she was confident she hadn't violated any other articles of the Criminal Code either, even if she was unfamiliar with it. Instead of saying this, though, she figured she would answer whatever questions these people had, and this misunderstanding would clear up by itself.

Yunusov, looking friendly but bored, asked her to talk about her family and what her childhood had been like. He recorded the conversation on his iPhone, scribbling notes on paper. Then he inquired about her teenage hobbies and what she'd studied at university. He asked her to name her friends from that time and describe them. Maya knew they were fishing for anything they could use against her later, but since there was nothing incriminating in her life, she answered every question truthfully.

Troitskaya interrupted every so often, barking "Last name! Address!" whenever Maya mentioned someone new, or "When was this? Provide a date!" if she referred to an event. It was hard to tell if Troitskaya actually believed anyone could recall such details from years ago. Either way, the look on her face made Maya feel like the lowest of the low. This didn't seem like a "good cop, bad cop" routine—she appeared to genuinely loathe her.

Since there was no clock in the room, Maya had no way to keep track of time. Hours crawled by. Around lunchtime, Troitskaya abruptly stood up, telling Yunusov to continue without her. She came back after a while in a much better mood, smelling deliciously of fried meat. Maya's stomach growled. Yunusov left at once, presumably to have lunch. Until his return no more than fifteen minutes later, Troitskaya watched videos on her phone, exploding in little bursts of laughter that sounded like someone gurgling after being shot in the neck and paying no attention to Maya. The noises coming from her phone were disturbing—someone either wailing or whimpering.

Once he was perched across from Maya again, Yunusov resumed the questioning, inquiring about her relationship with alcohol and controlled substances over the years. Gradually, they moved to her work in magazines—both officers were especially interested in Maya's contacts with the foreign press and foreign celebrities—then to her time in the film program.

It was likely around three or four in the afternoon when she began describing her professors and classmates. By this time, Maya was so exhausted she could barely keep herself upright. Then Yunusov remarked, in the same vaguely pleasant tone, "It sounds like you had a very nice life. Why would you want to destroy it by creating a document urging people to revolt against the government?"

"What?" Maya stared at him, instantly sitting up straighter. "I'm afraid I don't follow."

"Your movie," he said, a small smile hovering over his lips.

"My movie?" She tried to comprehend what he might possibly mean but couldn't. "I made two shorts, both of them family dramas.

And a feature, which is a funny weird horror movie. It's not finished yet. But there's nothing even remotely political in any of them, so you must have someone else's movie in mind."

"I'm referring to your movie," Yunusov insisted. "The funny weird horror one, as you call it. According to our sources, your film portrays our country's leadership as a dark force—an army of zombies, so to say—and those who fight against it as heroes."

Troitskaya made a little gloating sound, *gotcha!* written across her face.

Maya blinked at both of them. It took her some time to grasp what they were implying, and when she did, her mind went blank. This wasn't a blankness she'd ever experienced before. There had been many occasions when she would forget a word or fail to come up with a witty response on the spot. She'd sit there dumbly for a few seconds, more than a little annoyed, then move on. But this was something else entirely. There was nothing inside her consciousness now, just emptiness—a totality, a vastness devoid of any color, object, movement, sound, or electrical impulse needed to produce thought. As the nullity overtook her, she felt that she might never be able to speak again.

"We don't have all day," Troitskaya said sharply, leaning her weight on the table. "Answer the question!"

Maya snapped to. "What's the question again?"

Troitskaya shot a withering look at Yunusov, who sighed like someone used to dealing with difficult people. "Why did you portray our country's leadership as an army of zombies—or infected, or mutants, or whatever you meant them to be?"

Maya focused on the mole on his thumb that had begun to bother her for some reason. For a moment, she became riveted by it.

"What you're suggesting is so absurd, I have no idea what to tell you," she finally said. "There's nothing in my movie to support that notion."

She checked the two officers' faces for any sign they might be joking. What they were saying was beyond ridiculous, and they had to know it. Yet they seemed to take both themselves and what they were doing quite seriously.

Maya thought of Lenin's resting place then, the mausoleum, planted in Red Square beside the Kremlin. She had actually wanted to shoot a few scenes there! It struck her now that it was a good thing she hadn't been able to secure permission. Otherwise, the case against her might have seemed at least somewhat credible—when viewed from the perspective of the deranged, of course.

Yunusov, sounding even more bored than before, asked, "How did you come up with the idea for the film? Who helped you write it?"

As Maya recounted how she wrote the screenplay—alone, at home or in coffee shops around the city—some cognitive processes began to stir inside her brain, perhaps miraculously.

"Have you actually read my script?" she inquired. "Have you seen the footage?"

"We will. This will be part of the investigation."

"Are you looking at every zombie movie that's being produced?"

"Are there any other ones?"

"No clue. I'm just trying to figure out what prompted you to investigate me."

"We received a signal." Yunusov twirled the pen in his hand.

That mole again. Why wouldn't he get rid of it? It was positively driving Maya crazy. Was this another device to make people collapse under pressure sooner rather than later? She seemed to be losing it already, as evidenced by this line of thinking.

"What kind of signal?" she asked, nearly adding, "From outer space?"

"A concerned individual submitted a statement to us, reporting a perceived crime."

The situation was taking on an aspect of a hallucination, becoming even more bizarre. If Yunusov wasn't making this up, someone had not only come up with the idea to snitch on Maya—why? what could their motive have possibly been?—but also presented their report in such a way that the Investigative Committee had opened a criminal case. It had to be pretty convincing.

"Can I see the statement?"

"Under ordinary circumstances, we would show it to you. However, the individual in question fears retaliation."

"From who?"

"From you."

"I'm not a mafia boss!" Maya couldn't help scoffing. "What is this person afraid of exactly?"

"Enough with the questions!" Troitskaya interrupted rather grandly. "You are the one being questioned here." Her formidable chest was rising and falling.

Yunusov bit on his nail, an absentminded expression plastered across his face, then consulted his notes as if to remind himself of what it was they were doing here.

Maya was experiencing a bit of dissociation now. She found it hard to believe that what was happening to her could have serious consequences. The idea that these two bureaucrats—utterly divorced from her world, their thinking so twisted they were capable of believing any harebrained theory—nevertheless had the power to completely derail her life seemed grotesque to her.

Yunusov continued the interrogation, asking if she was dissatisfied with the government, whether she or anyone she knew had been unfairly treated by the authorities, and if she had contacted any organizations opposing the current leadership. He was searching for malicious intent where there was none, making it easy for her to say no to all. They clearly had nothing against her except for the alleged report. They'd launched the early-morning raid hoping she would break down under stress and confess. But the ordeal ended up having the opposite effect, desensitizing her to all the uncontrollable emotions she was supposed to feel.

"This was a preliminary questioning," Yunusov explained, wrapping up. "We opened the criminal case not against a specific individual but based on the occurrence of a crime. For now, you're a suspect. But once we collect enough evidence, we will press charges against you."

He took a long look at Maya, letting his words sink in. "We won't place you under arrest today, but you're not allowed to leave the city. You'll be called in for questioning again. I'd say a few times."

When he turned off the recording, Maya glanced at the time on his screen: fifteen to six. She was being let go because their workday was ending. Yunusov handed her another protocol to sign, just as undecipherable as the first, but she had no strength left to decode what it said.

"Will I get my phone back?" was all she could muster.

"We're keeping it as part of the investigation."

"But my whole life is in it!"

"There's nothing I can do," Yunusov said, spreading his hands in a gesture of resignation, his face communicating something like commiseration.

With a horrible noise, Troitskaya pushed her chair back and left the room without acknowledging Maya in any way.

Maya passed through the checkpoint and stood on Arbat Street, watching people walk past, enter and exit restaurants, and gather around street performers. She heard laughter and snippets of conversations. After spending a whole day in the interrogation room (they'd only let her out once to use the bathroom), she felt as though she had lost touch with the real world and didn't belong among regular people anymore.

When the wonderful aroma of something buttery and warm suddenly reached her, Maya realized she was starving. Entering the first fast food outlet she saw, she ordered a baked potato topped with chopped ham, double cheese, and relish, then wolfed it down while standing by a high table, watching a young couple outside belt out Sia's "Chandelier."

As she was finishing the gigantic portion of food, a memory surfaced in her mind. She remembered Lena telling her why she'd stopped loving Moscow. Her overwhelming feelings for it had been the reason for her return from America, but these had eventually thinned and evaporated. Because, Lena had said, she realized that she'd lost her city, which was taken over by ghouls. This was the exact word she used. By ghouls, she meant the whole state apparatus, including all the law enforcement agencies (whose only enforcement was of deceit and corruption) and various businessmen associated with them who were collectively siphoning money from the country and funneling it into their private accounts, using violence to suppress dissent.

Suddenly, Maya felt her hair stand on end. If Lena had come up with this image, it could have occurred to others as well. Because it was apt, Maya understood just now. And someone had interpreted her film as being an extension of that metaphor, had maybe seen in it a reflection of their own secret grievances. But who could this person be? It had to be someone who hated her. Who wanted to see her being seized by the ghouls and ripped apart.

She had to talk to Belov as soon as possible. He had connections and surely knew people high up. The best way to resolve this situation was to appeal for protection to someone with real power, like an FSB general. That was how things were done here—you had to follow the logic of the system. When a monster seized you, you found an even bigger one to fight it off.

But that would only be tomorrow, when she could reach Belov through his office. For a moment, Maya considered going home, but the thought of the mess the police had left—her belongings scattered in piles on the floor—filled her with dread. She was too exhausted to even think about cleaning, so she decided to go to Lena's, hoping she'd be home.

Lena opened the door, alarmed. "What the hell happened? You haven't answered my texts! I was starting to think the worst."

"I don't have my phone."

"Have you lost it?"

Lena led her into the living room. Half of the furniture was already gone; she'd been selling it or giving it away in preparation for her imminent departure to America. She had promised the couch to Maya, along with a lamp and some art. They settled onto the couch, and as Maya briefly recounted what had happened, Lena grew increasingly pale.

"I'm sorry, but I need a drink," she said when Maya was finished. "I decided to lay off alcohol, but this definitely calls for some wine."

After returning from the kitchen, Lena took a sip from her glass and mused, "If they accused you of defamation, like insulting Lenin's legacy or something, that would make at least partial sense. But inciting extremist activities? They're basically calling you a terrorist."

"I know, it's batshit crazy."

"Lenin as a stand-in for Putin! I didn't know those people had imagination."

"It's not them, it's whoever wrote that denunciation."

Lena shook her head incredulously and demanded more details. Maya shared her impressions of the search operation and then the interrogation, recalling each moment as best she could.

"You have copies of the protocols?"

"No. Why would I?"

Lena appeared flabbergasted. "You were supposed to ask for them if they didn't give them to you! They can add whatever they want in there now, you know that? They might be forging your confession as we speak! And you had the right to refuse to be questioned without a lawyer."

"How was I supposed to know all this?"

Lena was silent for a few moments, sadness washing over her face. "You know how I know these things? I read about what to do in situations like this because they can come for literally anyone, anytime."

This was the equivalent of Lena saying, *I told you. Why didn't you listen?*

"I just thought that if I did nothing wrong, nothing bad would happen to me," Maya said, feeling foolish and ashamed of her naivete.

Lena squeezed her hand. "We need to find you a lawyer."

"I don't have money for a lawyer."

"There are some who work pro bono. Don't worry, I'm on it. I'll start looking first thing in the morning."

"You have too much to worry about already." Maya gestured at the few remaining pieces of furniture, the empty spaces on the walls where pictures had been, and the cardboard boxes piled in the corner. Lena's living room looked desolate and strangely impersonal, deepening Maya's sense that something ominous was about to happen, or was already happening.

"You have an idea who ratted you out?" Lena asked.

Maya shook her head. "I mean, I don't have enemies—not that I know of. I kinda fell out with Ksenia, but it was silly, really nothing."

"It might not seem like nothing to her. I never liked her, you know."

"I'm also thinking about Alex?"

"Yeah, that psycho creep! Who else?"

"I can't think of anyone else." Maya felt genuinely at a loss. It didn't seem like anyone she knew would be capable of something so low as creating a bizarre theory for why she had to be labeled an extremist and submitting a written report to the authorities. Yet why would a total stranger do this to her?

Lena found a SIM card she no longer needed and an old, beat-up mobile phone. "I'm glad I didn't get a chance to throw this out yet," she said, giving them to Maya.

Turning the apparatus on, Maya saw a list of unfamiliar contacts. *Anya GROM Media*, *Pyotr Fazenda*, *Anatoly Anatolyievich K*, etc. How could she retrieve her own contacts, she wondered, if she didn't have access to any of her devices?

"Here's Ilyusha's old laptop," Lena said, emerging from the doorway again with an ancient-looking computer in her hands. It was as if she had read Maya's mind. "You can reach people through social media. Or email."

"How do I log into my accounts, though? It's not like I remember any passwords."

Lena stopped in her tracks. "I always write things down. Like my passwords are on multiple Post-it notes hidden in various places. Don't you?"

"I don't," Maya mumbled. "I bet those guys are looking through my Facebook right now. Or will be tomorrow at the latest. I hope they won't write to my friends, pretending to be me."

She'd heard this was a technique the FSB regularly used.

Lena let out a long exhale. She didn't have to say anything—Maya knew she was an idiot. She had ignored what Lena had been telling her for years, had preferred not to pay attention to what was happening in her own city.

Side by side with the loveliness—the glorious architecture, the immaculately clean streets, the trendy cafés and new cultural spaces—there were bulky, flat-faced men everywhere, looking at you as if you were a second-class human. There were black, ultraexpensive cars, out of which these same men materialized, accompanying smaller, balder men to spaces you couldn't go to make deals you weren't supposed to know about. There were policemen fondling their batons, and you knew what these things could do if you happened to be dragged to a police station.

When you were constantly surrounded by intelligent and sophisticated people, you tended not to notice all this, and it was easy to pretend that it had nothing to do with you—until, suddenly and shockingly, it did.

CHAPTER 10

The next day, Maya opened her front door to find her apartment in much worse shape than she remembered: it looked as if a bomb had gone off inside. Drawers and cabinet doors were flung open, items of clothing pitifully hanging from them; the floors were covered with piles of books, garments, shoes, and papers. Plants had been scooped out of their pots, which were now empty and overturned, soil peppering almost everything in sight, including her favorite jacket. In the kitchen, all the spices and grains had spilled out of their containers. The policemen had evidently helped themselves to food from her fridge, judging by the empty plastic packaging and wrappers scattered here and there.

The task of cleaning felt insurmountable, so Maya simply cleared the kitchen table, sweeping all the debris off it, and settled down with Ilyusha's laptop.

On the Mosfilm website, Maya found Gazarov's secretary's number and called. The woman answered in an indifferent voice, showing no recognition of who Maya was. Maya asked her to inform Gazarov that she'd been running a high fever yesterday and wasn't in any condition to make calls, but she felt better today and would try to come to work tomorrow. Lying made her sweat, but she saw no other option. Next, she called Belov's production company. His assistant refused to connect her, so Maya raised her voice, nearly shouting, "This is about me being investigated by the police! Because of the movie!"

In a moment, Belov picked up. Maya began to tell him about the search operation and the interrogation but broke down halfway through.

"There, there," he said. "Take a deep breath. Why don't you come to the office? In the meantime, I'll try to find out what's going on."

He didn't seem particularly perturbed. Maybe her situation wasn't as completely out of the ordinary as she thought. Maya gave him her new number and said she'd drop by later today.

She had to reach out to her parents in case they'd called and were now losing their minds over her whereabouts. But she couldn't remember any of their numbers. She called the clinic where her mother worked but was told she hadn't come in that morning. Then she tried her dad's institute and learned that he'd called in sick. Maya broke out in a sweat again. What if this was serious? What if one of them had fallen ill and been rushed to the hospital? Her connection to them suddenly felt tenuous. It all came down to keeping track of a few digits, and if they were lost, her only option would be to go to their apartment and wait by the entrance.

Maya spent at least fifteen minutes trying to retrieve from the deepest layers of her memory the name of the company her sister worked for. There was a star in it somewhere. Comstar, Allstar, or—Starlight? She googled them all but found nothing. Then the name abruptly resurfaced. Alfa Star!

"Where the hell have you been?" Polina hissed, skipping any greeting. "The police searched our parents' apartment yesterday! And they got a summons to go to the IC for questioning!"

A minute ago, Maya couldn't have imagined feeling more miserable than she already did. Apparently, misery had depths she hadn't been aware of.

"Where are they now?" she asked meekly.

"At home, cleaning up! You have any idea what those thugs did to their apartment?" Suddenly, Polina suspected something. "Wait—why are you calling me at work? Dad told me it might've had something to do with you."

"My phone has been confiscated. And my home has been searched, too."

"Huh," Polina said. "Well. At least I managed to throw out some junk Mom and Dad have been holding on to. I'm going there tonight to throw out some more."

Maya knew she had to go see her parents and help with the cleanup—after all, it was her fault their home had been raided—but she just couldn't do it right now. Feeling monstrous, nauseous with guilt, she called her father on his mobile.

"Who is it?" he demanded.

"Dad, it's me, Maya!"

"Honey, what happened? They told us you've been arrested!"

She had been pacing the apartment, but her legs gave out, and she had to lower herself onto a heap of clothing in the front hall.

"No, they just took me in for questioning."

"But why? What did you do?"

Maya was at a loss for words. Not only had she proved herself a narcissistic asshole who thought she could spend her life making art, milking her parents for money whenever she needed it, but she'd also implicated them in a criminal investigation—something her poor father had never imagined.

"Dad, I'm really, really sorry. I can't tell you how sorry I am. It's because of the movie I made."

There was a stunned silence on the other end, then her father said, "I don't understand. What am I supposed to say at the questioning tomorrow? I don't know anything about your movie."

"Then say exactly this."

"Have you been involved in something . . . unappetizing? Tell me the truth."

"No, Dad. I've done nothing wrong. This is all a crazy misunderstanding. I'm going to find a lawyer, and we'll get this sorted out."

"Are you coming over? We need to discuss this. Your mother is going insane."

Maya could hear her mother's voice in the background. "Give me the phone!" she was yelling. "I want to talk to her!"

"Dad, I really can't. I'm afraid I'm not myself right now. I'm very sorry this happened, and I'll call you tomorrow."

In a few minutes, Maya peeled herself off the clothing pile and slowly made her way around the apartment in search of something passable to wear. She didn't want to appear in front of Belov as a sad sack, broken down and pathetic. At last, she found a sweater that wasn't too crumpled, put it on, and used concealer to hide the awful bags under her eyes. It took her a while to leave the house because she kept feeling like she'd forgotten something important. Then she kept checking to make sure she'd locked the front door—checking, and checking, and checking—until she cried from exhaustion.

Her visit with Belov didn't turn out to be very productive.

"I haven't been able to find out anything yet," he said. "Please, help yourself."

He gestured at his desk, atop which sat several take-out containers. Maya took half a mozzarella and pesto sandwich and munched on it while he speculated about what actions could be taken.

"My guy is working on it. If we could track down whoever wrote the statement and convince them to take it back . . . You have any idea who it might be?"

Maya said she didn't.

"We need to figure out if he—or she—is even real. Then what drives them. I mean, if it's some sort of lunatic who sees enemies everywhere, there's not much to be done. People like that usually can't be swayed by money."

Belov appeared almost cheerful, as if he was enjoying this unexpected distraction from his daily routine.

"You don't think this is serious?" Maya asked.

"Nah. These organizations, they need to create the appearance of work. For reporting purposes, they have to open and solve a certain number of cases each quarter. They don't really believe in this shit; this is all playacting."

Some playacting, she thought afterward as she walked along Chistoprudny Boulevard. It was a game for them, but she could go to jail if she didn't play it right. She felt on the verge of tears again, struggling to believe that what was happening was really, truly happening. It couldn't be, right? Looking around, Maya marveled at all the strangers going about their business—holding hands, talking on the phone, scolding their kids, laughing at silly memes—while her own existence had been ripped open, leaving her feeling as if she would never be able to laugh again. Then the thought suddenly occurred to her that for years she'd led a charmed life: meeting up with friends, having nice meals, going to the movies, traveling. Never once had she stopped to consider that many people might be going through a tragedy at the same time—losing a loved one to cancer, having suicidal thoughts because of a bad breakup, or losing all their savings to a scam. Or even losing their limbs in battle.

When your own life was proceeding as expected, with regular problems that were no more than hiccups, you almost never reflected on the fact that something enormous and horrible might happen to you at any second.

That evening, Lena came by after work to help Maya with cleanup.

Mopping the floor, she relayed what she'd learned about some recent political cases that the FSB and other agencies had hacked together.

"They don't care if there's even a semblance of plausibility," she said. "They get away with making the most outlandish claims, which the court then somehow legitimizes. Like in Serebrennikov's case. The prosecution says that the show thousands of people have seen never existed and that he stole the money the state gave him to make it. Can you believe this? I've seen it twice. I was invited to the premiere, and I liked it so much I bought myself a ticket and saw it again a month later. People made videos of it and posted them online! I have videos of it on my phone."

"I don't get it. How can they claim it never existed, then? What's their evidence?" Maya said, climbing a chair to put some pots that had survived the search operation back into the top kitchen cabinet.

"They don't need evidence, that's the thing. The judge simply doesn't accept evidence collected by the defense, so it all works out nicely for them."

After lugging a bag full of trash to the front hall, Lena took up the mop again. "As you might've noticed, the truth doesn't matter anymore. We're living in the world of an absurdist novel."

"You should write about this."

"I will. As soon as I get away from here."

The next day, Maya arrived at Mosfilm half an hour late. She'd missed her stop and then struggled to find her way back, which was puzzling given that she'd navigated the metro by herself since she was seven. She figured this was the effect of the sedatives she'd taken the night before to fall asleep. Her office looked the same, and she found comfort in this small bit of stability, was grateful for it, even. Logging into her work inbox, she took her time sorting through emails, downloading a couple of scripts before heading to the kitchenette to make herself a cup of tea. When she returned, her landline blinked, and she was asked to see Gazarov in his office. This was surprising, considering his well-known germaphobia; usually, he told sick employees to stay home until they fully recovered.

"How are you?" he asked, gesturing for her to sit down and avoiding looking her in the eye.

"Much better, thank you. Totally fine, actually. It was a quick bug."

"Uh-hum," he said. Then, after a pause: "Listen, I really hate to tell you this, but we have to let you go."

"What?" Maya hadn't expected this at all. "Are you dissatisfied with my work? I mean, I haven't done much, but I've only been here a few weeks."

Gazarov tapped his fingers on the desktop, still avoiding her eyes.

"I'm sorry I missed two days," Maya said. "It's really unlike me. I promise I won't do this again."

"It's not your work or the sick days. It's the other thing."

"What other thing?"

He squirmed in his seat and took a deep breath, then stared at his hands. "The accusations against you. We can't be associated with something like this, it's bad for our reputation. I'm sure you understand."

He looked at her for the first time, waiting for her to say that yes, she understood.

Maya was rendered speechless. The news had traveled fast. But it made sense, of course—Gazarov knew everyone in this business. Also, he couldn't have occupied this position unless he was friends with some high-ranking FSB and IC people.

"We're giving you two weeks' notice," he said. "You'll be employed for another two weeks, but we'd prefer if you didn't come to the office."

Maya attempted a smile but felt her face contorting into a grimace.

"It's very unfortunate." He clasped his hands in front of him, signaling the end of their conversation.

As far as Maya could see, Gazarov's standing was rock-solid. Even if she were found guilty, it would have no bearing on him personally or the enterprise he was running. He didn't have to get rid of her; moreover, she had hoped to appeal to him for intervention if Belov's efforts proved fruitless. But maybe that was naive. Perhaps everyone in this system, no matter how high they had climbed, felt vulnerable, scared, and replaceable. She recalled Gazarov saying "better safe than sorry" on more than one occasion, like a mantra. It was hard to believe this was the same man whose most famous character had said, "Here, you can have my coat. Dream of something big instead." She used to love that movie. She would never be able to watch it again.

Maya returned to what used to be her office and collapsed into her chair. Her thighs were tender from all the pinching, but she pinched them again before she could begin to think clearly. Her first impulse was to leave immediately and slam the door behind her, but she didn't want to go home and had no idea where else to turn. Instead, she decided to stay, at least until the evening. Gazarov wouldn't dare throw her out, and she had things to do.

Can you call me when you have a minute? she texted Lena. *I just got fired.*

Lena called back immediately.

"That fucking prick!" she said, meaning Gazarov. "Covering his ass at the first sign of trouble! Though I must say, this was to be expected."

"I didn't expect it," Maya said.

"Anyway, I've talked to not just one but three lawyers. They are ready to represent you. Meet each of them and see which one you like best."

"I don't know how to thank you—"

"Stop it. Also, a friend of a friend is a big shot at Google, and I have his number. Call him right now, he'll help you get your Gmail account back."

"Oh my god, really? You're amazing!"

"Just don't mention the case. I told him that you're an important journalist and filmmaker and that your things were stolen."

After speaking to this friend of a friend, who sounded pompous and toothachy, Maya spent an hour and a half on the phone with another Google employee, who said he needed to verify her identity. The verification process turned out to be unexpectedly tedious. On his end, the guy perused her inbox and outbox while she recounted everything she could remember about their contents. She described a silly exchange she'd had with Lena about an ex-colleague of theirs—she'd kept it because it was hilarious. Then a long conversation with one of her professors about unjustly forgotten Soviet films. A thread that included all her ex-classmates, about their various upcoming projects. Maya detailed the projects as best she could remember. She proceeded to catalog the contents of her photos folder: her picture with Alicia Keys in Cannes and another one with John Malkovich, in London; a shot of her swimming with dolphins in the Dominican Republic; her portrait against the background of Paris in springtime; and so on. After a while, Maya began to suspect that the Google guy was enjoying peeking like this into her life, satisfying his voyeuristic tendency rather than simply doing his job. It was okay, though—she understood this. She liked glancing into other people's windows and eavesdropping on conversations at restaurants and on the metro.

He confirmed that her account hadn't been active for two days, which meant that the hackers at the IC hadn't been able to access it yet. At last, he let her reset her password, and she logged into her Gmail. There were dozens of new emails there. She opened the top one, from Sanya.

Where are you? Are you safe? I must've called you a hundred times. Did they arrest you? it said.

The IC could still get access to Maya's email through a court decision, Lena had warned her, so she asked Sanya for her phone number without giving her any details in writing.

"It's me!" Maya said. "They didn't arrest me, but they confiscated my phone. How did you find out, though?"

"You're all over the news."

"Wait, what? Let me check."

Maya entered her name into a search engine and saw a barrage of articles with headlines like "Horror Movie Director's Apartment Raided Amid Chilling Allegations!" She felt the blood drain from her head, pooling in her midsection. How did these things operate? Did tabloid reporters pay off the police for inside information?

"You okay?" Sanya asked. "Do you need help?"

"Well. If you hear about a job opening . . ."

"No! Don't tell me you got fired!"

"I did."

"What a cowardly bastard," Sanya tutted.

CHAPTER 11

Over the next few weeks, Maya kept being hounded by journalists. This time around, however, they weren't interested in hearing her views on the role of violence in contemporary Korean cinema or her own evolution as an artist, and none of them suggested a fancy photo session with her. All they wanted to know were the details of the case opened by the IC, the specifics of the search operation, and how she was holding up under the pressure. The reporters came from both pro-regime and oppositional media; some were quiet and polite, while others were pushy and loud. She had no idea how they'd gotten her number—this truly boggled her mind. It was Lena's old SIM card, which no one was supposed to have been able to trace!

A few of them even went as far as staking out her building. Maya dreaded returning home now, expecting someone to jump out of a parked car and stick a microphone in her face as she neared the entrance. All she could say to them was "no comment." Her lawyer, Lilia, had instructed her not to speak to the press just yet.

"When we feel we need publicity, we'll contact them ourselves," she'd said. "First, we have to collect as much information as we can and work out a strategy."

Maya had liked her from the moment she first saw her at a café in the city center. Lilia approached and held out her hand, looking at Maya with a calm and penetrating gaze.

"What a shame," she said. "They are going after creative types. Anyway. Have you been here before? The fried mushrooms are out of this world. But let's talk first."

She was Maya's age and dressed smartly in a dark-green suit. A redhead, she looked striking—like someone Maya would want to cast as a heroine in one of her movies. Maya was surprised by her beauty, to say the least, and couldn't help wondering if Lilia's appearance wasn't a handicap in her line of work. She'd heard from one of the other lawyers she'd met that most judges in Russia were now female. Which, considering the widespread sexism and rampant inequality in every profession, might seem odd but really wasn't. Most new judges were recruited from the ranks of judges' assistants and secretaries, traditionally low-paid positions occupied by women.

Maya recounted her story to Lilia, who was recording their conversation and jotting down notes, then asked, "What do you think? Is there a chance of winning?"

"Depends on what you mean by winning," Lilia said. "Just so you know, only point two percent of cases end in acquittals. So we're not aiming for that. Our goal is for you to remain free."

"Okay." Maya still had a hard time believing that anyone would want to put her in jail. "Is prison really a possibility?"

"Oh yes. Unfortunately. People are sent to jail for as little as liking a post on Facebook. If they don't accuse you of being part of a group, Article 280 of the Criminal Code sets a maximum sentence of five years in prison."

"But if acquittal is unlikely, how can I avoid jail time?"

"They could sentence you to community service or a fine. Or give you a suspended sentence."

Maya liked how direct and matter-of-fact Lilia was. She didn't sugarcoat or try to reassure her. Somehow, even though what the lawyer was saying wasn't particularly uplifting, Maya felt a renewed sense of hope sitting next to her.

After they'd ordered food, Lilia continued explaining.

"The outcome will depend on a lot of variables. Whether or not the case goes to trial, the kind of witnesses they bring in. What they find in your computer and how badly they want to lock you up. It will also depend on the judge we get, obviously. We'll do the best we can with what we have."

Maya struggled to articulate what she felt was amiss with the picture Lilia was painting. "It should really all depend on one thing—whether or not I committed the crime. And I didn't."

"What you have to understand—oh, this is so good!" Lilia closed her eyes, savoring the mushrooms, which were amazing indeed. Maya was glad she'd ordered them, too. Lilia was proving a great counsel. "This isn't a fair game where everyone follows the rules. They can do whatever they want, essentially. But there's a degree of unpredictability to what they do, and that's where our opportunity lies."

After that initial meeting, Maya had hired Lilia and insisted on paying her. A few days earlier, she'd had a long face-to-face conversation with her parents, during which she did her best to explain the situation. They said they supported her and followed through with a generous sum. Belov had offered to cover half of the legal fees as well, and he'd uploaded the rough cut of Maya's film to a video hosting service and sent her the link. She went to Lilia's tiny office above a dental clinic on the outskirts of the city to watch it with her.

They brewed some tea and had a blast. By the end, they were both laughing so hard they were crying. Stripped of special effects and music—elements that played a huge role in building suspense and terror—the zombies' misadventures came across as comical and almost pathetic.

Afterward, Lilia said, "There's nothing in this film to suggest that by Lenin and his demented army you meant Putin and his circle. Or that this has anything to do with real life."

"Exactly! Then why do you think they went after me?"

"They want to send a message to everyone else. You're just an instrument to them."

"But I'm not even famous, like Serebrennikov."

"That's the point. The message they're trying to convey is that everyone is a potential target."

When Maya came home, she was too exhausted to shower and wanted to go to bed immediately. Instead, she felt compelled to turn the movie on again. While watching it with Lilia, a vague suspicion had taken shape within her. Now, as she rewatched it, that suspicion solidified into a hard certainty. Her film had never been, and would never be, interesting or innovative. It was mediocre—not even particularly entertaining. If it had been any of those things, Belov would have found a way to finish it. As it stood, not even considering the case against her, just the Krasov conundrum, it was easier for him to scrap it. A seasoned professional, he'd clearly realized that no amount of graphics or editing would save the movie.

Moreover, it dawned on Maya—the thought exploded in her brain—that the Putin metaphor was what had been missing all along. It was the element that could have elevated her film and transformed it into a piece of art. But she didn't have the imagination or the insight for such an idea to form within her. In retrospect, it was too obvious: a high schooler could've thought of it. And, as if that humiliation weren't enough, someone else had noticed the missing metaphor in her movie and was now mocking her with her own failure. If she had been the one to create it, this grotesque and terrifying situation would've been easier to bear. What could she possibly say to all the independent journalists eager to make her a hero, another victim of the bloody regime? She wasn't the brave artist they wanted her to be, the one suffering for her sharp, uncompromising vision. She was an imposter.

During the next few days (she couldn't say how many, as the cycle of day and night had lost all meaning to her) she first crawled into, then plummeted down, a vast black space. With her phone turned off, she wandered aimlessly through her dark apartment or lay in bed, the sheets sticky with sweat, or else on the floor, uncomfortable but unwilling to move. Emptiness howled inside her. Time passed, or something like it. She didn't know who she was anymore, or why she needed to exist.

One morning, a stabbing pain in her side jolted her awake, and her first thought was *Appendix!* Then she remembered it had been removed years ago.

She dragged herself into the shower and stood under the water for so long that the pain eventually dissipated. It took her a while to dry off, untangle her hair, and get herself dressed.

Maya stepped out into the courtyard, squinting against the sunlight. Spring had arrived, bringing warm air and the frantic chirping of birds. Half-melted patches of snow lay scattered everywhere, stained black by soot. She made her way to the coffee shop in the next building to get a fresh cinnamon bun and a latte, then sat outside, relishing the weather. There were nearly a hundred messages on her phone, including several from Mark. She called Lena first.

"I was close to coming over and breaking down your door!" Lena said.

"No need for such drama! I was taking a few days off, that's all."

"Right. You have to see a doctor. You need help."

"I'm fine."

"The first thing depressed people do is deny they're depressed. Look, it's nothing to be ashamed of. Especially in your situation."

"I'm not ashamed of anything. Well, maybe a few things, actually, but this isn't one of them. I promise you I'm okay."

Maya spoke to her parents next, assuring them that everything was fine, then called Lilia. Lilia informed her that the Investigative Committee had filed charges against her and that the preliminary hearing was scheduled for April 25. Today was March 23.

"They don't seem to be in any hurry," Maya complained. "The wait is going to drive me nuts."

"You need to be patient, is all I can say. A trial can last a long time."

"How long?"

"Months. Or years, if they're interested in dragging it out."

"But you said the accusations were baseless!" Maya realized she sounded like a child throwing a tantrum, her voice whiny and high.

Lilia clearly had experience in dealing with emotional outbursts. "From the point of view of common sense, these legal proceedings cannot exist," she said in a soothing tone. "Because there is no corpus delicti, the body of the crime. But this system is not governed by common sense. So, be patient. And I'll do my job."

Lilia's last words reminded Maya that she didn't have a job anymore and desperately needed to find one. She not only had to feed herself, she also wanted to pay her parents back, even if it was in small increments. She ordered another latte and spent an hour writing to everyone she knew, including Belov, her ex-classmates, and her professors, saying that she needed work and that she was ready to do anything, as long as it had some relevance to cinema. After a moment of hesitation, she texted Mark to ask if he'd let her know about any gigs he came across.

He texted back immediately, wanting to know how she was doing and if she needed any other kind of help. Also, he did have a gig in mind: an Instagram influencer with millions of followers was branching out into singing and wanted to shoot a music video.

They scheduled a meeting with the aspiring singer two days later, and just before that, Maya met up with Mark in Hermitage Garden. They embraced like old friends. There was no sexual energy between them anymore, Maya noticed with relief. After her romantic feelings for Mark faded, she had mourned the loss of his companionship. He was someone she enjoyed having around, even if they couldn't be together. Now, friendship felt like a possibility. He smiled at her, looking genuinely happy to see her. His newly grown beard made him appear older, almost his own age now.

"How are you holding up?" he asked.

She told him she was fine, all things considered, and he began to fume about how fucked up it was that the state went after her, of all people, how this was the new low they'd hit, picking on someone who clearly had done nothing wrong and had no power to defend herself.

"Are you still volunteering for FBK?"

Mark replied that he was and that he'd learned a thing or two from working with them. He offered to organize a protest in her name to make her case as public as possible, putting pressure on those assholes who were trying to earn extra stars for their epaulets and stopped at nothing, despite the absurdity of their claims. He had a whole plan worked out.

"We'll make a long video—a documentary, basically—about you, and it'll go viral! You're gonna blow up!"

"No, no!" Maya interjected. "I don't want to sound ungrateful, but I have to lie low, at least for now. My lawyer is against going public, and she knows what she's doing."

Mark looked deflated. "That's too bad. But we can start making the video now, and then, when she feels it's time, we'll release it."

Maya said she would think about it, just to change the subject.

They met with the influencer, Nyasha, a beautiful twenty-two-year-old whose appearance had clearly been enhanced by invasive procedures and who had arrived in a Bentley, at an expensive restaurant of her choice. Having studied Nyasha's Instagram, Maya had to admit she couldn't figure out why this person was so popular and rich. Most of her videos consisted of her making various facial expressions, yet they somehow amassed millions of views. She also had a cosmetics line and a range of inexpensive accessories. Nyasha paid for their lunch (Mark went wild with scallop sausages and a porcini bake, while Maya ordered a grilled salmon) and made them listen to her song, a catchy but generic tune. It was called "Crazy About You," and she wanted the video to be set in a psych ward. She'd agreed to pay Maya an exorbitant fee. (Mark had told her to name a ridiculous number—ten times what was reasonable—because, according to him, Nyasha had no idea about money. Maya named three times the reasonable amount.)

Heading home afterward, Maya felt a renewed sense of hope, ready to dive into research and write a brilliant treatment for the video. Maybe this could be the start of a whole new career, she thought—creating music and advertising videos. Nyasha was big, and working with her could bring tons of exposure.

But the next day, after Maya had spent hours watching every clip she could find set in environments similar to a psych ward, and also a few unrelated ones—she had stumbled upon music videos made by Michel Gondry and was blown away by them, especially the ones he'd done for Björk—Nyasha's assistant called to say they wouldn't be able to work with her.

"Nyasha is very sorry," the assistant added. "She really liked you."

Maya's lips started to tremble, but she managed to say, "I understand. Not a big deal."

Why was she lying? This was a huge deal! Maya nearly started to hyperventilate. She texted Mark, who quickly replied that they'd already told him.

Is it because of the money? she asked.

No. They googled you.

No one would hire her now, Maya was beginning to realize. She was under investigation for political motives, which was worse than if she'd been accused of murder, dismemberment, and disposing of a body in a garbage bin. People were terrified of the state coming for them. It was a kind of primordial fear: of something vast, irrational, and therefore unpredictable. They avoided her as if she were contaminated, capable of ruining their lives just as she'd ruined her own.

Mark advised her to take a pseudonym, assuring her that plenty of other gigs would come her way.

But he was wrong. Over the next few weeks, nothing else came her way, at least not anything substantial or connected to film. Most people she'd reached out to didn't reply at all. A few texted back, saying they'd keep her in mind, to never be heard from again. Sanya referred her to a company that filmed birthday parties and weddings, while Lena gave her two writing assignments, sending her to interview two up-and-coming filmmakers. Maya found them so cocky and intolerable that she seethed with anger the entire time she spoke with them and while transcribing the conversations the old-fashioned way—using her outdated Dictaphone, which had somehow escaped the attention of the police. She couldn't relate to these people at all and had to tell Lena she wouldn't be taking such assignments anymore.

For hours, she browsed listings on job search websites, hoping to find something that fit her skills. Many remote jobs she would gladly accept, like film editing positions, required a powerful computer—

something she currently lacked access to. Lilia had told her she would likely never see her laptop again, and that thought weighed heavily on her as she scrolled through the limited options.

One night around midnight, an ex-colleague from her magazine days messaged Maya unexpectedly on Gchat, offering her a writing project. It was another interview, with someone Lena would never consider granting further publicity to. Nikita Goncharov was part of a famous dynasty—specifically, he was the younger brother of the director who had once urged Lena to quit doing the shit she was doing and devote her life to literature, the necessity to feed her child notwithstanding. Their father had been the most celebrated Soviet poet, the author of the official anthem of the USSR, as well as a good friend of Stalin and every subsequent leader of Russia.

Goncharov began his career in the fifties and went on to establish himself as one of the finest actors and directors of his generation. His films from the seventies bordered on genius—a widely held opinion that Maya herself shared. After his movie won the Best International Feature Film Oscar in 1994, however, both his artistic prowess and his connection to reality started to decline. Over the next decade, he made several high-budget films whose sole purpose appeared to be his own portrayals of Russian tsars, prompting speculation that he was laying the groundwork for a presidential career. He'd likely toyed with the idea but ultimately yielded to his rival.

Goncharov had been licking Putin's ass since day one, without shame or measure—hence his collection of titles. He was now head of close to thirty organizations (the Cinematographers' Union, the Moscow Film Festival, etc.) and had amassed an astonishing fortune, including some diamond mines. His last few movies had been so ridiculously crude and formulaic that he became a running joke among professionals and more discerning members of the public. In an effort to stay relevant, Goncharov, now in his seventies, launched his own

YouTube show, where he ranted about the stupidity of film critics and the perceived threat from the West to Russian traditional values.

The interview, scheduled for the next afternoon, was in connection to his upcoming documentary about his father. The journalist assigned to the task had fallen ill, and Maya agreed to step in. In addition to needing the money, she was also curious to meet this once-legendary figure and see for herself what had become of him.

She had to endure the documentary first, however, and it made her cringe.

At midday the next day, a black SUV pulled up by her building. It was Goncharov's own car and his own driver, who silently opened the door for her. In forty minutes, they were on Rublevo-Uspenskoye Highway, along which the wealthy and the famous had been acquiring properties since the Soviet times. Maya had never been here before and looked out the window, fascinated by the luxurious mansions hidden behind tall fences, the lavish restaurants, and the billboards aimed exclusively at those who didn't know what to do with their money. ITALIAN CASTLES WHOLESALE, one of them read.

A solid metal gate slid open, and the car glided down a paved road. The estate was enormous, with multiple buildings, farm animals in livestock pens, and workers bustling in gardens that were in full bloom now. It took the car more than ten minutes to reach the main house, where a young woman was already waiting for Maya at the entrance.

The house was decorated in a style reminiscent of nineteenth-century country residences belonging to noblemen, featuring ornate wooden furniture, heavy brocade upholstery, crystal chandeliers, and large oil paintings. In each room, a corner was adorned with Orthodox icons depicting various saints, with candles flickering in front of them.

Maya was led to a room with a dinner table in the center set for two people with a variety of appetizers like pickled mushrooms and pirozhki spread across it. Since her fridge was empty, she had only had a cup of coffee in the morning and was now starving. She tried to ignore the hunger, studying the still lifes on the walls until the host finally appeared many minutes later.

"Hi there!" Goncharov said in his characteristically husky voice that she knew from countless films. "Welcome, welcome. So great to have you."

Maya sat across from Goncharov, who looked remarkably good for his age, dressed in a velvet blazer with a silk neckerchief tied in an intricate knot. There was a spark of curiosity in his eyes, as if he wasn't used to having visitors. Two uniformed women brought more dishes and set them on the table.

"We make a phenomenal kulebyaka here," he said. "With eight different fillings. Chicken, mushrooms, potatoes, eggs, buckwheat kasha—I can't even remember all of them. Look at the cross section."

One of the women, as if on cue, cut the huge, glistening kulebyaka in half. The cross section had many different layers indeed. It looked like a work of art.

"I'll have some," Maya said, and immediately, the woman cut a smaller piece and put it on her plate.

Maya was unsure about when she was supposed to begin the interview. For a while, she just ate and listened to Goncharov speaking at length about his gardens and the winery he had down south, the beautiful wines he was making from heirloom grapes passed down for at least a hundred years. His voice had a deliberate cadence that lulled her into a state of being charmed, and she had to remind herself that he'd been trained to do this. The food was seriously amazing, though. Soon, she'd eaten so much her stomach started to ache.

After what felt like an hour, Goncharov invited her to leave the table and move to the armchairs by the fireplace on the other side of the room.

Maya began by saying she'd found his documentary fascinating. She couldn't admit what she really thought—that Goncharov Sr., dead for several years now, had struck her as utterly loathsome. The film revealed him as a terrible husband and father, obsessed with his career at the expense of everything else. In his quest for fame and power, he hadn't hesitated to do despicable things. He'd taken part in the persecution of Pasternak, Brodsky, and other dissident writers, only to deny his role after the fall of the communist regime, claiming he'd done nothing of consequence. If Maya were braver, this was what she would say. But instead, she stuck to what was expected, asking Goncharov if his life had been about proving himself to his father and seeking his approval.

"Yes," he replied. "All my life, I waited for him to recognize what I'd done and, in some way, show me—I knew he'd never say it out loud—that he loved me."

"Did he, eventually?"

"No." Goncharov stated this simply, and Maya felt a pang of empathy for him. Even in your seventies, it was still possible to long for your father's approval and to grieve the fact that he had never loved you.

"Do you disapprove of some of the choices he made?"

"Who am I to judge him? He was a great man. But I do wish he'd been a better father."

"In the movie, you mention that he often spanked you when you were young. Sometimes you couldn't even walk afterward. How do you feel about this, being a parent and a grandparent yourself?"

Goncharov appeared puzzled and a little put off by this—one might think he'd been asked something completely irrelevant. "I spanked every one of my children. How do you raise a child if you don't spank them? A belt is a parent's best friend."

Maya couldn't believe her ears. She was a journalist, recording this conversation. Did he not have the slightest idea how his words might sound if she decided to make a headline out of them?

Goncharov had four children, two sons and two daughters. The oldest son was in his forties, and the youngest daughter was thirty, if Maya remembered correctly. At six, Nadya had starred in his Oscar-winning film, and he brought her onstage at the Dorothy Chandler Pavilion to receive the golden trophy. Photos of Goncharov holding Nadya, the statuette in her hand, circulated around the world, touching everyone who saw them. Maya struggled to reconcile that image with the reality that he had beaten Nadya with a belt, perhaps for years. He'd made a film about his other daughter, Nina, titled *Nina from 6 to 16*, and Maya could still vividly picture that girl, vulnerable and shy. That child had also endured physical abuse at the hands of a father who claimed to love her.

Goncharov clearly read Maya's expression and volunteered, "I can see you've been spoiled by Western ideas. Fortunately, it's not too late, and we can set you straight."

While Maya wondered how exactly she'd managed to set him off, he launched into a tirade about the great Russian traditions that "our great ancestors passed to us" and about the detrimental impact that the immoral, perverted Western values were having on the minds of young people. According to him, concepts like democracy and personal liberties undermined the very fabric of community and family bonds—and everything that Russia stood for.

"You know what the UN's secret plan is? I'll tell you," he said, holding up his finger like a professor from an old movie. "To destroy our country! We have to fight with all our might. It's our mission—not to let the whole world go to hell. I don't doubt that we'll prevail!"

Maya slumped in her armchair, her mind empty of ideas on how to steer the conversation back to the documentary or at least something related to cinema. She shouldn't have eaten so much; her brain now felt sluggish, weighed down by the heavy meal.

Meanwhile, Goncharov gestured toward her Dictaphone perched on the coffee table between them. "This means you're not hopeless. We actually have something in common."

Out of his pockets, he produced two ancient mobile phones—scratched, bulky things the likes of which Maya hadn't seen for at least fifteen years.

"See, I don't use any of those new gadgets. Especially iPhones."

"What's wrong with iPhones?" she croaked, bracing herself for what she was about to hear.

"Ah!" Goncharov's face lit up, as if they'd stumbled upon his favorite topic. "You know why Bill Gates got into pharma? So that he could control the population on Earth."

They had obviously reached a dead end. Maya tried to interject with some questions, but to no avail—he continued to expound on the greatness of Russia and the nefarious schemes the collective West was plotting against it for another half hour.

At home, despite her fatigue, she transcribed and edited the interview at once, not wanting to spend any more time with Goncharov beyond today. In any civilized country, he would be condemned after a confession like the one he'd given her, but in the Russia he so loved, his right to abuse his family was protected by law. *I don't know what you're going to do with this*, Maya wrote in the accompanying email to the ex-coworker who'd hired her. *He's really out of it. I did what I could.* They must've known the guy was unhinged when they sent her to interview him.

The next evening, Maya visited her parents, who she'd started seeing more often lately because, at their place, a meal was always waiting for her. She'd somehow stopped caring that her mom's cooking was greasy and hard to digest. One could marvel at how quickly she had let go of the habits and attitudes that once defined her.

"You've lost more weight!" her mother exclaimed, meeting her in the front hall.

"It's all the stress."

"It's not just the stress, I can see it." Her mom, who had never shown concern about Maya's health, not even when she expressly requested treatment, suddenly appeared worried. "You look gaunt! Why don't you come to the clinic tomorrow? We'll do a complete physical."

But Maya had no desire to go to her mother's clinic and talk to her friends, the doctors. She didn't want to be the subject of scrutiny; she had enough of that already. And frankly, she was afraid of what they might discover.

At the table, as Maya ate, Polina and their dad recalled the time, just a few years ago, when Moscow had been overrun by feral dogs. These dogs had roamed in packs throughout the city, terrorizing residents and even killing a few people. Polina claimed that some still inhabited isolated industrial areas and had recently mauled a woman to death. Although it wasn't a pleasant topic, at least they weren't discussing Maya. She had set a condition for her visits: no talk of her movie, her criminal case, or her current situation. If she had any news, she would share it herself.

But, of course, they breached the agreement twenty minutes into dinner.

"Have you found a job yet?" Polina asked.

"I'm basically unemployable now."

"That's in your world. In my world, no one cares. Take an accounting course, and I'll set you up with some clients. You can even work from home."

Their parents perked up at this, and the whole family began brainstorming employment ideas for Maya.

"We need a receptionist at the clinic," her mother said. "The pay isn't great, but if they see that you're smart, they'll promote you."

Maya's dad suggested that she try dog walking instead. "I heard you can make a lot of money this way. Also, we can help you out if you need it."

Maya was broke, but she had sworn to herself that she wouldn't accept anything more from her parents. She left right after dessert; being with them and seeing the sympathy in their faces was unbearable.

Slowly, she began to unravel. It seemed that she'd lost the ability to sleep for good. The medication no longer helped. A few months ago, one pill had been enough to send her into a sticky, unsatisfying, yet unmistakably unconscious realm, disconnecting her from external stimuli. Now, she took six at a time—only to find herself spending hours in an intense, claustrophobic, nauseating state that provided no rest. She couldn't tell whether things were whirring inside her head or outside of it.

It took her a while to realize that her body had developed a tolerance to the drug. Taking more than six pills was dangerous. What if she died and everyone decided it was a suicide? No, she couldn't let that happen. So, around one or two in the morning, she started dragging herself to bed unmedicated, pulling the blanket over herself, hoping for something she couldn't quite define. Inevitably, the moment would come when lying in bed awake became unendurable, and she would get up, sobbing.

She began roaming the streets at night. Anything was better than staying home, where the bed seemed to stare at her. At first, she stuck to well-lit, central avenues, where cars whooshed by and people went about their business. But soon, she got the sense that no one could see her, that she had somehow become invisible, as no one addressed her or even glanced in her direction. She ventured into darker side streets and courtyards, discovering that she preferred them. As she walked quickly, she fell into a rhythm that hypnotized her into a state of reduced awareness, for which she was grateful.

Sometimes, Maya mulled over the roads not taken. There were so many things she could've done differently. She could've applied to a master's program either in Europe or the United States and then made her films there. True, it would have taken her much longer; it was almost unheard of for a director to make their own feature right after graduation in any other country. "Most people are held back by their inability to learn a new language," Lena had told her more than once. "And you already know five. You could go anywhere."

But Maya hadn't wanted to go. She used to love her country, her people. She'd felt she belonged here.

CHAPTER 12

It was a radiant, sunny morning when Maya left her apartment for a meeting with Lilia. Trees had already sprouted tender-green leaves; the sun felt warm on her face. Music wafted from someone's open window, and people in the street looked surprised by how nature was treating them, breaking into tentative smiles. In her previous life, a morning like this would have filled her with the sense of how amazing it was just to exist in the world. But that was in the past.

She and Lilia were meeting to discuss their strategy for the trial. In truth, Maya was only there to listen—she had very little to contribute. Sleep deprivation had taken a toll on her; she could no longer sustain complex thoughts or absorb most information. Even reading had become nearly impossible; often, by the time she finished a page, she couldn't remember a single thing she had just read.

The preliminary hearing had taken place last week. First, they waited outside the courthouse because the judge hadn't arrived by the scheduled start time. Maya had begged her family not to come, and they'd complied. Both Sanya and Mark had wanted to show up but couldn't get off work, so Lena was her only friend there, having taken the day off. After almost three hours of waiting, they were led into a stuffy room that quickly filled with people, most of them reporters and photographers. Then they had to wait another hour inside, where the heat became intolerable, forcing some to leave for fear of fainting. There was no air conditioning in any of the rooms, the bailiff clarified, wiping sweat from his face with his sleeve—not even in the judges' chambers.

Finally, Judge Dondurova—a woman with a heavy face who didn't seem to be having a good day—arrived and started the proceedings. The prosecutor turned out to be a dashing young man with a nice smile whom Maya had initially mistaken for a journalist. She briefly wondered what he was doing in a job like this and, for a few moments, clung to the hope that he might be an agent of sensibleness.

The prosecutor, Kryuchkov, began by reading the indictment, which claimed that Maya held extremist ideological beliefs and that her film was made with the intent to incite hatred for the current government and encourage viewers to overthrow it. There was no irony in his voice, and no conviction either, but from the look he shot at Maya, she understood that he believed she stood no chance.

"Maya Evgenyevna, do you understand the charges?" the judge addressed her.

Maya had gone through this with Lilia, but instead of simply replying "yes," as they had rehearsed, she said, "I understand the words that have been read, but I don't understand what they have to do with me."

Dondurova wasn't impressed. Maybe murderers and drug traffickers all said the same thing. "How do you plead?" she asked.

"Not guilty."

"Sit down, please."

After Lilia made her statement, elaborating on the absurdity of the charges, Kryuchkov launched into presenting the evidence collected by the investigative team. He invited a member of the team, an officer in his thirties, to read the document that had triggered the investigation. Its contents were more or less the same as the text Kryuchkov had read earlier and written in similar legalese, which prompted Maya to wonder once again if her snitch was even real. Perhaps that character had been invented by the operatives—a theory she and Lilia had discussed.

Lilia asked the man to explain why they had classified the informant's name—if they hadn't, she would have had the chance to question that person in court. "What is he—or she—so afraid of?"

The man replied that the informer believed Maya might be connected to Ukrainian terrorists and was therefore afraid of becoming their target. Maya felt her face split into a smile against her will. The claim was so preposterous it seemed impossible anyone wouldn't recognize it as such, then inevitably realize that all the charges against her were equally nonsensical. But no, people were listening to this with straight faces, even nodding.

The same man went on to read another statement, allegedly provided by one of Maya's ex-classmates, whose name was also classified for the same reason—fear of retaliation from her or whoever stood behind her. According to this person, whether real or fabricated, Maya had supposedly declared on more than one occasion that she was against Putin personally and the regime he'd installed. The lie was so blatant that she let out a yelp, causing Lilia to place her hand on her arm.

Another man, portly and short, replaced the officer on the witness stand and was introduced as Ivan Rubin, a film expert asked to provide an artistic examination of Maya's film. She'd never heard his name before. It transpired that he was employed at GITR, the institute Mark studied at, where he held the position of Vice-Rector for Youth Policy and Educational Work.

Rubin announced that he didn't know Maya personally and that his expert review was therefore objective, based solely on the rough cut of her film he'd been requested to watch. He took out his glasses from a protective case that hung from his neck on a cord, put them on, and commenced reading aloud from a printout.

First, he summarized the plot, mocking the lead characters and the premise, saying that it stretched credulity to its breaking point.

"The storyline," he continued, "unfolds with such implausibility that it undermines any attempt at genuine horror or suspense. The cinematography often relies too heavily on clichéd techniques and fails to build tension. Despite a few strong performances, the characters lack depth and fail to evoke empathy. The execution lacks coherence, with erratic, uneven pacing and predictable plot twists that leave the audience indifferent to the unfolding events. Overall, the film disappoints with its inability to deliver a compelling narrative."

"But more important"—Rubin took a breath and peered over the audience above the lenses of his glasses, then continued—"is the intended message of this film, its underlying metaphor. There is no doubt that its depiction of Lenin and the group of zombies under his command is a thinly veiled commentary on contemporary political figures. By conflating historical figures with current political personalities, the film misses an opportunity to engage in nuanced social commentary. Despite this allegorical approach feeling heavy-handed and lacking in subtlety, this movie is dangerous due to its implicit suggestion for viewers to overthrow the government, symbolically represented by Lenin and his zombie followers. This narrative choice could be seen as incendiary and provocative. By using horror elements to allegorize political upheaval, the film encourages radical interpretations, leading to a potentially inflammatory viewing experience. From all of the above, it is evident that this film is harmful and could have a particularly strong influence on young people."

When he finished reading, an overwhelming sadness washed over Maya. This was, essentially, her first review—and possibly the only one her film would ever receive. It had come from a no-name in the business who had likely been paid for collaboration with the authorities or at least promised some perks, but it still stung. Her mind almost completely blocked out the second half of the review, fixating on the first. She couldn't help but take Rubin's critique to heart. She wallowed in this feeling for a few minutes, nearly missing what happened next.

As it turned out, Kryuchkov filed a motion requesting that she be placed in custody of the state pending trial.

Lilia had warned her that this might happen, explaining that when someone was accused under Article 280, it typically landed them in jail right away. Maya had spent several evenings reading everything she could about life in SIZOs—pretrial detention centers—and watching videos by incarcerated women. Overcrowding was common, with up to fifty people in a single cell. She could be placed with inmates charged with anything from theft to murder. Some would likely have untreated infectious diseases, including HIV; others would be mentally ill. Hygiene conditions were abysmal: toilets inside the cell, sometimes just a hole in the floor; cold showers once a week; cleaning done by inmates themselves. Smoking was widespread, and with windows sealed shut, cells were thick with smoke. In many ways, SIZOs were worse than correctional colonies, and the worst part was the uncertainty: no sentence, no timeline. Detention could stretch on for years.

Maya didn't think she could last more than a week in a place like that. Maybe someone with a stronger character could, perhaps even coming out tougher on the other side, but not her. Watching the videos, she'd had to pause frequently, feeling suffocated by what she saw. She could hardly believe her eyes. For years, she'd walked by the SIZO Matrosskaya Tishina—"Sailors' Silence," what was up with that name?—located right in the city center, on her way to and from her editorial office. She could never have imagined what went on behind those walls.

And now, she was confronting the possibility of being locked up in a place like that herself. As Maya sat in the courtroom behind a cheap desk, she felt the duffel bag Lilia had advised her to pack pressing against her leg. It contained basic necessities: a change of clothes, underwear, lotion, toothpaste and a toothbrush, tampons, wet tissues, and sanitizer—in case she was taken into custody at the end of the hearing.

Lilia began to argue against the necessity of detention, presenting evidence to counter Kryuchkov's claims that Maya was a flight risk, a danger to the community, and likely to pressure the witnesses if not detained. With her back as straight as a dancer's, Lilia addressed the court in a voice that brought to mind an eager student who took pleasure in studying for exams. She looked radiant in her elegant navy suit, her hair in a messy bun. Pointing out that Maya had no history of violence or misdemeanors, Lilia concluded with "Please take a look at my client. Maya Evgenyevna couldn't hurt a fly. It's absurd to claim she's dangerous or could coerce the witnesses."

Maya was unsuccessfully holding back tears, clearly presenting a pathetic enough picture.

The court secretary announced an hour-long break for the judge to make her decision, and Maya followed Lilia outside with Lena. They found some shade at the back of the building, away from the cameras. It was uncharacteristically hot for late April, yet Maya was trembling as if she were freezing, her teeth chattering. Lena hugged her and made her drink some water.

"I have a protein bar. You want it?" she offered.

Maya shook her head. She couldn't bring herself to eat, even though she hadn't had a crumb since last night. Her stomach was in a knot.

"I really hope the judge didn't take the Ukrainian terrorists thing seriously," Lilia said. "That would really hurt our case. These people just say whatever comes to their sick minds. They have no filter."

"Aren't you used to this?" Lena asked.

"You kidding? I'll never get used to it. Day after day, I make myself say, 'Your honor, pay attention to such and such article,' or 'I ask the court to consider the constitutional court's position on this issue.' But inside, all I really want to do is scream, 'Are you fucking serious?! You must be insane!'"

Maya was just starting to wake up to the fact that many people seemed to be operating in a realm where completely deranged things could be true, or at least believable. And they dared to say that her film, a piece of entertainment, stretched credulity! Maybe this was how the human mind worked. When you witnessed the ruling class amassing staggering wealth, treating the country as their personal property, and killing citizens—including children—by the hundreds, all the while lying about it, you learned to ignore what was actually happening, and then your brain lost the ability to tell what was real from what wasn't.

Lena said, "As I listen to them, I keep asking myself—how come people with such limited intelligence are wielding so much power?

But I already know the answer, of course. It all starts with that one person who has an enormous amount of power he doesn't deserve."

From around the corner, a bailiff appeared and stared at the three of them, his eyes small like pencil erasers. "You're not supposed to be here," he said glumly.

Since none of them wanted to make a scene, they returned to the courtyard in front of the building, where everyone else was smoking and looking at their phones. They couldn't even talk there for fear of being overheard.

Once they were called back inside the building, Maya felt close to fainting. She leaned on Lena for support, past caring about how it looked. But then, suddenly, she entered a state of detachment, as if she'd lost the ability to feel anything. It was as if her brain, having reached its limit, had decided to stop caring. Everyone rose as Dondurova began to read her decision. Maya's attention wandered; unable to concentrate on what the judge was saying, she observed the others in the room. Some appeared incredibly alert, hanging on the judge's every word, while others, like the prosecutor, seemed bored, their minds elsewhere. Lena's face was tense, and she was biting her lip. One of the bailiffs, who looked no older than eighteen, had fallen asleep, his face sweet and childlike.

Dondurova's statement went on for some time, but Maya was able to grasp the gist of it: there was enough evidence to proceed to trial. However, Kryuchkov's request for detention was denied.

"Yes!" Lilia exclaimed and threw her arms around Maya. But Maya felt so empty inside that she couldn't share in the happiness.

Afterward, as their trio walked toward the metro, Maya's sensations began to return. She was going home. She would unpack her bag. She would sleep in her own bed, alone in her beautiful, quiet apartment, free to come and go as she pleased. Tomorrow, she would spend a whole day walking around the city and visiting lush, green parks, inhaling the wonderful smells of flowers and cut grass, then have a nice meal, either at home or in a café. She would watch a movie—or two. From now on, she would savor every minute of her life.

Meanwhile, Lilia was saying, "We really got lucky. Honestly, I didn't expect this from Dondurova. I didn't mention it earlier because—I didn't want to make you feel worse than you already did."

"You know her?" Lena asked.

"Yeah, I've been involved in a couple of cases where she was presiding. Usually, she's ruthless. I don't know what happened today. Maybe she was in a good mood. Maybe her kid got into MGIMO or something."

"It's too early for that," Maya said. "The results come in around midsummer."

"Maybe her husband got her a present?"

Their spirits lifted, and they began speculating about what Dondurova's husband might have gifted her.

"A Cartier brooch," Lilia suggested. "In the shape of a snake! With emeralds for eyes."

"A romantic getaway to the Maldives! Just the two of them, gorging on all kinds of food and getting massages nonstop," Lena said.

Maya offered, "A pigsty with twenty little piglets, all pink, with cute little snouts."

Their hypotheses grew increasingly bizarre until they were in hysterics, laughing uncontrollably.

Later, alone, Maya tried imagining all these people—Dondurova, Kryuchkov, Rubin, the officer who'd read the anonymous testimony—away from their jobs, at home with their families. What kind of lives did they lead? The judge probably enjoyed her dacha with its rosebushes. On summer weekends, she marinated pork in her special marinade and made shashlyk. She had an eggplant recipe passed down from her grandmother. Her mother-in-law had dementia, and her husband was a small-time businessman who collected swords. When she looked at herself in the mirror, she saw a woman whose looks were fading, who needed to lose some weight and do something about her hair. She was perfectly normal, in other words. How was it possible that she didn't see the accusations against Maya for what they were? Why hadn't she dismissed them right away? Had she developed a tolerance for the grotesque, for lies and shoddy work, over the years? Perhaps she didn't care either way; it was just a job. She was paid for it and did what was expected without getting into the nuances.

That had happened last week. Today, Maya met Lilia at a bistro on Sretenka. Lilia wanted to sit outside, enjoying the early May sunshine, and Maya insisted on taking the table farthest from the entrance, partly hidden from view by a hedge. After they ordered, Lilia opened her old-fashioned notebook.

"I thought our main line of defense would be that your film was never made public," she said. "So no public calls to extremist activity could have taken place. But as you know, they've dealt with that. We need to regroup."

During the hearing, the investigators had presented evidence that some footage from the film had been leaked and was available online. It was, of course, possible they'd leaked it themselves. What Maya had posted on Instagram was also conveniently counted as circulation. Then there was the fact that plenty of people outside the crew had read her script—this, too, was considered a form of publicizing. And finally, there was the supposed ex-classmate who claimed Maya had denounced the regime and said it needed to be overthrown. All of it, the prosecution argued, showed a pattern of extremist intent. The judge agreed.

Their strategy now, Lilia said, would be to contradict the prosecution's narrative completely: to demonstrate that the film contained no subversive message, and that Maya was apolitical and had never said anything incendiary.

Presently, they tried to come up with a list of witnesses and experts they could call upon for the defense. Lena was unfortunately out of the question: she was leaving for the States in August, and no one knew how long the trial would last. At Lilia's urging, Maya had reached out to several ex-classmates who she thought she'd been close to but received only polite refusals. Among her professors, only one had agreed to testify. Perhaps coincidentally, he was both very old and a drunk.

So far, they had three names with a checkmark across from them: Rytvin the professor, Sanya, and Mark.

"I hope they know what they're getting into," Lilia mumbled.

Maya herself didn't fully comprehend the ramifications her friends might face. If their names became associated with the trial, they might have difficulties finding work in the future—or worse. How much worse, she had no idea, but she was infinitely grateful to them. Who could have predicted that the only people willing to stand by her in this difficult time would be these three? A very old man with nothing to lose and two very young ones, still acutely aware of the world's injustices, unafraid of the potential fallout.

"I thought I was friends with half of Moscow," she said bitterly.

"You know the saying, a friend in need is a friend indeed?"

Maya sighed. "Shouldn't Belov be our witness, too?"

Lilia had already thought of him, of course—his name was in her notebook. In fact, she'd spoken to him, and he'd promised to think about it.

"What does he mean, think about it? It's his movie, too!"

Lilia shrugged. "Let's just hope he doesn't say he gave you the money without knowing you were an extremist."

As for the experts who could testify that the movie was purely entertainment and had no political meaning, Maya promised to come up with some names, even though she knew it wouldn't be easy. Why would anyone risk their career for a stranger?

"The good news is, we have plenty of time, which is not always the case," Lilia said, wrapping up. The date for the next hearing was set for June 4. "I'm sure we'll find someone. There are still some decent people in the world."

She left immediately after, since she was busy with other cases, and Maya stayed behind. She figured she could hold down the table for at least another hour without having to order anything else.

Dato had sent her a video of himself making his first short film in English. He was thriving in Berlin, where he'd landed a fellowship at a university. He had also applied for political asylum. The video ended with "Come here! I'll help you settle." Maya texted back, explaining that she was banned from leaving the country.

She'd sworn off social media because she couldn't stand seeing her peers' successes, but sometimes she couldn't resist taking a peek at Instagram. As she opened the app and scrolled through the stories, she saw Dato again, embracing a tall, handsome guy in a gay bar in Berlin. Ksenia was taking a bow on a theater stage after a performance, surrounded by flowers. Vova was filming with Bondarchuk. And then—Agatha popped up in a tiny white dress in front of the Palais des Festivals in Cannes, announcing that her feature had made it into the lineup for the upcoming festival! Maya checked the festival's website and confirmed it was true: Agatha's movie would be screened in the Out of Competition section. While it wasn't the same as being in the official selection, it was still incredibly prestigious. Maya felt like she was going to be sick.

She was startled by a man's head appearing from behind the hedge. "Hello!" the head said amiably. "I hope I haven't caught you at a bad time."

"What do you want?" Maya blurted out, though she already knew who it was and what he wanted.

Among the reporters who kept pursuing her, one was especially relentless. His last name was Bobrov, and he worked for an online outlet known for its sensational stories. He kept "running into" Maya at all hours and in various places, reminding her of Alex.

"I'm not talking to you," she said. "I already made that clear."

"Just one comment, please? I'll let you see the article before it goes live. If you're not happy with it, we can change it."

Maya knew this was a trick meant to lure her into telling him something she would later regret. Lilia had been clear that they shouldn't talk to the press. Since Dondurova hadn't sent Maya off to a SIZO, they needed to avoid antagonizing the authorities.

"You'd be wise to keep a low profile," Lilia had said. "Unless you want publicity no matter the outcome. Be remembered as a hero, a victim of the bloody regime."

This made Maya pause for a moment. As a matter of principle, she felt she had to let the world know about her case. People—not just in Russia, but everywhere—needed to hear about the injustice, to learn her story and become outraged at how Putin's system, driven by its own vicious and convoluted logic, persecuted innocent people. It was the right thing to do, and that was reason enough. After all, hadn't she become a journalist all those years ago because she wanted to make a difference? Yet instead, she had turned into one of those people who were too scared to speak the truth, too scared to even recognize it. It was time to toughen up and make the choice to stop being afraid.

But Maya knew she didn't have it in her. Other people were brave, and she admired them, but she just couldn't do it.

"I don't want to be remembered as anything," she nearly whispered. "I can't go to jail. I want my life back."

And so, she escaped from Bobrov and hid out in her apartment.

The next few weeks blurred into an endless stream of days, almost indistinguishable from one another. Obsessed with finding a job, Maya kept reaching out to people who promised to get back to her but never did. She managed to feed herself by doing freelance work for a company that organized weddings. With the season in full swing, there were plenty of them, and luckily for her, most clients preferred themed celebrations, which was where she came in.

Some couples wanted to imagine themselves in the world of *Pirates of the Caribbean*, with the groom as Captain Jack Sparrow and the bride as Elizabeth Swann. Others saw themselves as Jay Gatsby and Daisy Buchanan, Elizabeth Bennet and Mr. Darcy, Han Solo and Princess Leia, or even Spider-Man and whoever his love interest was. Maya was amazed at how deeply movie characters were embedded in the popular consciousness. These were all middle-class couples; the wealthy had far more developed tastes and would just rent a mansion on Lake Como and fly in Anna Netrebko or Jennifer Lopez. That meant Maya had to work with tight budgets and often dealt with complaints from customers who, despite their modest contributions, still expected elaborate details and a high level of authenticity.

Only once did she refuse to take part in the wedding planning: when a couple asked her to stage a raid by OMON, the riot police, in the middle of their reception as a surprise for their relatives. She couldn't go along with it. "Why?" the bride asked, genuinely puzzled. "It would all be in good fun! Imagine how relieved everyone will be when they realize it's just a joke!" But most of the time, Maya did what was asked of her, repeating a phrase she'd often heard but never had the chance to use: "As long as you pay, you can have it your way." No suggestion, no matter how ridiculous, was off-limits. If they wanted to make fools of themselves, that was fine by her. She spent the events glued to her walkie-talkie, giving instructions and feeling relieved not to be directly witnessing the hope and joy of the couples and their families.

Sleeping only four to five hours a night and still losing weight, she knew she was depressed but didn't want to see a doctor. She just needed time to get through it on her own, she reasoned. Eventually, she'd metabolize all the anger, resentment, despair, and helplessness she'd been carrying. The constant anxiety would fade, because the trial had to end at some point. She'd emerge from the darkness, a better version of herself. She'd stop grieving her old life and finally start a new one.

Granted, this was hard to imagine right now. No matter how much Maya tried to push these thoughts away, she kept coming back to a mental list of people she knew, running through it and trying to figure out who the squealer might be. She even started suspecting improbable candidates, like her own sister, who Maya believed had always been competitive and jealous of even her smallest successes.

When Maya set off on this train of thought, it sometimes took her to very odd places. She pictured Polina going to the IC's website and filling out the special form they had for reporting potentially criminal activity. Maya had seen this form herself—they really made it easy for you to slander anyone you chose. There was a phrase at the end that warned of criminal liability for knowingly making a false denunciation, but you could always claim you did it unknowingly, right?

Ksenia was the most likely snitch, of course, given her scheming nature. Maya had glimpsed the workings of her mind during their time in school, and it hadn't been pretty. Once Ksenia saw that her own movie was coming out, she might have decided to eliminate the competition. Or it could have been Nikita. A few times, Maya had been curt with him, and actors were touchy.

Krasov—where would she even begin with him? She'd had to confront him about sending his dick pics to Sanya, and he surely had taken offense. Then there was that conversation when Maya told him she didn't want to get involved in politics. What if he'd decided to teach her a lesson? Or maybe he'd written the statement to save his own ass, hoping the authorities would let him go. She'd heard he left Russia and was living in Spain now.

All of this was destroying Maya's brain and who she was as a person. She desperately wanted out.

One particularly miserable day in early June—she'd just learned her first trial session had been postponed to July—she met Sanya for lunch in town.

"I have fantastic news!" her friend said brightly. "Gosha Tychinkin is making another movie and looking for an AD. I recommended you!"

Tychinkin was the incredibly self-absorbed young director who Sanya had worked for and who they used to have a great time making fun of.

"Why aren't you taking the job?" Maya asked, unwilling to accept charity from Sanya or anyone else, no matter how difficult her own situation was.

"I accepted another offer. Anyway, Gosha said he'd be excited to work with you."

"Why would he be excited? He's never even met me."

"Well," Sanya chuckled, "this is just a theory, but he likes to think of himself as progressive and opposed to the regime, even though he takes state funding and is careful not to say anything provocative. Working with you would send a signal to the right people about where he stands."

"I'd be bettering his image without him actually having to do or say anything. Smart."

"Who cares, though? The money is very good. Also, after this, people might be less scared to work with you."

Sanya was right, of course. Maya would be an idiot to pass up this opportunity.

For a while, they spoke about how various people in the industry justified their involvement with the government. The reality was that most films received funding from the state-backed Cinema Foundation or the Ministry of Culture, otherwise they would never get made.

"What I've heard from a few directors," Sanya said, "was, basically, 'I'm not happy about this, but I have to make movies somehow, and this is the situation we live in. As long as they're not making me support their patriotic initiatives or say something that's against my beliefs, it's fine. I'm just taking their money.'"

But Maya wasn't sure she was buying this argument. "If you're against the regime only in your own head, what value does that have? In the physical world, you're using it for your benefit. It's cynical. And you're normalizing the situation by signaling to others that it's okay to do this."

Sanya shrugged. "I know what they would say to this. 'What am I supposed to do? Forget about making movies and go to a remote village to raise cows?'"

Maya didn't know what anyone was supposed to do. She'd thought so much in recent months about how authoritarians thrived on their subjects' moral paralysis, how passivity in the face of evil helped cement their power. Yet she felt endless empathy toward people who simply tried to live their lives, who minded their own business because they didn't want to get hurt. Every step of the way, they made a choice not to ask for trouble. What was so wrong with that? It was so human, so understandable. But to actively support the regime, to become part of the system—that was a different matter altogether.

One night, she'd gone into a deep dive researching the people her life, inexplicably, now depended on: Dondurova, Kryuchkov, and Yunusov. She found them on social media—VKontakte and Odnoklassniki. Yunusov was from Myshkin ("Mouseville"), a small town about three hundred kilometers north of Moscow. From what she could gather, he had relocated to the capital after high school, having been accepted to Moscow State Law University. She assumed that, from then on, his career had been straightforward. He was thirty-four, married with two kids—a boy and a girl. Together with his family, he went camping and mushroom foraging; they also took vacations in Sochi and, recently, Crimea. He was a man like so many others.

Dondurova wasn't open about her private life, and there was little Maya could find on her, aside from a few photos with a man who looked about twenty years her senior and a teenage boy. There were no vacation shots or dacha pictures. Kryuchkov, on the other hand, stood out as the son of a high-ranking official. His life was extravagant; it took him on trips around the world, including a stay at the famous giraffe hotel in Kenya. He posed beside luxury cars and in lavish interiors, surrounded by model-like women and food that looked expensive, if not particularly appetizing.

Maya had gone digging in hopes of understanding them better but ended up understanding as little as when she'd started. What she saw were people without much imagination, who likely viewed state work as the surest, and perhaps easiest, path to success. Maybe this was their own version of choosing the safest option at every turn. Everything happened incrementally, and if they encountered something unsavory along the way, they simply pretended not to see it. Eventually, they were in too deep to even recognize that they'd chosen the dark side.

CHAPTER 13

In retrospect, Maya shouldn't have accepted the job, even if it was the last one left in the world for her.

At their initial meeting, Tychinkin—his eyes bright with curiosity, hanging on her every word—peppered her with questions about her movie and the upcoming trial. Then he said, pompously, "Know that I'm on your side. If you need help . . ." but trailed off without clarifying what he would do if such a need actually arose. In any case, she got the impression that he valued her, even if for completely the wrong reasons, and that, on the set, he would have her back.

His screenplay was about a young film director who went about his days, tortured by it wasn't clear what—some sort of internal conflict the audience wasn't privy to. The idea it seemed to want to drive home was how hard it was to be a young and talented director whose life revolved around going to clubs and restaurants and having sex with attractive women. It was poorly written, with unrealistic dialogue and awkward transitions. How he'd managed to find the cash to turn this nonsense into a movie was beyond comprehension.

But Maya wasn't going to ask questions—she was in it for the money.

She had other reservations going in. The weddings she helped organize were one-off events, allowing for breaks in between, but film shoots demanded a different kind of endurance. Production days stretched from twelve to sixteen hours, with the first AD being the busiest person on set. She had to be the first to arrive and the last to leave. How she would manage, considering her impaired health, she wasn't sure.

As production began, Maya quickly grew so exhausted that the word "exhausted" didn't do justice to her state. She would arrive on set, her stomach flipping and her head pounding as if about to burst. Despite her best efforts, she became increasingly weak and confused. The support she had expected from Gosha didn't materialize. He showed up late and in a sour mood, then remained capricious and petty throughout the day. He treated Maya not as his right hand but as someone insignificant, like an intern responsible only for bringing him coffee. It soon became clear he treated everyone this way except for the cinematographer, an older man who was somewhat famous, and the principal actor, who essentially played a version of Gosha.

Somehow, Maya kept going through the motions of running the production, consuming every stimulant she could get her hands on while constantly terrified that people would notice her condition. She became prone to sudden bouts of nausea and vomiting. Instead of saying "Quiet on set!" or "Mark it!" she shouted "Roll camera!" which only made the other crew members laugh. Every day, she contemplated quitting but convinced herself to hold on until tomorrow. By the fourth week, she began having panic attacks at inopportune moments—mid-conversation or during crucial shots. At night, her nightmares felt so real that, speaking to an assistant, she once referred to a fire on the set that had occurred in her dream, believing it had actually taken place. By the time production wrapped, she was in such a brittle state that she was physically unable to attend the wrap party—or do anything, really, even walk from her apartment to the nearest grocery store.

Finally, on July 20, Maya stood in front of the courthouse once again. Her first trial session had been postponed twice due to the prosecutor's illness, but she couldn't shake the feeling that it had been deliberate, keeping her in limbo. Sanya and Mark were present as witnesses for the defense, while Lena, who was leaving in less than a month, was there solely for moral support.

"What a turnout!" Lilia smiled, looking at them. She was less pleased, however, with the TV crews that had tried to approach them. Despite her efforts, the trial had become somewhat high-profile, and the courtyard was so packed that Maya thought she caught a glimpse of Alex in the crowd.

The hearing started almost on time. They were ushered into a cramped, stuffy room—much smaller than before. Most of those who wanted to attend couldn't get in. Bailiffs began circulating, asking anyone without authorization to leave, and Lena had to go since she wasn't a witness and hadn't applied for a press pass.

"Urgh, this is another one of their tricks," Lilia muttered under her breath. "They have plenty of bigger rooms. They just don't want any extra pairs of eyes and ears in here."

Maya's mood darkened immediately. "Why? What's going on?"

"I guess we'll find out."

The session began with the prosecutor motioning to the judge to present a new witness who had not been disclosed to the defense. Kryuchkov, sporting a fresh haircut, explained that this individual had come forward with new and relevant evidence. He also requested that the interrogation occur under conditions that excluded visual observation, as the witness had asked to keep their identity secret.

Lilia sprang to her feet to object. "Your honor, this sudden appearance of a witness several months into the trial seems highly suspicious. In my opinion, the purpose of this interrogation is to cover up the investigation's errors in obtaining evidence. The prosecutor is abusing his authority."

"This person came forward to express his civil position—that this film justifies extremist activities against the state," Kryuchkov said resentfully. "Nothing suspicious about this."

Today, Dondurova appeared to be in pain that made it difficult for her to concentrate on the proceedings. She was pale, and her eyes were glazed. She took a sip of water and allowed the new witness to be questioned.

It turned out that the witness, who would be listed in the official records of the hearing under the pseudonym Gleb, was somewhere inside the building but would testify via video connection to prevent anyone from seeing his face. His voice would be digitally altered.

"This is certainly new," Lilia said. "Haven't seen that before."

But she sounded as if nothing could really surprise her anymore.

Two large LCD monitors mounted on opposite walls flickered to life. The screens remained black, but a faint scratching and wheezing sound came from the speakers.

"Gleb, can you hear me?" Kryuchkov said.

Fragments of words emerged from the speakers, but the scratching and wheezing persisted. The prosecutor began his questioning, apparently satisfied with the quality of the connection. Meanwhile, Gleb's responses remained unintelligible, and Maya was scandalized. She couldn't believe that a roomful of people were sitting there, playing along as if this was acceptable. How long was this going to last?

"Louder, please!" Dondurova finally interrupted, wincing—either from Gleb's garbled voice or from whatever she was privately experiencing. "Witness, try to speak slowly and clearly into the microphone."

Over the next few minutes, the quality of the communication gradually improved, or perhaps Maya's brain had learned to decipher the sounds she was hearing. Gleb's voice was that of a typical man, but the unnatural pauses between his words made it seem as if his speech had been chopped into fragments and reassembled.

At the prosecutor's request, Gleb recounted his experience reading Maya's script, which he found "questionable" and didn't like at all. He didn't say how he had come across it. He then mentioned being on set for most of the production and secretly recording some scenes and conversations. His impressions of Maya's film were similar; he thought its main idea was that the Russian state and society were rotten and needed to be torn down.

"Have you ever been threatened?" Lilia asked Gleb when he was handed over to her for cross-examination.

"You mean, in my life? Yes."

"Have you been threatened by Ms. Kotova?"

"No."

"Then why did you want to keep your identity a secret? What are you afraid of?"

After some wheezing, Gleb replied, "I work in the film business, right? Not everyone shares my opinion on this. I fear for my reputation."

"So, you're afraid for your reputation, but no one has threatened you and there was no violence against you?"

"Not only for my reputation. My career, my financial situation."

Maya was surprised to hear this, as she hadn't received any support from the film community. Was it possible that people believed she was being unjustly prosecuted but were too afraid to say so? Or was Gleb just making this up to make himself look good?

Lilia asked him how he had come to be on the set, but he refused to disclose that information, saying it could reveal his identity. She then pressed him to identify which phrases or scenes in the script suggested that the zombies represented Russian authorities.

"The script doesn't rely on isolated phrases; it's a complex piece," he said. "It works as a whole, but the impression it leaves is undeniable."

"Why didn't you come up to Ms. Kotova and inform her about this impression of yours? Tell her how her script could be misinterpreted?"

"I had contradictory feelings about this. If I started to formulate them, there was a chance that I myself would've been misinterpreted."

Lilia asked Gleb why he hadn't gone to the law enforcement authorities right away. Why had he waited several months?

"It's not an easy thing to do," he replied. "Different things happened to me, I experienced mental distress. I thought, there's this film that promotes radicalism. My conscience tormented me. Do something, it was saying."

The cross-examination lasted about forty minutes. Lilia was thorough and precise in her questions, but Gleb was so vague and evasive that it was impossible to determine if he was telling the truth—whether he was genuinely familiar with the screenplay or had really been on the set. Maya remembered that many random people had come to the set during filming, including those who helped out for free and others who just came to watch. He could be any one of them. Maybe someone had printed out the script, and he'd seen it lying around and taken it. Or perhaps he was an operative posing as a witness. Anything was possible.

After Lilia finished with Gleb, Kryuchkov announced that the prosecution was done presenting evidence and that the defense could now call their witnesses. But Lilia suggested screening the rough cut of Maya's film together first. Kryuchkov suddenly looked alarmed by this idea.

"This isn't necessary," Dondurova said, sipping water. There was a greenish pallor to her skin. "We can form our opinion based on the written descriptions."

And with that, the hope that the film itself might unravel the accusations vanished, leaving Maya feeling as though her best chance had just slipped away.

Sanya came up to testify and was articulate and confident. She answered every question, supporting her arguments with facts, which she listed in an organized manner. She seemed to remember everything about the production, and, at cross-examination, no trick question could stump her. She insisted that there were no extremist ideas in Maya's script and that none had appeared during filming. The movie was simply a piece of entertainment with no hidden meanings. Maya couldn't have testified better—in fact, she was sure she'd do much worse on the witness stand.

Mark was up next and did brilliantly as well. He described several meetings between Maya and other crew members where they discussed the precise nature of the zombies. Nothing inappropriate came up in any of those meetings, according to him. Maya was as far from politics as you could get, he said, recounting several conversations that revealed just how little she knew about the current political situation. Maya felt her cheeks burn at this, ashamed of the clueless person she used to be.

Kryuchkov took a very long time cross-examining Mark. It felt personal, as if he'd taken offense at Mark's age and boundless self-assurance. However, nothing came of it: Mark dodged every attack, an amused smile hovering on his face all the while.

Then two film experts testified that Maya's movie wasn't extremist at all. They argued its message was actually humanistic, highlighting universal themes like compassion and resilience, and stressed that the film dealt with the characters' personal experiences rather than any political agenda. One of the experts was Rytvin, her ex-professor, who looked frail but competent. The other was someone he'd recommended, an ex-student of his who had made a name for himself in academia. Belov was supposed to show up too but bailed, claiming he was sick.

An extended break followed, during which Sanya and Mark had to leave because they both had early days tomorrow. It was nearly nine when everyone who remained was called back into the room, and Dondurova began reading her decision in her usual drone. Exhausted, Maya had an extremely hard time focusing and extracting meaning from the torrent of legalese. She was able to grasp that Dondurova found the prosecution's arguments that her film was harmful to be justified and the testimony of the defense witnesses to be uninformative. According to her, they were incompetent and clearly not objective. At this, Maya wanted to turn to Lilia and throw a WTF look at her but realized she wasn't even a little surprised.

Afterward, as the two of them waited for their taxis, Lilia asked, "How are you feeling?"

"Like an idiot."

"Because you can't understand how they can do this?"

"No. I keep asking myself, how could I have been so stupid? I thought nothing could happen to me. I'd just live my life, make movies, and everything would be great."

Maya's shame at hearing what Mark had to say about her still hadn't passed. It stayed inside her like a pressing heat, making her sweat.

"Don't beat yourself up," Lilia advised. "If it makes you feel any better, most people think like this. It's normal in a situation where you can't control anything—your brain is just trying to protect you. You ignore reality because it's too awful to contemplate. If you face it, it can destroy you."

And if you don't, Maya thought as she sat in the car on her way home, *it still comes for you and destroys you.* Suddenly, it occurred to her why the horror genre hadn't really caught on in Russia. The reality was so horrifying that viewers didn't need to be scared. They already had too much of that.

It was Friday night, and the city streets were almost empty. Those who hadn't left for the summer had left for the weekend. The car drove fast, and Maya's favorite neighborhoods rushed by one after another.

Even a few weeks ago, she would have mentally appealed to Lena, asking how she could bear to leave all of this behind—all these places that held so much of their shared history. Kitay-Gorod, where two girls they knew from work had opened a charming vintage store in a quiet courtyard off the main drag. They'd celebrated the opening, and so many cool people came; there was music, and someone brought out a stove to cook tacos. And that bar on Lubyanka, where they got drunk many times, including once with a cute psychiatrist who turned out to be a musician. And this apartment in Pechatnikov Lane, this square, this park, this theater . . . Nearly every corner held significance here. For the longest time, Maya couldn't fathom how Lena could willingly part with all this. But now she understood. For Lena, there would be other streets and squares, other courtyards and bars and coffee shops. Maybe she would fall in love with them, or maybe she wouldn't. The main thing was, she would feel safe where she was.

When Maya got to her building, two men stood up from the bench by the entrance, and she was momentarily gripped by panic. *What now?* But she didn't have the chance to get properly scared, recognizing one of them as Alex. The other man was in his thirties, broad-shouldered with an anxious expression and small, widely spaced eyes. He looked like a stock Russian thug from an American action movie—the kind who gets killed off early because he's all bulk, no brain.

"What are you doing here?" she demanded, keeping her distance.

"I wanted to talk to you before but couldn't work up the nerve. I know all about the trial, I follow it closely."

Was it just a coincidence that he was in Moscow on the exact day the new witness appeared in court? She studied his face. These past few months must have changed something in her perception; she couldn't understand now why she used to feel so threatened by Alex. He seemed small. Trivial. Pathetic, even.

Since he didn't say anything else, she had to ask again, "What do you want?"

"To help you."

"I don't need your help. Is that all?"

She moved toward the door, but he stepped in front of her, blocking her path.

"I have a plan, but we can't talk here. Can I come up to your place?"

"Out of the question."

"Then can we go somewhere quiet?"

"No. If you've got something to say, say it now."

Alex looked briefly desperate, then drew a breath. "Okay. This is Mikhail," he said, nodding to the other man. "He has a Toyota RAV4 that can get us to the Belarusian border in under five hours. There are no checkpoints there. If you've still got your travel passport, we can try to cross into Lithuania. Maybe your name's not in their system yet—it happens. But even if it is, I've got a plan B."

"You're saying you want to smuggle me out of Russia?"

"Yes. And then I'll take you to Stockholm. I have a great apartment—you'd like it. Money isn't an issue. You could apply for asylum. They'd love you there. You'd get grants, make films . . ."

Out of nowhere, Maya was overwhelmed with excitement. Could this be real? Was this why she'd studied Swedish at university, the cosmos preparing her for this turn of events? And she did still have her travel passport: during the search, it had been in her Mosfilm office, so it hadn't been confiscated. Maybe that happened for a reason! She pictured herself in Stockholm, walking by the water, surrounded by beautiful people and clean architecture, eating pastries in sunlit cafés, making friends, writing again, breathing freely.

During the brief moments she lived in this fantasy, she felt amazing, but then she had to return to reality. Her whole life was here: her parents, her sister, the apartment she loved. If she left, she might never return—not until the regime fell, and there was no sign of that happening anytime soon. Besides, she wasn't cut out for a spy-thriller escape. She'd fall apart under the gaze of the first official, give herself away without even meaning to. Then she'd be arrested, dragged back, and tried for a fresh offense. And this time, there'd be no way out—she'd be locked up, maybe for a very long time, held up as a showcase example of an enemy of the state.

As her mind ran through all the options, Maya kept looking at Alex. He was definitely not someone she could entrust with her life. An office-job holder, a man as ordinary as they came—and now he thought of himself as some kind of mastermind?

"Are you Gleb?" she asked, hoping to catch him off guard.

"Am I Gleb? What does that mean?"

"Was it you who snitched on me?"

"What? No!" He looked stunned.

"Did you write anonymous letters and drop them in my mailbox?" Maya pressed.

"How can you— No! I would never—"

"Did you ring my doorbell at night?"

"Of course not! Why would I do that?" His eyes were wild now.

"Fine. Thank you for the offer, but I don't need more complications in my life. So I'm asking you one last time: leave me alone."

And with that, Maya went inside, ignoring his pleas.

CHAPTER 14

On the morning of August 1, the day of Lena and Ilya's flight to America, Maya arrived at their apartment and helped bring their luggage downstairs. They took a taxi together to Sheremetyevo, where Lena checked their bags and got their boarding passes at the Aeroflot counter. With two and a half hours left until departure, the three of them headed to an overpriced self-service café to grab a bite, but really just to spend a few last moments together. Maya had no idea when, or if, she would see Lena again.

As they settled into a corner table and set their plates down, Maya focused on holding back tears, taking deliberate, slow breaths. She stayed quiet, knowing that if she tried to speak, she'd start crying.

Lena looked paler and thinner than usual. The past few months had been tough on her, too. Her syrniki sat untouched on her plate.

"We should've left a year ago, or even two," she said. "Why did it take me so long? You could've come with us. My parents have two extra rooms. You could've stayed in one of them as long as you wanted."

Maya contemplated this. A year ago, she had just turned thirty-six. She could've easily started a new life in the States. Okay, maybe not easily, but she would've had a decent chance of making it work. She'd always wanted to visit New York City, having seen countless movies set there. On the other hand, had she left, she might never have tried her hand at filmmaking. She knew it was infinitely more difficult to debut with a feature in America. There was much less gatekeeping in Russia and far less competition. Practically anyone could make a movie here, if you thought about it. And what if those weeks spent making her own movie turned out to be the highest point of her life? She often found herself revisiting that period, trying to relive it. That heightened sense of creating art, of being alive three hundred percent, would always stay with her. She was grateful to have experienced it. Whenever things got unbearable, she could return to that feeling. At least she'd had that in her life.

Ilya hadn't touched his food either. He was engrossed in a game on his phone, and the long diner-style seat he and Maya were perched on rocked with his energetic movements.

"That's it!" Lena snapped at him. "Stop immediately!"

"What?"

"When was the last time you read a book? Or listened to a podcast? Or something?"

He put his phone away and sulked. Maya hugged him. "Your mom is stressing out. Don't be hard on her. Take care of her, okay? She's doing this for you."

He bristled. "For me? I don't want to go! All my friends are here."

Lena rolled her eyes. "You're at home playing games all the time. You don't even hang out with them anymore."

Maya looked into Ilya's face. "You know what happened to me? To my movie?"

"I heard about it."

"I might go to prison, and I didn't do anything. This is why you have to leave. So nothing like that can happen to you."

Soon, it was time for Lena and Ilya to head to their gate. Maya walked with them to the security check.

"Promise me you'll be okay," Lena said, wrapping her arms around Maya. "I'll come visit as soon as I can."

When Lena took off her shoes and waved at her one last time, Maya finally started to cry. She sobbed all the way home and kept crying even after she arrived. What did she expect? Lena couldn't stay here with her. She was physically removing herself from this place, where basic human rights weren't respected, where anyone could slander you, where the court had the power to send you away somewhere near the Arctic Circle, ignoring all the evidence of your innocence. Where you could be crossing the street during a protest and the next thing you knew, you were in a police cell, your spine broken and your anus ripped. Where you couldn't say what you thought and always had to look over your shoulder. Who could blame Lena?

Maya felt bereft and obliterated. Her tears ended quickly, giving way to numbness. She stopped leaving the house and eating. Even taking a few sips of water felt like a monumental effort. She expected this to pass, as it had last time, when her depressive episode kept her hiding from the world for several days. But this time, the days stretched into weeks, forming a continuum of viscous, slippery gloom. She could hardly stay awake, spending most of her time sleeping, emerging from oblivion weak and disoriented, or else in a stupor where she felt and thought nothing. During brief moments of what passed for sentience, she would sometimes talk to Lena, who called to update her on how she was settling in New Jersey. When they spoke, Maya managed to impersonate someone capable of delivering convincing lines, even if they were just a few words. In truth, her mind was in a place where it couldn't function with any degree of coherence.

With Lena, everything seemed to be going well. Her parents were happy to have them; Ilyusha had been accepted into an excellent high school and was excited to start. He'd even shown interest in joining the swimming team. Lena had begun applying for jobs and was considering getting a master's in something, maybe social work. In any case, she had enough savings to last them about a year.

After one of their conversations, Maya realized: she didn't care that Lena was now living across the ocean. She was starting to like this muffled state she was in, as if wrapped in layers of bubble wrap. She survived on protein shakes, a batch of which she'd had delivered, since food tasted like cardboard anyway. Lena's old laptop sat untouched on the kitchen table, gathering a fine coat of fuzzy dust. Most texts went unanswered for days, and when Maya did manage to reply, who knew if she even made sense?

She barely registered that her next trial session had been rescheduled to September 26—a detail as irrelevant as everything else.

When she wasn't asleep or lying in bed with her eyes shut, trying to pretend that she was, she parked herself in the window seat, staring down at the street below. She watched cars zip by and pedestrians scurry around, transfixed by their relentless motion. There was a time when she'd been a sucker for the drama unfolding beneath her window, the plots playing out in real-time. But now? Now it was just noise. Who cared about those minuscule people?

Occasionally, Maya would peek into the world through social media, but the people she followed felt increasingly distant. Their faces, their words, the photos they shared—it was as if they inhabited a realm she no longer understood, speaking in a language unfamiliar to her. She'd stare at the images, scroll through the captions, trying to latch on to some meaning, but it all slipped past her. Her own sister, in particular, was becoming harder to recognize. Polina had two Instagram accounts: one for herself and one for her dog, Nini. On the first, a woman with a flat, vacant expression posed with her mouth slightly ajar or posted pictures of whatever she was cooking: zucchini casserole, cheesy squids. On the second, the dog appeared in a series of unflattering shots, its gaze deranged. Maya vaguely remembered that Polina's posts used to fill her with acute agony. Now, she looked at them without a trace of emotion.

All of this changed one day when Maya saw Ksenia's post announcing that her striptease movie was headed to the Mostra—the Venice Film Festival. There was a picture of Ksenia with her lead actress and Dennis at the airport, about to board a plane, followed by another shot of them in the lobby of the Hotel Excelsior, just after their arrival.

With a jolt, Maya snapped back to something resembling her full self and wiped the dust off her computer. As she checked the festival program, she saw that Ksenia's film was listed among the main contenders. She also found a couple of rave reviews online, in English, from critics who had already seen it. "An emotional roller coaster that will leave you breathless!" one exclaimed. "Incredibly moving and beautifully crafted. An extraordinary film that blends heart, humor, and humanity," said the other.

A dull ache started in Maya's sternum. She sank back into her chair, suddenly transported to the Excelsior—a place she'd never actually stayed. During her trips to Venice as a reporter, her editorial office had always rented cheap lodgings for her in Castello or Santa Croce, and every morning, she'd had to take a crowded vaporetto to Lido and then walk to the Palazzo del Cinema or another venue where screenings were scheduled. But she knew the Excelsior well. Right this moment, she could picture the Blue Bar, with its Murano glass counter and black-and-white portraits of Hitchcock, Mastroianni, and Deneuve. There, she'd interviewed Tilda Swinton and Diane Kruger and had drinks with a handsome French journalist whose name she couldn't recall now.

At the Adriatico Terrace, she'd had lunch with the head of some film company and a bunch of other reporters. Obscenely expensive carpaccios and risottos. In the banquet hall, Sala Stucchi, she'd attended a dinner for four hundred people. This was where the famous scene from *Once Upon a Time in America* had been filmed, when Noodles takes Deborah on a date to an opulent restaurant—supposedly in Long Island. The dinner was hosted by a prominent jewelry brand, an advertiser at the magazine Maya was working for, which was the reason she'd been invited, even if she had to sit at a corner table. Next to her was a Russian film critic who tried to hit on her. Later, he was accused of rape by multiple women, and he was now editor-in-chief of a pro-Kremlin film magazine.

Maya remembered how she'd raced between theater venues, trying to catch as many screenings as she could, drunk with joy. Back then, the idea of making movies herself was beyond anything she dared to dream. But the photo calls, the press conferences, the red carpet events—they were intoxicating. Once, she even asked Jude Law a risqué question, and the way he smiled at her!

How was it possible that she'd ended up here, locked in her apartment that she'd stunk up with her sweat?

Having emerged from her comatose state, inexplicably energized, Maya began binge-watching the festival livestreams like it was her job. Each morning, she rushed to her laptop to devour the latest reviews and videos, scanning for any sign of Ksenia. In photos, Ksenia looked anything but glamorous: boxy outfits she'd clearly picked herself, and a stiffness that contrasted sharply with her radiant actress in clingy dresses. "You should've hired a stylist," Maya muttered, gloating.

On the third day, Ksenia's film screened, which Maya knew from both the official schedule and Ksenia's Instagram post from the auditorium. Unable to watch, she paced for two hours, tearing at her cuticles. Soon after, she found videos of the standing ovation. Though she was aware that every film received one if the crew was present, it still hurt. Ksenia was crying with joy. Maya cried a little, too, though not for the same reason.

The next day brought the main reviews. Some were tepid—"familiar tale," "predictable," "shallow exploration"—and Maya relished those. One even called the direction "exploitative." But most critics loved the film.

At the press conference, Ksenia spoke through a translator while her producer and actress fumbled through English. Maya felt smug watching her former friend give bland, generic answers. Then a reporter finally asked about the film's silence on Russia's political situation. Ksenia faltered, then offered a canned response about focusing on "small but important personal choices." "Seriously?" Maya scoffed.

Two days later came the award ceremony. Maya, nauseated with anticipation, watched as time dragged. Minor awards passed. Then came the Coppa Volpi for Best Actress. Maya froze—Ksenia's actress had won. The camera caught them both in shock, then rising from their seats to accept. But why was Ksenia going up too? It wasn't her prize. Still, there she was, in emerald silk, holding the award alongside her actress. Maya could barely breathe.

She knew the Volpi Cup could change everything: press, distribution, career offers. Though Ksenia's film didn't win anything else, that one award was enough. Maya slammed her laptop shut, furious.

She still had some vestiges of self-reflection and critical thinking left. This was a moral challenge she should have risen to, and one she'd failed miserably. She couldn't summon even a shred of happiness for her once-upon-a-time friend. Instead, she was consumed by jealousy. Did she truly believe she should've been there instead of Ksenia? No. But she could have been. She was a narcissistic asshole—of that, she was certain. Life hadn't taught her anything. Humility was what she needed to work on.

Maya berated herself endlessly, but it did nothing to alleviate the pain of Ksenia's win. She couldn't stop imagining all the opportunities that would come her way now—European producers taking notice, perhaps even inviting her to direct; magazines featuring her; brands reaching out with offers. There would be glamorous parties, yacht cruises, all of it. And Maya—she didn't deserve any of that. She'd been given her chance, and she'd blown it.

Removing her T-shirt, she headed to the bathroom to brush her teeth but felt too drained to do it. Instead, she went to bed, stewing in envy and bitterness, and drifted into a fitful sleep.

When Maya woke up the next morning, the room was spinning—not just a little, but a lot. She felt more or less okay lying flat with her eyes closed, but even the slightest movement or opening her eyes just a crack sent everything around her rotating violently, making her want to vomit. Standing or sitting up was out of the question. Something strange was clearly afoot, but she couldn't determine what it was. She couldn't even Google it.

For a while, Maya lay on her bed, debating her next move. Suppose she called her parents—no, that was a bad idea. They would barge in and create a flurry of activity aimed at helping her, but it would ultimately lead nowhere. Her mother was a doctor, yet Maya had never found her to be much help. She'd probably call an ambulance, which Maya could do herself. What if she contacted Sanya instead? Sanya could Google this for her, but then what? She'd likely insist on calling an ambulance anyway. That was people's typical response to any medical situation.

There was always hope that this thing, whatever it was, would go away on its own. Maya had heard of incredibly strange symptoms that suddenly developed in people, only to disappear without a trace. Lena had once started seeing double out of nowhere. She had her eyes checked, but nothing was wrong, and her vision returned to normal a few days later with no explanation. Maya herself had experienced bouts of pain that left her unable to function for a day, only for the pain to vanish the next morning. This could be a migraine of sorts. On the other hand, could it be a stroke? She had once worked on an article about how strokes or infarctions presented in women, and sometimes the symptoms were so unusual that they could be completely misleading. Though she couldn't recall now which it was—strokes or infarctions.

In the end, Maya decided to do nothing. She spent the entire day in bed, bored out of her mind. Occasionally, she tried opening her eyes to see if her condition persisted. It did, so she shut them again. At one point, she crawled to the bathroom to pee and drink some water, but the effort left her so disoriented that she could hardly find her way back to bed. Once she settled down again, her thoughts drifted back to Ksenia. She kept picturing her in that stunning emerald dress, laughing and gripping the award, the entire audience focused on her.

The next morning, the room was still spinning, possibly even faster than before. There wasn't much else to do but call for an ambulance. But this was easier said than done. Maya had to unlock her phone, navigate to the dialer screen, and press 0-3-handset, each action triggering a wave of nausea. She wasn't sure about this, but progress needed to be made, and she could see no other way.

In a mechanical tone, the operator asked Maya about her symptoms and then advised her to seek help at her local polyclinic. The condition had clearly failed to impress her. This forced Maya to raise her voice, explaining that she couldn't even make it to her own bathroom, let alone the polyclinic. Now that she was being denied treatment, she found herself wanting it. Their back-and-forth continued for another ten minutes before the operator relented and told her to expect a crew.

It took Maya a tremendous amount of willpower to put on some clothes, grab her bag, and meet the paramedics at the door. She had to lie on the floor while she explained her condition to them. The paramedics were two young women who briefly conferred on how to proceed. One of them then went downstairs and returned with their driver, who seemed very small, judging by where his voice was coming from. The three of them attempted to lift Maya onto a stretcher and carry her down the stairs, but that didn't work out. Ultimately, she had to creep down the steps on her own two legs, with her eyes closed, the women supporting her on either side. With the siren blaring, they drove to a hospital on the other side of Moscow, where the system had dispatched them.

The ride felt interminable, the wailing like a hole being drilled into her skull. Once at the hospital, Maya underwent some tests and briefly blacked out during a CT scan. Finally, two or three hours later, she found herself in a ward occupied by two older women, who were engaged in a lengthy conversation, sharing detailed stories about their families and lives at home. This became her entertainment for the day as she lay in bed with her eyes pressed shut, now surrounded by a medical environment. At least this had to be an improvement.

Her actual treatment started in the evening, just before the quiet hours, with the nurse giving her some pills to swallow and administering an injection in her right buttock. The next morning, she felt better, her dizziness reduced by about half, and she managed to eat some sweet kasha for breakfast. However, throughout the day, she was nearly driven mad by her two wardmates, who repeated the same stories to each other in a different order, seemingly forgetting they had already told them. There was no treatment again until the evening, when the routine of pills and the injection was repeated.

On the morning of the third day, Maya's vertigo was almost completely gone. As the head doctor and his entourage of interns made their morning rounds, she asked him about her diagnosis and how long they planned to keep her.

"Have you been under a lot of stress lately?" he inquired, eyeing her dubiously, as if she were occupying someone else's place, someone who needed it more.

"I guess you could say that. Yes."

"You're going to have to manage it," he said. "You're fine physically, just undernourished. Eat well, exercise, and see a doctor who can prescribe antidepressants for you."

"Antidepressants? I'd rather not take them."

"I strongly recommend that you do. Otherwise, something bad might happen." With that, he took off, the interns trailing after him.

Maya pondered what he'd said. She had no idea how long the trial would last, and the waiting was killing her soul. She would have preferred it to be over already, even if this meant going to jail. The possibility of a prison term was always hovering in the back of her mind, and random images—of being pushed face-first into a wall, hands behind her back, or of a violent inmate scowling toothlessly, signaling the beginning of a fight—kept popping up in her consciousness. Maybe she underestimated herself. Perhaps she could survive it and come out stronger. If this wasn't material for a screenplay, then what was?

Then she received a message from Lilia.

I have news. It's something we have to discuss in person.

CHAPTER 15

Lilia arrived at the hospital during visiting hours. Maya met her at the entrance, and together they wandered into the park on the hospital grounds, searching for a quiet corner to talk in private.

"This is quite nice, actually," Lilia remarked as they strolled down a path lined with blooming hydrangeas and pansies. "Better than some parks I've been to."

Two young women were filming themselves doing a dance routine, their iPhone set on a tripod. Nearby, two older ladies in whimsical hats walked arm in arm, listening to music on the radio. When they'd passed, Lilia asked what had landed Maya in the hospital.

"We could use this," she said. "I doubt it would make much difference, but maybe it's worth a shot."

Maya told her that her diagnosis seemed to be depression.

"I guess I'm not surprised," Lilia said. "Anyway, the reason I'm here is they're offering us a deal."

"Who is?"

"The IC. Though I'm not totally sure. I got the impression that maybe some other agency got involved and they came up with this plan."

Lilia went on to explain that the authorities—whoever they

were, though she'd heard this from Yunusov—were offering Maya a sentence of one year of probation in exchange for her cooperation. "Looks like someone's decided to make an example out of you."

"An example of what?"

"Active repentance, I suppose."

"Jesus. What do I have to do?"

Lilia said they'd go over the details during a meeting with Maya, to be scheduled whenever she was ready. From what Lilia had gathered, it sounded like they wanted Maya to make a movie for them. "This deal's off the record," Lilia added. "No paperwork, no signatures."

Maya struggled to process it. She knew her country ran on backroom deals, from small businesses greasing low-level officials to quiet arrangements made at the highest levels. Just recently, she'd skimmed a piece in an opposition outlet about Mount Athos—*Afon*—a monastic retreat that had become a discreet fixer's office for the elite. Businessmen, government insiders, anyone under pressure flew in on private jets to meet the elders and get a blessing. The story went that the elders had a "direct line" to God, or maybe to someone even more useful. Calls were made. Problems disappeared. It was everyone's modus operandi: the real decisions always happened behind closed doors.

She knew she should feel relief—after all, it meant she might not end up in jail—but all she could think about was how deeply cynical the offer was. They were basically telling her that independent justice didn't exist, that the judge was just a pawn controlled by people higher up. If she accepted their offer, she'd become a collaborator. They weren't offering her a way out—they were making her one of them.

"What do you think I should do?" she asked.

Lilia shrugged. "My guess? If you turn them down, they'll almost definitely send you to jail. Just to make a point, you know? So it's not really a choice. I mean . . . you could take the risk and see what happens—"

Lilia studied her closely, as if trying to decide whether Maya was the kind of person who would risk everything to prove that some people out there still cared about principles. But Maya wasn't.

The last day of the trial began with Kryuchkov delivering his closing argument before the court. He went on for about fifteen minutes, listing all the egregious things Maya had supposedly done in her movie and beyond, like criticizing the government in private conversations that made the people she talked to suspect she was up to something subversive. Yet it was obvious his heart wasn't in it. Maya tried to analyze his performance from a director's perspective; his stiff body language and indifferent tone of voice betrayed a lack of conviction. She could've given him some pointers on how to appear more persuasive and make this hearing seem less orchestrated. But it was clear to her that none of the people in charge cared about how this whole thing looked.

By the end of his speech, the judge propped her chin on her hand, reminding Maya of nineteenth-century paintings of merchants' wives having tea. A gentle melancholic expression lingered on Dondurova's face, until a large flying bug zipped into the room seemingly out of nowhere, buzzing in circles above the audience and prompting squeals and bursts of laughter. Kryuchkov stopped talking and glanced quizzically at the court clerk, a blond woman who looked no older than sixteen, who then appealed to the bailiffs, "Please restore the room to order."

Two bailiffs—one short and pudgy, the other tall and skeletal—rose from their seats, their faces bewildered. They began circling the room, waving their arms and trying to swat at the bug. Their efforts were awkward and utterly ineffectual, prompting even more hilarity from the audience. Maya thought this scene could be filmed exactly as it was. Even without directorial input, it was perfect—straight out of a Chekhov story or a Charlie Chaplin movie. On one hand, it was too easy, an archetypal slapstick routine; on the other, it was nearly impossible to recreate on a film set these days, since there were no contemporary actors trained in physical comedy to the necessary degree—at least none that she knew of. Yet here were these two people, doing it without actually trying to be funny.

At first, Dondurova's face wore an expression of deep detestation as she watched them, but then her features softened, turning into a smile that she clearly tried to suppress. A few members of the audience stood up to help the comical duo, and finally, a reporter crushed the bug between the pages of a magazine.

The court clerk announced the defense attorney's closing statement. Lilia, ravishing in a black pantsuit and white blouse, rose to her feet. Maya couldn't help but think how much she wanted to emulate her style. Lilia argued that Maya's movie had never been intended as a political statement, methodically presenting the evidence while striking the side of her hand against her palm. In a film, this might seem cliché, but in real life, it worked beautifully. She then laid out the flaws in the prosecution's case, from intentional misrepresentations and unreliable witnesses to crucial evidence being conveniently overlooked. Her sharpness and command of the case were so impressive that even Kryuchkov appeared visibly stricken by the end of her speech.

Maya had been offered the chance to make her final address to the court. Political opposition figures often used this moment to air their grievances, their statements then quoted in the press or sometimes even printed in full. Today's hearing had been moved to a bigger room to accommodate the extra reporters, all likely expecting something provocative from her, or at the very least, something emotional. The trial had already given them plenty to work with, and they were ready for a memorable finish. But they were about to be disappointed—Maya wasn't going to throw her life away for the sake of drama. She had decided to pass.

When Dondurova retired for deliberation, Lilia escorted Maya to a waiting area—a room with a window and a cooler, which Maya was grateful for. She wasn't in the mood to fend off journalists or endure their stares. She didn't feel fully in control of herself. Something trembled anxiously inside her, and her breath came in uneven, shallow bursts. As Lilia tapped away on her phone, Maya dug out hers and tried to check her email. But nothing made sense, not a single word. The same thing happened when she scrolled through Facebook—everything blurred together. It was humiliating, how she couldn't get ahold of herself.

When they returned to the courtroom, Maya felt goosebumps crawling over her skin, and her nose tingled like she'd just stepped in from the cold. What if they—whoever "they" were, the masterminds behind the deal—had backed out, or if their whole proposition had been a setup? What if they just wanted to mess with her? She didn't trust anything they'd said or would say. As she settled into her chair, she glanced around the room, lingering on Kryuchkov and the court clerk, trying to see if they knew something she didn't. But their faces just showed they didn't like their jobs much and would rather be somewhere else. Kryuchkov stifled a yawn, then pulled out his phone and started typing something furiously under the table.

Looking at the sun-dappled leaves of a maple tree outside the window, Maya couldn't help wondering if these were her last moments of freedom. It was possible that, after the judge announced the verdict, these same bailiffs, the hapless twosome, would handcuff her and take her outside, where a police van was probably waiting. But there would be nothing comical about that, at least not for her.

Dondurova entered the room through her own side door, and everyone rose to their feet. Complete silence fell upon the room, everyone hanging on her words. It was clear she was relishing this moment, a ghost of a smile hovering over her lips even as she tried to look severe.

"The court hereby announces the verdict in the name of the Russian Federation."

She then began reading from the document in her hands, naming the court, identifying the defendant, listing the charges brought against Maya, and outlining the court's findings. This went on for nearly an hour. Maya hoped the judge wouldn't read the entire thing, as according to Lilia, just the delivery of the verdict could sometimes take several days. Finally, Dondurova got to the most important part.

"Based on the above, the court rules as follows: to find Maya Evgenyevna Kotova guilty of committing a crime under Part 2 of Article 280 of the Criminal Code of the Russian Federation."

A sound came from the audience, like that collective gasp when a villain suddenly appears in a horror movie, startling everyone in the theater. Maya, barely registering her own disappointment, found their reaction puzzling—did they really think she'd be acquitted, given the statistics and all? But the crowd was murmuring, talking about what they'd just heard. Maybe they were just getting ready for what was coming next.

Raising her voice, Dondurova continued, "Taking into account the nature of the offense, the personality of the defendant, and the circumstances of the case, the court imposes a conditional sentence of one year of imprisonment, with a probationary period of one year."

After this, mayhem erupted, forcing the clerk to call for order. While the judge droned on about the appeal process, the audience buzzed. They hadn't expected this—none of them had. They'd been waiting for Maya to be sentenced to jail time, at least a couple of years. Wouldn't that have made for a great story? The so-called patriots would've been pleased she got what she deserved, while those against the state would've felt confirmed in their beliefs about the iron-fisted regime. Now, everyone seemed dissatisfied and taken aback by the court's decision. And Maya was surprised too—especially with herself. She'd thought she'd be delirious with relief, but instead, she felt nothing.

Outside, as the flashes started going off, she tried to arrange her expression into one of contentment. But her muscles wouldn't cooperate, leaving her face stiff like a mask, lips pinched in a grimace. It was Lilia who smiled radiantly for them both, tossing out short, snappy comments into the microphones shoved in her face: "We disagree with the verdict, but we're glad the sentence is lenient" and "We're considering an appeal. Need to go over it with my client first."

After they made it out of the gates, Lilia asked, "Want to celebrate?"

Maya paused, taking in the street in front of her, bustling with city life. That horrible world she'd been reading so much about lately was fading, slowly moving out of view. She wouldn't have to strip down in front of guards and inmates, then take a deep squat to show any objects she might've hidden in her body. She wouldn't have to writhe in pain, trying not to soil herself, because in some women's penal colonies they only allowed one or two ten-minute bathroom breaks a day, with way too few toilets for everyone. She wouldn't have to make sanitary pads from scraps of fabric and wash them in the sink, since the state provided only five regular ones a month. She wouldn't have to clean herself with cold water from an aluminum bowl. She wouldn't have to spend years surrounded by others, craving even a few minutes of solitude, or endure endless hours of nonstop radio blaring Russian pop.

She'd been spared all of that. Wasn't that reason enough to celebrate?

"Sure," she said. "Let's celebrate."

The production office was pleasantly warm and smelled like a bakery. Maya had just come in from the cold. Her coat was immediately taken from her and hung on a standing hanger.

"Maya Evgenyevna, please follow me." A young woman guided her to a row of desks set up like a committee and pointed to the chair in the center, where a neatly printed sign read MAYA KOTOVA, DIRECTOR.

The production office had a lot of staff, most of whom she hadn't met yet. Another young woman asked with a note of reverence in her voice, "Would you like tea or coffee? We can also order food from any restaurant you choose." Maya thanked her and requested a cappuccino.

Soon, others joined Maya at the table: her first AD, her casting director, and their assistants. Then a man in his late sixties or early seventies walked in with a military gait and was introduced as Vasily Vasilyevich Tushkov, a retired FSB general.

"So glad to meet you," he said, breaking into a smile. "I'll be your consultant. Looking forward to working together!"

The lines around his eyes and mouth gave him a kind, gentle look, and Maya realized he reminded her of Toni Morino.

Today, she was auditioning actors for the lead role—men between thirty and forty. The producers wanted this to be a modern-day version of *Seventeen Moments of Spring*, rumored to be one of Putin's favorite movies. It was a Soviet classic from 1973 that everyone had seen, regardless of age—a dramatic miniseries about Stierlitz, a Russian intelligence officer operating undercover in Nazi Germany. Vyacheslav Tikhonov, who played Stierlitz, had had a distinctly un-Soviet face—a patrician and highly intelligent one, despite not being the sharpest in real life. Maya was sure the success of the original show had had a lot to do with that face. But now, there were no visages even remotely like his among the actors who'd sent in their self tapes, or anywhere else they'd thought to look, for that matter.

After the first round of auditions, the general offered an explanation. He said there were very few actors in this age bracket because of two economic crises in Russia—one in 1998 and another in 2008—that had made pursuing acting careers absolutely impractical for young men.

"Maybe we could send scouts all over town and just grab people off the streets?" he suggested.

Maya pictured "scouts" as uniformed men with guns at their sides.

"I don't think someone with no acting training could pull off the lead role," she replied.

Even people who lied as part of their job couldn't do it convincingly, she nearly said. She was thinking of those two dummies, Boshirov and Petrov (not their real names), the GRU agents who had traveled to Salisbury, England, in March to poison former Russian officer Sergey Skripal and his daughter with Novichok. When the details of their operation came to light, they gave a high-profile interview to the head of a Russian propaganda TV network, claiming they were just regular tourists visiting the famous cathedral. They came off as pathetic and laughable, portraying themselves as victims of a smear campaign and making every sane person cringe. They'd botched the poisoning, too, killing an innocent civilian and making themselves highly visible. There was incompetence all around.

Some of the actors who'd come to audition today actually resembled those two—not just in appearance, being completely unremarkable and lacking charisma, but also in how they read their lines, with a flat, robotic affect and vacant expressions. For all Maya knew, real-life agents might be like that—so bland they could blend into the walls. Maybe that was a prized quality in an intelligence officer, but it could never work on screen.

The second batch of hopefuls was proving equally underwhelming.

"Please tell us a little about yourself," she said to the next actor, who was making himself comfortable in his chair. He was sweet-looking, with a broad, ruddy face and a mop of light-brown hair.

"Makar Chyorny, thirty-seven," he replied cheerfully. "You might've seen me in a Kiryanushka commercial."

"What's that?"

"Pelmeni."

"Anything else we should know about you?"

"I got married two weeks ago."

How this was relevant to the part he was auditioning for, Maya had no clue. "Congratulations!" she said anyway. "Please read the scene you prepared."

He started reading, suddenly becoming very animated. His delivery was exaggerated—eyes bulging, face muscles visibly flexing—so she asked him to tone it down. He did, just by a notch.

It was clear he was a no-go, but Maya was feeling generous and decided to give him another chance. "Improvise an action scene, please. You're chasing a suspect, but someone else is actually chasing you."

Makar jumped up, brandishing an imaginary gun. Eyes darting wildly, he started running around the room—falling to the floor, rolling, jumping up again, seeking cover. He fired everywhere—left, right, ceiling—so fast Maya's head spun. He ducked behind a chair, fired—shouting "Bang! Bang!"—and then kicked it like it had slept with his wife. The grimaces he made were so grotesque Maya clamped her hand over her mouth, praying she would keep it together. And she did—until the general, seated somewhere to her left, let out a tiny, helpless squeal. Just then, their entire table exploded in laughter.

Makar stood still at last, an uncomprehending look on his face.

"Sorry about this!" Maya said, wiping away tears. "You were a little . . . extra. Thank you so much! We'll get back to you."

"Oh, god," the casting director groaned next to her. "He was referred to me by an acquaintance. I don't know what they were thinking."

Maya sat back in her chair. She could do this all day. Even if nothing came out of this project, even if it became a total disaster, what did she care?

After her trial ended, she'd passed through several stages. During the first, she was in what she later came to identify as a state of dissociation. It was like the whole ordeal she'd been through hadn't happened to her but rather to someone else, or maybe she'd just hallucinated it. As far as hallucinations went, it lingered as a series of disturbing images, but no more than that. She was able to ignore them and do things like clean her apartment, visit her parents, see some Louis de Funès comedies and actually laugh at them.

But then the reality collapsed onto her in a heap, all at once, almost stifling her, and she had to find her way through it to the surface. She became possessed by rage. She was furious at the judge, the IC, the operatives, and anyone else who belonged to that great repressive machine governing the country, collectively known as a bunch of "crooks and thieves," as per the famous expression coined by Navalny. She was angry at most of her colleagues, who had disappeared from her life the moment they heard of her predicament. And at herself, for making that film that wasn't even worth all of this. She developed a new tic where, instead of pinching herself, she bit the inside of her mouth raw.

For a while, Maya couldn't stop thinking about her snitch. At their last meeting with Yunusov, she'd asked him to name the person who'd triggered the investigation. "Petr Ivanov," he'd replied. The name sounded so generic it had to be real, but for the life of her, she couldn't remember ever coming into contact with him. It turned out he was an actor who'd auditioned for a minor part in her movie and been rejected. She watched every video she could find of him—just a regular, forgettable face with no standout acting skills. There wasn't much about him online; he graduated from the Yaroslavl State Theater Institute and played small roles at the local theater in Yaroslavl. He seemed like an affable guy. Had she been harsh with him? No memory of his audition stuck with her. Determined to figure this out, Maya reached out to Belov to get the audition tapes, but he never replied.

Then, as her anger faded, she found herself trying to think about the future. Tentatively. Since she hadn't heard from the IC or anyone connected to them in weeks, she started to hope that this was it—the end of the story. Maybe they'd forgotten about her, caught up in new schemes and trials. Perhaps she could finally move on and start planning the rest of her life. As part of this fresh start, Maya went in for a physical. The kind doctor prescribed her an SSRI.

It was early November, a month and a half after the verdict, when her illusion of freedom vanished. She was summoned to the office of a production company called Bereg, where a contract was already laid out for her. None of the familiar faces were there, but it was clear to everyone that she couldn't say no. She was assigned to direct a series about a fictional intelligence officer, and his portrayal was meant to flatter the state agency he worked for. The agency, which just happened to be the FSB, would oversee the project to make sure she stayed in line. This was her part of the deal, the condition on which she'd avoided prison: making a propaganda piece as someone who had supposedly seen the error of her ways and repented.

Maya signed the document and returned home, feeling crushed. But by then, her antidepressant was kicking in, and in a few days, she stopped caring.

At six, after the day's auditions wrapped up—disappointingly, with no one showing even a hint of promise—Maya quickly went over tomorrow's round with the casting director, a birdlike woman in her fifties, then headed to the bathroom to wash her face. The space was large and brightly lit, and she noticed she looked much healthier than she had even a month ago, her eye bags nearly gone, her face filling out. She debated what to do next. It was late November, the most depressing time of year, and she didn't want to spend the long evening at home. It was too cold for a walk. Maybe she could go to the movies?

Outside in the corridor, the general was waiting for her.

He cleared his throat in what she thought was pretend embarrassment. "Would you be open to having dinner with me?"

When, momentarily stumped, Maya didn't reply, he added, "Nothing funny—I'm a happily married man. My wife is visiting her sister in St. Pete, so I don't have dinner plans."

They were trying to feel her out, that's what it was. But Maya didn't care; she had nothing to hide. In fact, this might even be entertaining. Anything was better than spending another night alone at her apartment.

"You have to forgive me. I'm retired and have more time than I know what to do with," Tushkov said amiably as they entered the elevator.

Outside the building, a black Mercedes was waiting. The driver, a tall man in a suit whose bulging muscles suggested vigorous weight training and perhaps other, more dangerous physical activities, opened the back door for them.

On the way to dinner, the general talked about his only daughter, who had always loved art and was now running a museum.

"Which one?" Maya asked, wondering if the daughter had landed the position on her own talent or thanks to her dad's connections.

"Mayakovsky Museum."

The one on Lubyanka. How nice—right next to the FSB headquarters. Maya actually liked the museum. It had that vibe of Mayakovsky's poetry: once avant-garde, now nostalgic. She hadn't visited in years, though.

"How old is your daughter?"

"Your age—thirty-seven."

It was spooky how he knew her age. But they probably knew everything about her.

When they arrived at a steakhouse with white tablecloths and soft lighting (Tushkov's choice), they were shown to a private room. "I get distracted by people talking," he explained. "So loud! People didn't used to be so loud thirty, even twenty years ago."

Over his bloody steak, he launched into stories from his days as a young officer. He seemed to have traveled all over the world. In some unnamed South American country, he'd been part of a hostage rescue. In Africa, he'd found himself stranded on a mountain, nearly freezing to death. Another time, he had to survive by scavenging and ended up on antiparasitic meds for months. Then he moved on to his time serving on the Soviet cruise ship *Mikhail Lermontov* in the seventies, which, according to him, shuttled back and forth between London and Australia under a British charter.

"The passengers were all foreigners—rich ones," the general said. "Naturally, I was curious about them and tried to befriend them. I wanted to understand their way of life, their way of thinking. In 1986, the ship sank near New Zealand, and I went there as part of the investigation team."

But Maya was more interested in the methods of intelligence agents. "Is it true you guys have a special technique to drink large amounts of alcohol without getting drunk?" she asked. She'd heard this rumor but wasn't sure if it was true.

"Not any amount, exactly, but yes, I could put away a bottle of vodka without showing it," he replied.

"Can we use this in the show?"

"Wouldn't be accurate now. People don't do this anymore, from what I've heard—it's a lost art."

"How come?"

"Guess there's not much need for it now. People drink much less these days. Look at this." He gestured to his glass of mineral water. "I haven't touched vodka in years."

"Have you ever killed anyone?" Maya blurted out, and felt herself blushing.

"I can't answer that," Vasily Vasilyevich chuckled, then quickly shifted the conversation to the script she was directing.

It was written by a man whose name she didn't recognize. The plot didn't make sense; it was so preposterous that the author clearly didn't care about plausibility.

"I don't get it," Maya said. "I was told this was going to be like *Seventeen Moments of Spring*. But in that show, Stierlitz mostly stays in his office, having tense conversations. The suspense is all psychological—you're on edge, worrying he'll get caught. Here, though, our agent is straight out of a James Bond movie. It's all chase scenes and shoot-outs."

"True. But that's what modern viewers want, I suppose. You have to compete with Western movies these days, right? Plus, in *Seventeen Moments*, Russian actors played Nazi officers and spoke Russian the whole time. That was a conceit we accepted back then. Not so much anymore."

Tushkov explained that the first version of the script had in fact followed *Seventeen Moments* quite closely. It featured an undercover agent in a foreign country, presumably the US. But the producers rejected it, deciding that Russian actors couldn't convincingly play foreigners. And what language would they speak, anyway? So the script was reworked to have the agent uncover internal enemies—people recruited by the CIA who were working against Russia on its own soil.

Maya suddenly suspected that the general's role might be more than just a consultant. "Did you help write it, by any chance?"

"Oh, no!" he laughed. "I only came on board two weeks ago. I'm just telling you what I heard through the grapevine."

Later, at home, Maya marveled at how much she'd enjoyed the dinner. It could be that Tushkov had been trained to put people at ease, or that this was a natural trait that came in handy in his line of work. Another possibility was that, being a decent person, he'd joined the KGB back in the day with idealistic hopes and then gotten trapped in the job. She'd heard that once you were involved with them, they never let you go.

This was what had surprised her most when she started working on this production—that she was surrounded by regular people, not the moral monsters she had imagined. There was her first AD, Danya, a foppish young man who was meticulous about schedules and had a great sense of humor. He'd already told her that he and his wife, a banker, were trying to have a baby. There was her casting director, Lida, who was maybe fifteen years older than Maya but looked out for her like a mother. Lida was crazy about her four dogs and spent her free time volunteering at animal shelters. There was Andrey, the cinematographer, a shy, modest man in love with his job. He seemed to know everything about movies and made exquisite little films from his travels to northern countries, which he was also entranced by. And many others like them. They were here for the simple reason that it was a nice gig that paid well.

To Maya, the producers were certainly paying a shitload of money. When she first got a text from her bank informing her of her new account balance, she was rendered speechless. Right away, she paid off most of what she owed her parents and sister and felt her body becoming lighter.

The first few weeks were filled with casting, scouting locations, and discussing set design. It felt completely different from working on her own movie. She wasn't invested in this project, and every task that had once felt exciting now seemed endlessly tedious. Like an automaton, Maya merely went through the motions, waiting for the moment when she could finally fall into bed and enjoy her luxurious eight hours of sleep. She could sleep now! Thanks to the antidepressant, no doubt. But this wasn't how you made a film, no matter how cringeworthy the script might be. She wondered if there was a way to work around it, to produce something at least halfway decent. First, though, she needed to rediscover a semblance of enthusiasm, perhaps by reconnecting with her love of cinema. She had thought she'd never direct a movie again, yet here she was, leading this massive production, with people calling her by her patronymic. Wasn't that something?

In December, after auditioning what felt like every available actor, they settled on Ivan, a Serbian who had come to Moscow years ago to study and never left. Although he had a slight accent, the producers accepted him as the best option. At least he had presence. Maya proposed a backstory for his character—that he was born abroad to Russian parents who were spies—and everyone agreed. They began rehearsing; Ivan was fine, though a bit self-involved. His numerous girlfriends often showed up to pick him up after their sessions.

Tushkov was present throughout the process, curious about the intricacies of filmmaking, and Maya found herself enjoying his company. He was soft-spoken and had a knack for making her laugh, which wasn't easy—she wasn't as quick to laugh as she used to be. He wore delicate cashmere sweaters and often brought her hot tea. The general seemed to genuinely take an interest in her. At one point, they began discussing books, and she discovered that he was reading Jonathan Franzen. This sparked Maya's interest in fiction once more, and they formed a sort of book club for two.

Every now and then, something would trigger a memory of when she was filming her own movie, and suddenly, a scene would flash before her eyes, so vivid it felt as though it had been captured on film. She would realize once again how much everything had changed. It wasn't just her circumstances that had shifted, but most of all, herself. She felt like an utterly different person now, as if she'd aged twenty years. Never again would she be so light-hearted, confident, and full of anticipation and awe.

She'd gone out with Sanya and Mark a few times, celebrating the end of the trial, but she had shared nothing about the deal. It wasn't just because she'd been asked to keep it a secret; she felt so ashamed that she couldn't bring herself to mention it. How could she? They'd put their careers on the line by testifying in her defense, and she had betrayed them by defecting to the other side.

In any case, they would find out sooner or later. The truth was bound to come out—this was going to be a high-profile series. But Maya couldn't bear to be the one to tell them. She had only hinted that she'd been hired for a film, dodging their questions and promising to reveal everything when the time was right. Eventually, Mark sensed that something was amiss.

I really hope everything's ok with you, he messaged her out of the blue one day. *That you're not involved in anything weird.*

She replied with a heart emoji.

Blink twice if you're being held hostage, he texted.

Haha, she responded.

It was best not to dwell on how her friends would react when she was exposed, she decided. She would handle it when the moment actually arrived.

Lena didn't know anything either. Maya had only told her she'd found a well-paying gig, and Lena was happy for her.

"Maybe you should start thinking about getting a US visa," she said when they spoke on the phone. "Come visit when your project is done."

Maya didn't want to point out that, as a convicted criminal, she'd probably run into trouble getting a US visa. Instead, she asked Lena if she was planning to visit Moscow in the summer like she'd said she would, mostly to steer the conversation away from her project, just in case Lena started asking for details.

And then, right before New Year's, a couple of trade publications ran a news item about the new series. Thankfully, not many people read them, so there was no immediate reaction from anyone she knew. But two days later, Bobrov, the journalist who had been her nemesis during the trial, published an article in a major media outlet with a wide readership. In it, he claimed that Maya, having undergone a personal transformation and rejected her previous beliefs, was now working for the good of the Motherland, filming a series about the great organization keeping all Russian citizens safe—the FSB.

Everything inside Maya went cold and brittle when she read this. The article reeked so much of Soviet-style propaganda that it didn't feel real. But it was real. It occurred to her that Bobrov was probably on the government payroll, though that didn't matter. What mattered was that she hadn't expected them to spin it this way, taking control of her story and trashing her name. Why was she still so naive? Of course, they were using her for their own purposes the way they saw fit. Had she really expected sensitive and nuanced treatment from the same people who had likely orchestrated her trial and tortured their opponents in baroque ways? She should've spoken to Bobrov before he had a chance to write his article. But he hadn't even contacted her for comments, so it was clear no one was interested in what she had to say.

The next day was the last day of rehearsals before everyone went on an extended vacation. Maya was in a dark mood, leaving most of the work to Danya. Tushkov had called in sick and stayed home, and she felt thankful for this—she might've said something to him that she would later regret. The team occupied a spacious room in Bereg's office outfitted with shaggy carpets, velvet couches, and low tables made from tree cross sections. They slogged through the day, making final adjustments to a few difficult scenes, with Ivan struggling and growing increasingly annoyed. As they wrapped up, Maya glanced at her phone and saw that Lena was calling. She never called without scheduling their conversations first, so Maya immediately thought it was urgent. She signaled for Danya to continue without her and answered the phone.

"Is it true?" Lena demanded.

"What?"

"That you're directing a movie glorifying the FSB?"

Maya panicked, trying to come up with something to say. Something other than "yes." She hadn't expected Lena to hear the news so quickly.

"I see," Lena said when Maya didn't reply.

There were people scurrying around in the hall where Maya was standing—she couldn't possibly discuss anything private. "Can we talk about this later?" she finally said. "It's not a good time right now."

But then they couldn't find time to speak, as Lena was traveling with her family for vacation. This would have to wait. Maya resented the thought that, until she could tell Lena how she'd been forced into this project with a choice between it and prison, her friend would keep seeing her as a despicable human being. But there was nothing to do but wait. She wanted to explain everything in detail, so Lena could see she wasn't exaggerating or lying just to cast herself in a better light.

In the meantime, there were other people's emotions to manage. Amid the holiday greetings, Maya was receiving texts from her aggrieved friends.

Did they make you do this? Mark's text read. *Did they hold a gun to your head?*

No greetings, no nothing, just this.

She typed a reply, then deleted it. Started again, then deleted it once more. She couldn't explain everything in a message—this had to be a face-to-face conversation. Besides, they might be reading her texts, so in the end, she said nothing, hoping Mark would suggest a meeting. But he never did, and she didn't have the wherewithal to do it herself.

Sanya called without texting first, and Maya told her she'd explain everything in person. "But I don't know if they're tracking who I meet with."

"I'm already talking to you, though. By that logic, wouldn't they be listening to us right now?"

There was an ongoing joke among regime opponents that the FSB listened to them constantly, and if you wanted to reach them, you could just speak into a potted plant and say, "Comrade Major, do you copy, over?"

They started giggling, then burst into hysterical laughter.

CHAPTER 16

For the first time since she was a teenager, Maya celebrated New Year's at her parents' house. This was the biggest holiday of the year, universally loved: if there was one thing the whole country agreed on, it was this celebration. She remembered how as a child, she'd start anticipating it in early December, her heart fluttering with excitement at all the magic it would bring.

Together with her dad and sister, she would go to the fir tree bazaar to pick out the tree that would grace their living room. In her Soviet childhood, the fir trees were thin and sparse, with few branches and needles, but their wonderful scent filled the whole space. After setting up the tree in a bucket of water, they would decorate it with ornaments her parents had inherited from relatives: quirky old animals, people, and cartoon characters mostly made of glass and porcelain, with a few very old ones crafted from fabric and paper. Then came the dinner, with dishes that never changed and signaled New Year's as much as the tree—Olivier salad, herring under a fur coat, duck with sour apples, red caviar sandwiches. They would watch all the celebratory television, switching between channels. Maya would drift through it all as if in a dream, enchanted. Sometimes, her parents would even hire actors from an agency who went door to door, impersonating Grandpa Frost and his granddaughter, the Snow Maiden. But this practice occasionally backfired, as previous households had often convinced the actors to drink vodka with them.

After listening to the bells on the Spasskaya Tower chime midnight, Maya would go to bed, knowing the best part would come soon. In the morning, she'd wake up first and run to the tree to discover her presents, nearly fainting with expectation. Unpacked, they almost never warranted this level of emotion (one year, she got a sweater and a tiny box of chocolates), but the experience was so intense that the magic of New Year's stayed with her through the following decades, nearly unchanged. This remained true even long after she'd learned that Stalin's propaganda had created this holiday for Soviet people by pasting some elements of Christmas onto a secular base.

When she turned seventeen, Maya began spending New Year's away from her parents: first with her boyfriends' families, then at parties filled with people her own age. Eventually, as everyone got fancier jobs, more parties appeared—lavish celebrations hosted by companies for their employees, partners, or both—turning the end of December into a nonstop celebration. Even last year, despite feeling weighed down by problems with her own movie, Maya had gone to several parties hosted by film and magazine people and had a great time.

This year, the only two invitations she had received were from her parents and from Bereg, the production company she was working for. Their event was scheduled for January 11, presumably for when the management would be back in Moscow from their various exotic vacations.

Presently, Maya was chopping boiled potatoes alongside her mother, having arrived early to help with the cooking. Polina stood at the sink with her back to them, cleaning the duck and rubbing it with salt and pepper.

"I don't know if I should get a Yorkie or a Chihuahua," she was saying. "I'm torn. Help me."

Nini had died, and she was heartbroken.

"Why don't you get a bigger dog? They're more intelligent," Maya suggested, before wondering if this was a quality her sister, who could spend hours doing nothing but cracking and eating sunflower seeds, held in any regard.

"They're a pain in the ass. They have to be walked twice a day!"

Nini had used pee pads and almost never stepped on the ground with her paws.

"Walking is good for you. You've been complaining that you've become completely sedentary."

Polina didn't reply, but her back radiated annoyance. She'd been complaining about everything wrong in her life for years, and she hated it when someone pointed out ways to fix the things she didn't like. Maya kept doing it on purpose. She was sick of the whining.

"Dear, getting some exercise wouldn't hurt," their mother piped up.

"You're saying I'm fat?" Polina whipped around, holding the raw bird in her hands. She'd been steadily gaining weight and was now at least twice the size she had been at twenty.

"You've been whining for literally years that you're getting fatter," Maya observed. "But no one else is allowed to mention it. Either do something about it or shut up already!"

Polina shot her a vicious look but didn't say anything, which was unusual. Maya was used to being bullied by her, but now their dynamics seemed to have shifted. She was starting to feel that her family was apprehensive around her. Could this be true? Did they think she was working for the FSB, as in reporting for them? It was better not to ask.

Later, at dinner, her dad kept offering her the most appealing caviar sandwiches and the juiciest parts of the duck. It was clear he was happy to be spending time with her, but they struggled to find topics to discuss. She didn't want to talk about her new job, and no one dared to ask about her romantic life or pressure her about starting a family anymore.

Soon, everyone but Maya became riveted by the TV. A New Year's program came on, featuring musical numbers in which Soviet-era songs were reimagined for the modern viewer. She never watched TV except when she was here, and what appeared on the screen now reminded her why. Pop stars and famous actors, dressed in tacky costumes, grimaced at the camera while performing dance moves so cheesy they seemed lifted from a dystopian comedy like *Idiocracy*.

"Can we watch something else?" she asked.

"Why?" Surprised faces all around.

"It's just . . . so tasteless and vulgar. It hurts to look at."

Polina pinched her lips, her expression conveying, *Our intellectual here with her refined tastes!* Their father looked hurt, as if Maya had insulted him personally, but started flipping through channels.

"Oh, *Home Alone*! Let's watch it!" Maya exclaimed, seeing Kevin's grinning face.

"I'm not watching an American movie," her father mumbled, switching to the next channel.

"Why not?"

He turned to look at her like she was a dimwit. "Let me explain, since you clearly don't get it. America's trying to turn our great country into one of their puppets. They're just parasites, draining our resources and causing trouble wherever they go. They're pushing their crap on us—movies, ideas, everything. It's infuriating how they think they can mess with us like this!"

He went on about how it was the US and its NATO allies—essentially its vassals—that were to blame for everything that was failing or falling short in Russia. Maya sat there stunned. They never discussed politics, and she had missed the moment when her father became so brainwashed by propaganda. This was what happened when you worked at a state institute, where you were constantly fed the narrative that Putin's government was excellent and devoted to improving your life while NATO was painted as the root of all your problems. Then you came home to get more of the same from state-run TV.

Meanwhile, her father said, "And that friend of yours, Lena—betraying her country like that! I can't believe we took her in like family. What a traitor. A swine!"

Maya's face burned at this. Her parents had once loved Lena, and Lena had always been kind and generous to them. She stood up. "That's enough. Mom, thank you for the lovely dinner."

She headed to the front hall, her mom trailing behind her. "I thought you were spending the night! Stay. Your father didn't mean what he said."

"I meant every word!" he shouted from the living room.

On the metro, the few passengers looked somewhat disoriented, as if they were on the verge of something momentous but unsure if they would be able to handle it. They kept wishing Maya a happy New Year. She got out at Tverskaya and walked down the boulevard to Patriarch Ponds. The city sparkled with festive lights, the elegant neoclassical buildings illuminated from below; the sidewalks were swarming with tipsy, laughing people. It was nearing midnight. She would be meeting the New Year alone, but that was fine.

On the ice in the middle of the pond, two stalls were selling drinks and snacks, and a bunch of people were crowding nearby, moving to disco music. Maya approached a group of well-groomed, stylishly dressed men and women who seemed like the kind of people she liked hanging around with—young creatives. It wasn't that she was going to join them specifically, but they seemed friendly and fun, and just being in their vicinity felt nice.

"Here." A young man from the group handed her a plastic champagne flute and poured from the bottle he'd just opened. She noticed the label—Dom Pérignon. Not bad.

"Make a wish!" said his friend, a blond girl with a delicate face.

Someone started a countdown on their phone. As it struck midnight, Maya made a wish. Everyone cheered and whooped, and the young man with the bottle suddenly leaned in and gave her a long kiss on the lips. When ABBA's "Happy New Year" began playing, she was swept into the thick of the crowd and danced along with everyone else. Her mind cleared of the thoughts and anxieties that had been torturing her, and for the first time in what felt like forever, she was genuinely happy.

She slogged through the mandatory eight-day vacation, wishing for it to end from day one. After meeting up with Sanya, her only remaining friend, twice, Maya found herself with absolutely nothing to do but read and watch movies. She even started exercising with some YouTube videos and took a day trip to Myshkin-Mouseville, the town that had stuck in her head since she learned that Yunusov was from there. Hoping to jolt her brain out of the near-coma it had sunk into lately, she set out in search of new impressions—only to discover that all the museums, including the ones dedicated to mice and felt boots, were closed. All that was left was to wander the quaint little historical town and eat pelmeni.

And so, Maya spent hours either in her living room or in coffee shops with her laptop, ostensibly trying to write, but in reality, contemplating what her life had become. The rift with her father felt like a laceration across her chest. Perhaps they could still be on speaking terms, but she knew there was no way to return to what they had been before. This was permanent. Her family had been stolen from her, along with everything else. Too late, she realized that she should've acted years ago, should've fought for them. But she had been too oblivious and self-involved to even notice that something was wrong.

How crazy it was that she now worked for the very system that had plucked her at random from among those trying to create something meaningful—and crushed her in the process, leaving nothing of her hopes, her work, her relationships, or even her sense of self. Had she really been given no choice? If she had broken her promise and refused to sign the contract with Bereg, then what? Would they have done anything? If they really wanted her in jail, wouldn't they have arrested her from the very beginning and kept her in a SIZO? But she had no way of knowing, of course.

In her search not for justification but for a way to orient herself, Maya looked for artists who had collaborated with totalitarian governments. Leni Riefenstahl was the first name that came to mind, but she was the wrong example. Maya was interested in those who, despite their choices, managed to maintain their good name and produce significant work. Like Sergei Eisenstein, or Dmitri Shostakovich, or Sergei Prokofiev. There were many others, less famous ones: writers, directors, dancers.

No, she wasn't comparing herself to the greats—of course she wasn't. By now, she knew her gifts were mediocre at best. That series she was about to shoot? It would be so many levels below *Battleship Potemkin* that Eisenstein wouldn't have deemed her worthy of a glance if he met her in another life. Paradoxically, jail suddenly didn't seem like such a bad option to Maya. Maybe there, through all the hardships, she could have become someone.

Around her, in the current film industry, Maya saw different forms of collaboration. Some people were cynics, driven by pure greed. They didn't care what they did for money, like her ex-classmate Stasik, now churning out nauseating propaganda for Channel One and flaunting his high salary and perks in his gleeful posts. Others tried to defend their actions, framing them in reasonable terms like "Don't hate the player, hate the game," or "Suppose I die on the barricades. Who's gonna feed my kids?" They were at least capable of feeling shame, though it was buried under these platitudes. Then there were those who scrupulously avoided anything state-related but were nonetheless complacent—and wasn't that a form of collaboration too? But Maya reminded herself she had no right to judge anyone. She was a second-rate artist and, as was now painfully clear, a second-rate human being.

Still, she set some boundaries for herself before filming began. She'd agreed to this gig, but she wouldn't put anything of herself into it. She would be just a hired hand, responsible for turning text into images—like an automatic transcriber converting one medium to another.

The script was ludicrous from beginning to end, full of arbitrary plot twists and underwritten characters with no discernible motivations. It relied heavily on coincidence, asking far too much from the viewer in terms of suspended disbelief and acceptance of events that made no sense in the universe she knew. Maya felt excruciatingly embarrassed for whoever had written it. She hoped she'd never have to meet him and look him in the eye, but maybe she could help him by representing this schlock with a certain level of craft.

On the first day, the crew shot the opening sequence in a restaurant. The protagonist, a master of disguise, was supposed to poison two American diplomats, causing explosive diarrhea in them and thereby thwarting their plans. Maya wondered how she was supposed to establish any level of credibility with this story when it struck her as utterly idiotic. She'd already tried to convince the producers to cut this sequence or at least have the diplomats faint rather than suffer an unstoppable bowel movement. But to them, making Americans shit their pants was the point.

The casting, which the producers had also insisted on, was equally bizarre. One diplomat was played by an actor known for despicable roles—a pustule of a man with a larger-than-usual head and nearly absent features; the other had a malformed arm and bulging eyes. Both had blindingly white false teeth.

She started with the kitchen scenes. Dressed in a white apron, Ivan played around with pots and pans, trying to channel the fancier food bloggers, she thought, and being coy with the camera. She made him focus on being more efficient and understated.

Later, they moved to the dining room for the diplomats' scenes. The two actors were supposed to chat in English while they ate. The producers' plan was to dub them later with native speakers and add Russian subtitles, but for now, the actors had to mimic the English sounds. Neither spoke the language, so they memorized the noises and tried to replicate them—badly. The first takes had the crew doubled over laughing. And visually, it was no better. The two of them, stiff in their suits at a table set with white linen and china, looked like scarecrows. You either had to have manners from childhood or the skill to fake them—and they had neither. Maya couldn't imagine anyone mistaking them for diplomats, foreign or otherwise.

All of this was beyond absurd, but hardly a shock. She'd long known that the state of Russian film and television was abysmal. The system was built for producers to make money before films even hit theaters or TV screens, leaving no incentive for quality, only the predictable churn of state-funded garbage.

Two weeks passed in much the same way. The villain finally appeared, played by Dmitry, a popular actor best known for his enormous mouth, which stretched halfway down his face when he smiled. It was unsettling, but perfect for the role. His character was a Russian bought by the CIA for an insane amount of money, though how he ended up with so many henchmen—who conveniently showed up when needed—was never explained. Presumably, he'd shared the cash with them. Wasn't the script basically saying that Russians would sell out their country for the right price? Luckily, no one seemed interested in that question. With the henchmen's help, the bad guy planted explosives under the Kurchatov Institute, which the hero defused in a dramatic, last-minute sequence.

More was to come—ridiculous gadgets, a femme fatale. Maya attempted to argue with the producers about altering the script in the direction of realism, but their strained conversations followed the same, more or less fruitless pattern. Then she noticed they started avoiding her.

She raised this again with Tushkov. "Weren't you hired as a consultant to make this at least somewhat plausible?"

But he only threw up his hands. "I came on board after the script was approved," he replied.

So far, the general had given her notes on some minor points, like the use of wiretaps or countersurveillance tactics, which, honestly, she could've done without. Maya began to doubt his role as a consultant; it occurred to her that his real purpose might be to keep an eye on her. Consequently, she declined a dinner invitation from his wife, citing exhaustion. Who knew—maybe it was a trap of some sort. After that, he began coming to the set less often.

And then, as Maya struggled to find her way through the script, longing to create some meaning for herself in all of this, it suddenly dawned on her: she could implement a little sedition without anyone realizing! When this hack job of a series came out, she would at least be able to say that she'd tried to do something subversive with it and thus make her position clear. She suspected, however, that she wasn't smart enough to pull it off on her own. The idea seemed great, but what did it really mean to be subversive, especially if she couldn't mess with the script?

Lena was the best person to talk to about this, but she'd distanced herself since learning about Maya's new job. They finally spoke during New Year's vacation, and Maya filled her in on the details of her deal with the IC. Lena had been sympathetic—how could she not be? She understood that it had been a choice between jail and freedom. Yet, somehow, they'd stopped speaking after that. Every attempt Maya made to reach out fell flat, and their texts dwindled to nearly zero. Maya couldn't tell if this meant Lena truly disapproved of her choice. Did she think Maya should have accepted prison instead? Was that the respectable thing to do, because anything was better than cooperating with the system?

Maya decided to contact Dato since he was also abroad and risked little by talking to her about this. She texted him but then realized it would be best not to discuss her ideas over the phone. She was a small fish, yet she might still be bugged. It was so easy to do nowadays, she'd learned from Tushkov, given the advancements in digital technology. If they found out what she was planning, they could easily undermine her cause. She would be better off speaking to someone in the open, like in a park, leaving her phone at home or at least far enough away so that her voice wouldn't reach it. After some deliberation, she texted Mark, asking to meet and discuss something important. They hadn't exchanged a word since he'd asked her if a gun had been held to her head.

In three days, neither Dato nor Mark had replied, even though her texts had been marked as read. Maya then realized that the people who once loved her, craved her company, and valued her opinions no longer felt she deserved a response—even a simple no. It was an awful, sinking feeling. The only person who reliably answered her calls and messages was Sanya, but Maya didn't want to drag her into something potentially dangerous. Sanya was too kindhearted and too invested in her, Maya felt, to make an informed decision.

Fine, she would do it on her own. At a library, Maya used a public computer to Google possible ways to incorporate subtle dissent while directing a movie, but there seemed to be none if you couldn't manipulate the script. She felt that her IQ had been reduced by the combination of months-long insomnia, stress, and medications taken without medical oversight, so whenever she tried to think intensely, hoping for a breakthrough, she ended up tensing the muscles in her forehead so hard they started to ache, with no effect on her actual thought processes. Several days passed with no progress, and she finally gave up.

But then—bam! Maya was in the middle of scrubbing her bathtub when inspiration struck out of nowhere. With her hands covered in goo, she began to panic because she couldn't reach for her phone right away. She feared the idea would evaporate from her mind before she had a chance to write it down, never to be summoned again.

The idea was this: previously, she'd seen her mission as reducing the amount of inanity in the project she was overseeing, but now she understood that she needed to take the whole thing in the opposite direction. By amplifying the senselessness of the protagonist's actions and the crudeness of his behavior, she would impart the impression that it was the secret agent hero who was the cretin. This would be subtle but powerful. Sneakily, she would introduce her own take on the subject matter, and those perceptive enough would pick up on it.

The following day, Maya requested an urgent meeting with the producers—two men who looked like twins with their soft brown eyes and immensely hairy bodies, as evidenced by tufts of dense black hair spilling out from under their shirt collars and covering their ears. She explained that she couldn't go on directing this script, whose idiotic peripeteia would put even Fred Olen Ray to shame—unless she was allowed to complicate the goody-goody main character. What if, every once in a while, he made a mistake? Mistakes were inherent in his line of work. What if, sometimes, he did something objectionable rather than being perfect all the time? This would only make him sympathetic to viewers, who were themselves far from exemplary. Think of Stierlitz, she said, certain that the producers had seen the movie as children and didn't exactly remember it.

They didn't explicitly say no. Clearly having no idea who Fred Olen Ray was, they were hoping to get out of the meeting with her as quickly as possible. Maya could tell she was like a toothache to them. They squirmed in their seats, casting longing glances at the world beyond the window and at their phones, quietly buzzing with incoming messages. To her, this was a victory.

The next morning, before the first take, she rose from her director's chair and approached Ivan. She'd already informed him of her intention to "complicate" his character and now used the few minutes while the cameramen were still setting up to give him further instructions.

"Remember what we talked about?" she said. "He's grown a bit overconfident over the years. And ruthless. It's like being a doctor—eventually, they get desensitized to human suffering."

Ivan was loving it. He was working his face as she spoke, a maniacal glint appearing in his eyes.

"Perfect!" she praised him. "This is exactly what I mean. Try to convey it as much as possible through your body language and facial expressions. Also, you can improvise some dialogue if you like."

"I'd really like that," Ivan said. From what Maya had gathered, he considered himself to be a major artist, so the script felt a little too tightly written to him.

They proceeded to film an action sequence in which the agent made a failed attempt to get his hands on a briefcase with top-secret information. He moved through enemy headquarters that masqueraded as a confectionary factory (Maya's idea—she'd convinced everyone that the body shop stipulated by the script was a tired cliché), knocking over vats full of syrup and multicolored caramels (luckily, she didn't have to think about how much the cleanup would cost) and hissing swear words (Ivan's improv). Distracted by the machinery, he missed a guard coming up behind him and had to deal with him using a crooked metal thingy (a piece of the factory's property no one knew the purpose of).

"What a horrible, useless death!" Ivan improvised. (Maya gave him a thumbs-up.) The antagonist, Dmitry, showed up because of another mistake the agent had made—namely, not listening to his superiors, who'd warned him that the main guy could be here. Both actors were deadly serious as they hurled large objects at each other. They then grappled in a puddle of purple syrup, trying to strangle each other, until Ivan rendered his adversary unconscious and retreated without checking for signs of life (more mistakes).

"Great job, everyone!" Maya said when the shift was over. As a reward, every crew member got to take home a box of chocolates.

Over the following two weeks, the agent hero alternated between impersonating a cancer surgeon, a taxi driver, a lab custodian, a paper goods salesman, and a nanny for a wealthy family. Despite his constant blunders, he managed to obtain the secret documents and deliver them to his superiors. Many people were killed in the process, including his potential love interest. He behaved like someone with no prefrontal cortex, guided only by his basest instincts. But unfortunately, what had seemed like a clever concept in Maya's head wasn't working out in real life. The project had devolved into an extravaganza of stupidity, and yet it was becoming clear to her that viewers would be unable to separate the main character from the noise of the ridiculous plot and perceive him as uniquely foolish and villainous. For that to happen, everything else would have to make sense. At best, she was succeeding in turning the material into a parody. No one, however astute, would be able to grasp her intention.

For a film to become a statement, everyone involved had to be in on the idea, and every aspect of the film needed to support it. Movies were ultimately a collective effort. She'd always known this, but only now was it becoming glaringly evident.

In the meantime, Maya's bank account kept fattening up. In February, she received twice the usual amount, which she was told was a bonus when she inquired. Before this, she hadn't exactly let herself dwell on where the money was coming from. But now, when the thrill of "getting back at them" had dissipated, the question presented itself—and wasn't going away. Bereg, the production company, was owned by a huge oil and gas conglomerate, which was in turn partly owned by the state. This was the money, then, that didn't go to old people living in near-starvation; to cancer patients treated with domestically made, nonworking generics; to children in homes with no running water and holes in the ground instead of toilets. And she was not only taking it, but also helping create something meant to strengthen the system that was sucking resources from those who rightly deserved them and funneling them into unimaginably luxurious yachts, stables, and villas for the select few.

When all of this had sunk in, Maya couldn't pretend anymore.

For long stretches of time, she felt dead inside. At work, her mouth produced the right words, and her body performed the necessary movements, but her mind was elsewhere, absent from what was happening around her. She spent her days calculating ways to simply last until the end of her shift, waiting out the hours she had to spend in the company of people she'd slowly begun to despise. Why were they taking part in this? They hadn't been threatened with prison. This wasn't the last job in the world, and they were doing it of their own free will.

And then, when the workday finally ended, the last place Maya wanted to be was alone with herself. The weekends had become especially hard, and she tried to devise ways to distract herself. She had now the means to travel, but her choices were limited. Her Schengen visa had long since expired, and, with her criminal record, she might not get it renewed—or else getting it would require energy she didn't have. So Europe was not an option. One weekend, Maya traveled to Istanbul and spent two days aimlessly strolling around the same three neighborhoods and eating overpriced eggplant dishes. The next, she boarded the Sapsan to St. Petersburg, where she checked into a Deluxe Historic Suite at the Belmond Grand Hotel with the vague intention of pushing her situation to an extreme, throwing it into sharp relief, as if it weren't stark enough already. She expected to be sickened by the opulence but found herself rather liking it and getting sickened by that instead.

As she entered the train car on her ride back to Moscow, Maya spotted her former classmate Petya, aka Broomstick, sitting in the back row by the window. He had put on some weight, no longer warranting the nickname, and had grown a beard. They had never been especially close, but she remembered catching him gazing at her on more than one occasion during the program with what she assumed was quiet attraction—something he was too shy to ever express. Stopping by her seat to put her weekender down, she raised her hand and smiled, genuinely excited to see him. What a lucky coincidence! She could now spend the long ride catching up with Petya, a kindred soul, trading stories and maybe hearing some gossip about their other classmates instead of stewing in her own gloom.

But then, in the span of a drawn-out second, she saw it: a flicker of recognition in his eyes, quickly replaced by a hardness that overtook his expression like frost. Her own body went rigid as Maya watched him turn toward the window in a deliberate show of pretending not to know her.

This hurt as though Petya had landed a fist to her jaw. In her seat, she tried to make herself small. The train was full, and for a moment, she contemplated moving to another car and begging someone to trade places with her. But, being a coward, she couldn't bring herself to do it and spent the next three hours and fifty minutes right where she was, her skin burning the whole time. She didn't even get up when her need to pee became overwhelming. She was unhandshakeable now, unacceptable, tainted—ostracized by her peers.

When the train finally pulled into the station, Maya waited until every last passenger had cleared out of the car. Only then did she slip out, her heart racing. She felt exposed, as if everyone's eyes were fixed on her with contempt and judgment. She couldn't remember ever feeling such profound shame in her life. In the station bathroom, the tears came, and she cried until she felt numb.

At home, Maya entered a sort of manic state. She spent an hour and a half texting nearly everyone she knew from her life before the trial: every single one of her former classmates, with the exception of Petya, her professors, her ex-colleagues from other jobs, Dennis, Belov, Gosha Tychinkin, and members of his crew she'd worked with. She asked how they were and suggested a meetup for coffee next week or whenever was convenient. At this point, she didn't care how pathetic or needy she appeared; she just wanted to know where she stood with them.

Over the next few days, she checked her messaging apps obsessively. Every time a notification chimed, her pulse quickened, but almost always, it was either her bank, spam, or someone from her new life, like Danya, who had a habit of texting her even while they were both on set.

A week passed, and out of the sixty-seven people she'd texted, fifty-nine had read her message. Of those, only seven replied. They offered noncommittal responses like *Yeah, I don't have time right now, but maybe in a couple of weeks*, which felt just as dismissive as no response at all. It was official—she was an outcast, expelled from the ranks of those she once respected. The feeling of otherness and loneliness that descended on her then was more than she could bear. It was soul crushing.

And then she became angry, choked with rage. Who did these people think they were? What gave them the right to look down on her? They hadn't walked in her shoes. It was easy to feel superior when you'd never had to make a difficult choice. Take Dato, for instance: he'd bought a ticket to Berlin, where he was thriving precisely because he had escaped from tyranny, using that fact to secure more opportunities. Some people like him, who fled to Europe, were later kidnapped by their relatives and dragged back to Chechnya, where they abruptly renounced their beliefs and sexual orientation, embracing traditional values. What would Dato do if he were brought back the same way? Was he a hundred percent certain he wouldn't break under torture? Was that why he felt he could judge her?

As for the rest, they weren't even in this kind of danger, yet they fed their egos by thinking they were better than her. What did any of them know about surviving a hellish trial like hers? Lena, too—she'd gotten out before anything bad could happen to her. If Ilyusha were taken hostage by the regime, she would do whatever it took—run Russia Today, Putin's main propaganda arm, or join Vladimir Solovyov's awful TV show, where he shouted pro-Kremlin slogans like a man possessed. Maya would bet that out of the sixty-seven people, sixty-six would crack when pressured. They dismissed her as morally bankrupt, but they'd never faced what she had. You didn't know who you were until you confronted that kind of choice. The only people Maya was prepared to take shit from were those who had chosen prison in a situation exactly like hers. But she didn't know anyone who had.

This rage boiled within her for days. She kept imagining what she would say to everyone who hadn't deemed her worthy of a response. At times, it made her feel murderous. Once, in the middle of the street, she couldn't contain it any longer and started yelling, startling passersby, who scattered and watched from a safe distance. When she was finished, she stormed away.

And yet, this didn't make her feel any better. She couldn't stand going to work anymore. Just seeing the crew and actors made her want to throttle herself—and them. The words they spoke, especially the ones they'd memorized, made her esophagus fill with bile. So, one morning in March, Maya turned around before reaching the set and headed to the Museum of Russian Impressionism, where she spent several hours with her phone turned off. When she emerged, she texted the producers, Goga and Vlad, to inform them she wouldn't be directing the rest of the project.

The next morning, Tushkov, who hadn't set foot on the set in the past three weeks, called and requested to see her, anywhere she chose. Maya didn't really expect him to do anything strange. What could he do—poison her in a public place? It wasn't inconceivable, but highly unlikely. She was no one important, even if she was somewhat notorious now because of all the trial coverage. Still, she offered to meet at the Moskva bookstore, figuring that if they had to stand, their conversation wouldn't last long. There were no places to sit there, if she remembered correctly.

"If you're here to convince me to stay," she said after making some small talk about the novels on the new arrivals table, "it's not going to work. I just can't."

She still had no idea what his role was in the project. He must have been a good spy back in the day, she thought, as it was impossible to tell how much influence he had, if any, by the way he carried himself—or whether he was involved at all in making decisions. Every time she'd interacted with him over the past few months, he'd been nothing but cordial and kind to her, or at least had appeared to be, and he was the same now.

The general opened a book, scanned the first page, and put it back down. "I guess you feel strongly about this. I'd rather you didn't quit, but it's ultimately your decision."

Maya wondered what they could do to her for not holding up her end of the deal. They couldn't try her again, could they? Maybe they could—anything was possible, she already knew. But she was beyond caring. Somehow, even prison didn't seem so scary anymore.

"I watched your movie last night," he said.

"What movie?"

"The Undead."

"You mean the rough cut. It's not a movie. It could've been, though."

"I realize this. Still, I liked it a lot."

Maya looked at him with curiosity. They'd never spoken about her movie before.

"I can only say that I hope you'll make more films. You're a very talented young woman."

Maya scoffed at this. “I don’t think I’m talented. As a matter of fact, I’m pretty sure I’m not.”

Tushkov raised his eyebrows. “I guess we mean different things by talent. I don’t think it’s a gift from the gods that you’re blessed with. You’re born—and then you start making great art. That’s bullshit. Talent is just the ability to teach yourself and hone your craft, nothing else. You just have to continue doing it.”

This was the nicest thing anyone had said to her in ages. Actually, out of everyone she knew, he’d been the nicest to her lately, perhaps with the exception of Sanya. Maya didn’t necessarily agree with what he’d said, but she gave Vasily Vasilyevich a hug before they parted ways. He smelled nice, like something with bergamot and fresh tobacco leaves.

CHAPTER 17

In June, exactly two years after she'd signed with Belov and the day after her thirty-eighth birthday, Maya started a new job as an administrator at a cosmetology clinic, essentially a beauty salon that also offered anti-aging lasers and injections. She had gone through a surprisingly rigorous process of interviews—first with the owner, then the staff manager, then the head doctor—and two weeks of paid training to finally land the position. At first glance, the doctors, nurses, and beauty specialists seemed like perfectly decent people with whom she could see herself getting along just fine. None of them appeared to have heard about her trial, and she told none of them about her failed film career. She found herself looking forward to normal human interactions: conversations about men, shopping, and celebrities; meals together after work; and gifts for each other on various holidays. There would be no talk of art and its purpose, which she welcomed. Now, the mere thought of that seemed exhausting.

The clinic was located in Maryina Roshcha, a neighborhood easily reachable from her place by bus, yet untrendy and far enough from popular spots that she didn't have to worry about anyone she knew walking in by chance. She worked nine to six on weekdays and every other Saturday from nine to eight. On slow days, she could do whatever she wanted at her computer, as management didn't care what she occupied herself with when the phone wasn't ringing. One day, a melancholy hairstylist, Gene, cut her hair out of boredom, and the result was stunning. She looked almost unrecognizable with the soft shag and wondered why she'd ever kept her hair long.

This wasn't what Maya hoped to be doing for the rest of her life, but it suited her well for now. She'd tried to find another job in the film industry. For nearly three months, she'd chased down every opening, even for lowly assistant positions, but never heard a word back. It was as if her phone and laptop only pretended to connect her to the world, while her emails and messages vanished the moment she sent them. The rumors about blacklists had to be true, then; the question was, could you get off them when enough time passed, or were you stuck there forever? And had she been blacklisted because she'd collaborated with the state or, conversely, because she was considered a dissident? Maybe both, depending on who was deciding. It was impossible to know—there was no one to ask. And even if she found someone who knew for certain, which was unlikely, they probably wouldn't tell her.

She rolled the idea around in her mind that she might never be able to break into the cinema world again and tried gauging how she felt about it. A bit sad, but also like it wasn't that big of a deal. The events of the past two years had taken such a toll on her that she wasn't even sure she'd have the energy to start over. And what she wanted to say now, she knew, would never make it onto film with the growing censorship. In trying to teach her a lesson, they'd ended up teaching the opposite.

During Maya's second week at the clinic, Sanya came in for a discounted facial she'd arranged for her. It was the last appointment of the day, and afterward, they went out to a nearby café for dinner. The place had a hipsterish vibe: white surfaces, farm-to-table food, obscure wines, that kind of thing.

Her face still splotchy and shining with lotion, Sanya raised her glass. "To your new life and whatever comes next! I'm sure it'll be amazing."

They'd both agreed that since there had been no fallout from Maya walking out on the FSB project, none was likely to come, and she could finally put everything that had happened behind her.

"What makes you think so?" Maya laughed.

"I just know. And also, you deserve it."

Over appetizers, Sanya described her new project, written and directed by Boris Mednikov, whose previous movie had played to great acclaim at European festivals and who, despite his oppositional views, had managed to stay on the good side of the regime.

"It's about a single mother somewhere out east trying to survive and her teenage son falling in love and getting bullied at school. A kind of low-key personal drama."

"Wait, that's it?"

"Pretty much."

"It's not a commentary on the current state of things, or how every state system is failing?" Maya clarified.

"The funding comes from Mincult, so."

"I see."

"Speaking about Mincult, you know who else is on their payroll?" Sanya's eyes brightened with the news she was about to share. "This is so good! Ksenia is making a movie about Ksenia of St. Petersburg."

"Who the hell is that?"

"It's a saint who lived in the eighteenth century. She helped the poor and performed miracles. Ksenia is in the starring role, naturally."

"Is she completely out of her mind?" Maya asked, aghast, and Sanya giggled.

It was clear this wasn't just a movie on a topic Ksenia happened to be inspired by—it was a strategic move on her part. When Putin, holding the rank of lieutenant colonel in the FSB, had come to power in 1999, he almost immediately made the Russian Orthodox Church one of his main allies in brainwashing the population. That wasn't accidental, either. During Soviet times, the church had worked closely with the KGB; most priests leading various dioceses and parishes outside of Russia were also secret agents. This fact was well established—there was plenty of scholarship on that. But over the last few years, the church's role had been growing more prominent, and its influence was expanding. Putin was good friends with its leader, Patriarch Kirill of Moscow, whose corruption and love of luxury were widely known. Maya remembered that Ksenia had been the first to be outraged by this clerical expansion, and now she was aligning with them by promoting age-old superstitions! She'd likely had to get their approval to make this film, lest the church try to ban its release on the grounds of an untruthful portrayal of a canonical figure or something. Unbelievable.

"Let me guess," Maya said. "She probably had no problem securing the funding?"

"I heard her budget is, like, crazy high." Sanya rounded her eyes.

"And this is the same person who lectured me about not having a political position!"

Maya had unfollowed Ksenia's Instagram last year, but she opened it now and looked at it together with Sanya. Sure enough, there was a post about the new movie. In the long-winded caption, Ksenia talked about how she'd written the script after discovering the story of Ksenia the saint and being deeply moved by it. Yuck. Even through her syrupy language, it was clear she wasn't sincere. This was all just a show.

You had to give it to her—she was skillfully navigating the currents of the moment. She could always claim she was making an innocent story about an admirable historical woman. Coincidentally, it aligned perfectly with the priority topics for state support in cinema, which Mincult published each year. Over the past couple of years, one of those had consistently been Culture of Russia: Preservation, Creation, and Dissemination of Traditional Values.

In another one of Ksenia's posts, there was a video taken on set where she was already filming. In the clip, Ksenia stood motionless for several seconds, her arms positioned awkwardly in front of her chest, her face conveying infinite sadness and perhaps deep contemplation about the state of the world.

"What's going on here?" Maya wondered aloud.

"She's petrified."

"Huh?"

"So, according to legend, this woman became petrified after her husband died, due to shock. She went through a spiritual transformation—while in this state, I guess. Then she gave up all her belongings and devoted herself to God."

Maya shook her head slowly. "Looks like integrity's just a word now."

Later that night, at home, she thought that maybe it was good she couldn't make movies anymore. She wouldn't be able to do it like Mednikov or, heaven forbid, like Ksenia—or all those others making all sorts of compromises to stay in their profession. She knew what they told themselves: "I've taken their money, but I still have creative freedom. Maybe I can even slip in a little critique here and there." It was ironic that these same people wanted nothing to do with Maya.

But she was grateful to the film world, if not to most of its representatives. It had given her a whole new life, richer and more fascinating than anything she'd known before. For a while, being part of it had felt breathtaking. The fact that she had that experience was more than most people could say about their lives. She often returned fondly to the memories of filming her movie. Despite the lack of sleep, the constant anxiety, and the never-ending problems that seemed to appear out of nowhere, she had enjoyed the process more than she'd ever enjoyed anything else. The intense intimacy she'd felt with her crew was something that happened only on set. Working on a movie brought people together like nothing else. Almost every day, after the camera had stopped rolling, they had found it hard to part and had often gone out for dinner or drinks, spending hours laughing and sharing stories. Maya had felt certain they would remain friends forever.

She climbed into bed with her phone and saw a video her mom had sent her via WhatsApp. It was a clip of a capybara bathing, and Maya replied with a smiley face. Her relationship with her parents had been slowly warming, but mostly through messaging apps. She had seen them only once since New Year's, when she had walked out.

Then her phone buzzed with an incoming call.

"I just bought myself a ticket! I'm coming in three weeks and staying for two weeks!" Lena said excitedly.

After Maya had quit the FSB series, they had started talking again.

"Do you already have plans?" Maya asked. "Anything specific you want to do?"

"Just some errands with my documents and a checkup. Nothing big. I mostly want to hang out with you."

"I'll see if I can get a couple of days off work. By the way, are you interested in facial rejuvenation? I can arrange you a few procedures at a great discount."

Lena said she would love that. They had talked before about how medical and beauty services were so expensive in the States that she couldn't afford them.

"What's new with you?" Lena asked. "Have you gone out on any dates?"

"Ha! When you come, you'll see for yourself what kind of guys are on Tinder."

Then, after a moment, Maya confessed, "I'm writing something."

A few weeks ago, she'd realized she wanted to tell her own story and started writing a screenplay. In fact, her first draft was nearly finished.

Lena was beyond thrilled. "I'm hoping to be your first reader! Whenever you're ready."

Maya didn't want to load her project with meaning and expectations. She could see no way for it to be produced in Russia, and producing it outside the country would be extremely difficult. But probably not impossible.

After Lena hung up, Maya turned off the lamp on her bedside table and lay in the darkness, listening to the sound of cars whooshing past on Novoslobodskaya. Her phone lit up next to the lamp, and she glanced at it, wondering if Lena had forgotten to tell her something important. But it was a message from Mark.

I'm so sorry, he said. *I was a total dick. I really want to see you. How about a coffee sometime?*

Maya smiled. She decided to reply in the morning—or maybe even the afternoon—so he wouldn't think she'd been waiting for his text all this time. But actually, she had.

ACKNOWLEDGEMENTS

Most of the events in this novel are based on real life, though I've taken some liberties with details, chronology, and names. For the criminal trial, which I didn't witness, I relied on reporting about the trial of Evgenia Berkovich and Svetlana Petriychuk, two extraordinarily brave women. Their story deserves a novel of its own, and I'm certain someone is already writing it.

I'm endlessly grateful to my amazing editor, Mike Lindgren. His guidance, his sharp eye, and his kindness shaped this book in ways I can't measure—and honestly, talking with him is better than therapy. Thank you also to Dennis Johnson and Valerie Merians, who believed in this novel and gave it a home, and to everyone at Melville House: Pia Mulleady, Katrina Weidknecht, Beste M. Doğan, Philip Velinov, Hanna Lafferty, and Jay Pabarue.

I'm so thankful to Julia Phillips, a dear friend and a brilliant writer, and to Madeleine Thien, Sam Lipsyte, Helen Phillips, and Paula Bomer for their generous words about this book. To my early readers, Andrea Somberg, Evan Rausch, and Julian Tepper, whose feedback helped me see the book more clearly, and to my MFA professors Joshua Henkin and especially Ernesto Mestre-Reed, an extraordinary writer and human being whose generosity knows no limits. To my beloved friend Sasha Vasilyuk, who has been there for me in ways big and small, coaching me through every corner of a writer's life. I don't know how I would have done this without her. The Jordan Center for the Advanced Study of Russia at NYU made my research possible. My heartfelt thanks go to its director, Joshua Tucker, who read an early draft and gave feedback that strengthened the book. And to the NYU librarian Alla Roylance, who always knew how to help, thank you.

I could never have written this book without the people closest to me. My parents worked hard to make life bearable, first in the USSR and later wherever I lived, and supported me even when we disagreed. My son Nikita—who appears in these pages under a different name—was one of the reasons I decided to leave Russia when staying there under Putin became impossible. And my husband, Sergey, who caught last-minute blunders, dreamed up Maya's zombie movie, and whose unwavering support—emotional, financial, and otherwise—carried me through: this book wouldn't exist without him.

SVETLANA SATCHKOVA is a Russian-born journalist and writer who immigrated to the United States in 2016. She covers culture and politics, with bylines in *The Rumpus*, *Newsweek*, *LARB*, *The Independent*, and others. Currently a research fellow at the Jordan Center for the Advanced Study of Russia at NYU, she holds an MFA from Brooklyn College and lives in Brooklyn. She has published three novels in her native Russian; *The Undead* is her first novel in English.